Sword and Song

Roz Southey

Also by Roz Southey from Crème de la Crime:

Broken Harmony †
Chords and Discords
Secret Lament

† Also available as an ebook

Praise for Roz Southey's richly inventive historical mysteries:

You can see and smell the city, feel the mystery and tensions, and become drawn into the pursuit... It remains absorbing to the end... a must-read.
– Historical Novels Review Editor's Choice

What really makes the novel come alive is its setting... she seamlessly incorporates the historical information into the novel... The dialogue, too, rings true: just ornamented enough to feel right for its time... A charming novel...
  Booklist, USA

A very entertaining story... Patterson is an engaging hero... growing and developing as a character as each novel progresses.
– Angela Youngman, Monsters and Critics

Original, unusual, and grabs your attention from the opening lines. The tension is maintained, the characters are engaging, and the reader is kept guessing right to the end.
– Sarah Rayne, award-winning crime writer

... plot as intricate as a fugue... wickedly pointed characterizations and the convincing evocation of the sounds and stink of a preindustrial city. Southey deserves an encore...
– Publishers Weekly, USA

... a masterpiece of period fiction that delights while it provides an intriguing puzzle that keeps the reader riveted until the end.
– Early Music America

First published in 2010
by Crème de la Crime
P O Box 523, Chesterfield, S40 9AT

Typesetting by Yvette Warren
Cover design by Yvette Warren
Front cover image by Peter Roman

ISBN 978-0-9550566-2-7
A CIP catalogue reference for this book is available
from the British Library

Printed and bound in the UK by
CPI Cox & Wyman, Reading, Berkshire, RG1 8EX

About the author:
Roz Southey is a musicologist and historian, and lives in the
North East of England.

My thanks ...

...to Crème de la Crime and Lynne Patrick for continuing to have faith in Charles Patterson and his friends. Also to my editor, Lesley Horton, for all her hard work and perceptive insights.

to Jeff for all his excellent company.

...to Jackie, Laura and Anu for their continuing friendship, and for their endless store of good stories. It will be a long time before I forget the story of Anu's proposal...

...to Matthew. Many's the happy hour we've spent swapping stories of musicians past – and, yes, there are one or two mentions of Handel.

...to all Crème's other authors, especially Maureen Carter, Mary Andrea Clarke, Kaye C Hill and Adrian Magson, from all of whom I've had useful and often humorous advice.

...to all my family, including my sisters Wendy and Jennifer, and my brother-in-law, John, for their encouragement and support.

...and particularly to my husband, Chris, who is still supplying me with restorative cups of tea, and ferrying me to various literary events without complaint. And he even reads the books!

For Kirsten –

even though she prefers the
seventeenth century to the eighteenth…

1

Every time I come to England, I am struck by the
dens of iniquity that exist in the dark corners of the cities.
[Letter from Retif de Vincennes, to his brother Georges,
10 August 1736]

"Three shirts at least," Hugh said, gulping down his beer. The din in the tavern was so loud he had to shout.

"I don't have three shirts," I shouted back.

"Devil take it, Charles, you musician fellows don't know how to dress!"

"And you dancing master fellows are damned peacocks."

He grinned. My friend Hugh Demsey likes his clothes and, unlike me, has enough money to indulge himself. Tonight, he was dressed in his best coat of turquoise blue, with a paler waistcoat and a cravat so white it must be brand new. Even at the end of the day, he looked neat and fresh. The clothes, and his black hair – he hates the itch of wigs as much as I do – always attract attention from the ladies.

"I've been to these country houses," he said, signalling to a serving girl for more beer. "The gentry wear a different suit of clothes every day. If you take one shirt and one coat, you'll feel like – like – "

"A tradesman? That's what I am, Hugh. I'm not going to this summer party as a guest – I'm going to work, to entertain the ladies and gentlemen."

"Make them see you as something more than a tradesman!"

I laughed. "How?"

He looked at me, began to speak, closed his mouth again, breathed heavily. "Marry the lady," he said in a rush, as if he knew he'd regret it.

"No," I said forcibly.

The lady he referred to is wealthy and of impeccable family, much too good for a lowly musician. And with the added disadvantage, in the eyes of the world, of being – at thirty-nine years of age – twelve years my senior.

"I'll wager you ten guineas you'll name the day before the end of the year," Hugh said.

"I will not."

"I've a feeling it's not up to you, Charles." He tossed the serving girl a few coins. "The lady's pretty determined."

It was then that the message came. Something gleaming slid along the wall to my right. A spirit. I tried not to flinch. Spirits cluster in alleys and streets and houses, on doors and window-frames and roofs, each tied to the place the living man or woman died. Three days after death the spirit disembodies, and they form a network we living men can only guess at. We see them when they choose to let us see; they speak when they wish and not otherwise. If they want to cause trouble it's difficult to prevent them; I've had recent experience of the havoc they can wreak. But this spirit seemed innocent enough; it was drunk – spirits in taverns tend to be – but it made sense enough.

"Message for Mr Patterson. One of you two gents, is it?"

"I'm Charles Patterson," I agreed.

"Message from the constable, sir. He wonders if you'll come down to the lanes by the Castle. To Mrs McDonald's in Walker's Wynd. Third house from the Black Gate. It's urgent, he says."

Hugh groaned. "Involves a dead body, does it?"

"Didn't say anything about that, sir. Just said it was urgent. Can I send a message back to say you're on your way?" Spirits can send messages from one end of the town to the other in less time than it takes for a living man to speak them.

"Do you want to go?" Hugh asked. "It's gone midnight. Aren't you leaving town early tomorrow?"

I shook my head. "The carriage is coming for me at midday. If Bedwalters is asking for my advice, he must be worried. He usually advises me to keep clear of these matters."

I'm a musician by trade and inclination but ten months ago now, last November, I was involved by chance in the machinations of a villain that led on to murder, and since that time two more such affairs have come my way. I seem to have a knack of unravelling crimes, of working out what happened, and finding the guilty party. I admit I like the feeling that I can mete out justice where others fail. Bedwalters the constable has inevitably been involved in these matters too and has had cause to be annoyed at my interference. But he's a decent fair man and I like him very much.

Hugh fell into step beside me as we went to the tavern door.

"Handkerchiefs?" he asked.

"Half a dozen."

"Neckcloths?"

"Another half-dozen."

"Stockings?"

"And that's another thing," I said. "Why the devil should such things cost so much?"

The night was cold; we hesitated on the doorstep of the tavern looking left and right. A few sailors were still about, and two apprentices walked on the other side of the road earnestly debating the appearance of the latest comet. Most of the lanterns in the street had burnt themselves out, or were guttering.

"I wish you wouldn't get involved in these things, Charles," Hugh said as we walked down towards the castle. "It's dangerous."

"It pays better than music," I retorted. So far I'd made sixty pounds from the affairs in which I'd been involved, more than my usual annual income.

The bulk of St Nicholas's church was black against the starlit August sky – a full moon was rising high above the mass of narrow lanes beyond Amen Corner. Over all loomed the castle's Black Gate.

"Sword?" Hugh asked.

"How can I afford a sword?" I protested. "I've been looking for a good cheap cane."

"I mean," Hugh said. "Are you by any chance totally unarmed?"

Belatedly, I saw why he asked. At the mouth of the alley leading up to the Black Gate, a pair of sullen lads were lounging against a wall, hands in pockets. One was smiling, unpleasantly.

"I'm unarmed," I admitted.

Hugh dragged his hands out of his pockets and showed me the dark gleam of a pistol. "I was teaching in the country today, and thought I might have to ride back to town in the dark."

"For God's sake, put that away! They'll attack us just to steal it."

The lads let us pass, although they eyed Hugh's fine clothes. This is the poorest end of the town, where thieves and thugs congregate, with probably not a penny between them. Hugh's clothes must represent a year's gin to anyone with enough daring. And they all clan up against outsiders, so if Bedwalters had a dead body in here, the chances of finding the killer were almost certainly remote.

The Black Gate obstructed the street ahead, ancient grimy stones topped with crenellations and pierced by tiny arrow slits. It was a long time since any warrior had defended this gatehouse and the stones were crumbling. We walked through the archway into another street and looked left and right for Mrs McDonald's. No torches here, and in the darkness all the houses looked much the same.

A young girl darted out of a door. "Mr Patterson?" She was no more than ten years old and dressed up in so many ribbons and flounces it was difficult to see her shape. Rouge disfigured her face. I began to feel uneasy.

Hugh frowned. "Doesn't Bedwalters's *inamorata* live somewhere near here?"

Bedwalters the constable is a respectable man, running a respectable writing-school and enduring a respectable marriage to a respectable woman who doesn't know what it means to be civil. And in the meantime, he conducts a liaison with a girl of the streets whom he patently adores, and who quietly heals all his worries and cares.

I've met her several times, a girl of eighteen or so, dressed in poor clothes but clean and tidy, her brown hair tied back simply. She plies her trade without complaining, accepting what is and what cannot be with equal stoicism. She once defended Bedwalters to me, passionately. A *good* man, she called him. Well, no one condemns a man for straying from home, especially not a man with so shrewish a wife.

The door was low enough to make both Hugh and me duck; we found ourselves in a bare, ugly hallway, hung with badly-framed engravings almost too embarrassing to look at. From upstairs came the sounds of several couples enjoying sexual congress; a murmur of voices filtered from the first room inside the house, immediately on the right.

The girl gestured to the half-open door. "Mrs McDonald's in here." I glimpsed the back of a gaudily-dressed woman, and pushed open the door.

Bedwalters sat by the side of a low bed; the straw mattress was torn and leaking, and topped by blankets stained by unimaginable activity. He was a man both feared and adored by his pupils, and so respected that the Vestry of All Hallows elected him constable year after year; he was known for his quiet and his calm, his decent demeanour. Now his middle-aged face was white as ice, his wig awry on his bald head, his clothes thrown on anyhow and mis-buttoned. He was staring into mid-air, like a man for whom the world is so painful it can only be ignored.

The woman glanced round, said in a broad Scotch accent: "Oh, thank goodness. Mr Patterson, is it? Pray sir, you do something with him for *I* can't."

I moved towards Bedwalters, hearing Hugh swear behind me. The constable was plainly not aware of my presence. His left hand clutched the hand of the girl who lay on the bed, staring at him with empty unseeing eyes. The girl Bedwalters so loved, who once told me she would do anything to protect him. A thin girl with dulled brown hair, dressed only in a thin shift.

A shift soiled by a browning stain of blood.

2

Shocking deeds are reported in the newspapers every day.
[Letter from Retif de Vincennes, to his brother Georges,
10 August 1736]

I bent to check for the girl's breath but she was patently dead; the flesh of her bare arm was chill. She had one wound, in the middle of her back, close to the spine. One wound and one wound only, but it had been enough.

"Stabbed from behind," Hugh said contemptuously. "She wouldn't have had a chance to defend herself."

Mrs McDonald had drawn back to give us room. "He won't let her go," she said, nodding at Bedwalters. She was an elderly woman but tall and upright; her dress was gaudy, her face sour, and she had one of the broadest Scotch accents I've heard in a long time.

"What happened?"

"She had a customer. One of the other girls saw her bringing him in the door. Next thing, she's screaming her head off."

"Screaming's not unusual in here, surely," Hugh said, bending down and shaking Bedwalters's shoulder gently.

"Not that kind of screaming," she said dryly. "You can tell when they mean it. When they're frightened. And Nell was."

Ironic, I thought – I never learnt the girl's name until after she was dead. "And?" I prompted.

"Nothing else to tell. When I got here, she was like you see. So I sent for the constable." She nodded at Bedwalters. "I knew he had an interest in her."

"He was in love with her," I said.

"He's a married man," she said, dryly. "Like all the rest. And he just sits there! Can't shift him, can't get any sense out of him. Not till he said to send for you."

I looked round, at the bare room, the thin body on the bed,

Bedwalters's bleak absorption in his grief. Over the past year I'd become all too familiar with this sort of scene. Death is an everyday event, but illness and the acts of God, perplexing though they may be, are only to be expected. The acts of men, however, all too frequently fill me with anger.

"I need to speak to the girl who saw Nell and her customer," I said. Mrs McDonald turned and bellowed into the back of the house. I knelt down in front of Bedwalters, put my hand on his arm. Recognition stirred in his eyes. He said hoarsely: "He didn't need to do this."

"No."

"When did she ever hurt anyone?"

"Never," Mrs McDonald said. "She's been here six years, since she was twelve, and never once said an unkind word. And always ready to help them as needed it." She added, "Wish I had a houseful like her."

"So can you think of anyone who might want to hurt her?"

Mrs McDonald laughed cynically. "There's some as like to do it for fun."

"This isn't a man going too far in the heat of passion," I said. "This is a deliberate act of killing."

"Maybe she recognised him," Hugh said. "Maybe he was someone well known in the town?"

I shook my head. "If he'd wanted to keep his identity secret, he wouldn't have come back here with her."

A woman hesitated at the door. She was wearing a shawl over a shift that was patched with blood and the leavings of her clients. Her gaze settled on the corpse on the bed then shifted away again.

"Mr Patterson wants to know what you saw, Maggie," Mrs McDonald said, jerking her head at me.

She shrugged. "I saw them."

"When?"

"Hour, two hours ago." Maggie had been born within a couple of miles of the house, to judge by her accent. How old was she? Three or four years older than myself – around thirty,

7

possibly? Getting dangerously close to the end of her attractiveness even to the most undemanding of men.

"Where were you?"

"In the kitchen having a bite to eat. Back of the house."

"And they were…"

"Outside her door."

"What did he look like?"

Another shrug. "A man."

"Young, old? Tall, short? Dark, fair?"

Eventually she decided he was youngish, shortish, dark. "He spoke nice," she said. "Reckon he was an apprentice." She waxed lyrical briefly. "Had a lovely waistcoat, embroidered, bright colours. Roses."

"God help us!" Hugh said horrified. "Apprentices never have any taste."

"Did you hear him say anything?"

Maggie pondered a good while then looked genuinely puzzled. "Well now, there's a strange thing. He asked her if she had the book."

"The book?" I echoed, startled.

"Aye. The book he'd given her to keep safe. And she said she had it and she'd be glad if he took it away with him. So he said he would."

"What kind of book?"

"Never said ought about that."

"Did they say anything else?"

She shrugged. "Never heard ought."

"Did the man see you?"

"Nah, never looked my way." She looked alarmed. "You think he might come for me next?"

"Not if he didn't notice you. But best keep quiet about what you saw just in case."

She nodded. "Think that's why she got killed – so she couldn't say nothing?"

"Possibly."

"Then you're looking for a fool," she said. "You learn to keep

8

your mouth shut in this business. Nell knew that. She'd never have said ought."

"Presumably he didn't know that."

"Didn't want to know, more like," she said. She seemed to be looking at Nell's body without much emotion. I said: "Doesn't it distress you?"

She shrugged again. "We all come to it. And the likes of us faster than anyone else."

"That doesn't mean to say the murderer shouldn't be brought to book."

She laughed. "For killing one of us? That'll be the day!"

"Very likely," I said. "I'd be grateful if you could ask the other girls if they saw or heard anything."

"Yeah, all right," she said. But I fancied she wouldn't bother.

I got up and looked about more carefully, watched curiously by Hugh and Mrs McDonald, and hopefully by Bedwalters. In an ironic sort of way, despite her poor station in life Nell had retained some pride. She had taken care of the home that was also her place of work. It was ordered and tidy; she must have dusted regularly – there were no visible footprints on the bare boards, no hand prints on the scarred table that held only a candle. A rag rug on the far side of the bed was rucked up as if someone had tripped over it. The bedclothes on the far side of the body bore a depression as if someone had knelt there. Nell's shift was pulled up above her knees and had slipped down from one of her shoulders.

With so little to go on, it was only possible to guess what had happened. Nell had brought her customer here, they'd lain together and he'd then stabbed her. She'd clearly put up no struggle – she must have been taken entirely by surprise.

"Would Nell have had a knife?" I asked Mrs McDonald.

"Maybe. Or maybe she borrowed one from the kitchen."

"Could you check if one's missing?"

She cackled. "Wouldn't do no good. God knows what's in there. There are twenty women in this house go in there to cut themselves a wedge of bread or cheese, or get a drink of ale.

Stuff's always coming and going."

I sighed. "It doesn't matter. He almost certainly brought the knife with him, anyway."

Hugh frowned. "How do you know that?"

"Because he took it away again. Maybe it could be identified as his – some people put their initials on their cutlery, or their coat of arms."

"Are you saying this is a man of family?"

"I'm not saying anything at the moment. Many men carry a knife with them – butchers for instance, or some other trades. Or – " I hesitated and Hugh raised his eyebrows. "Maybe he came prepared," I said. "Maybe he always intended to kill Nell." I looked down on the girl's body. One stab – a cold calculating gesture rather than a frenzied, impulsive attack. This looked carefully planned.

"But why, for heaven's sake!" Hugh demanded. "Because of a book!"

I looked down at Bedwalters. "Had she mentioned a book to you?"

He shook his head.

"He did take the book, I suppose?" Hugh asked.

There were few places in the room where a book might have been put away. A small clutter of feminine things – a gap-toothed comb, a few hairpins, a ribbon – lay on a table and, on a chair, a neat pile of clean clothes. With great reluctance I slipped my hand beneath the mattress on which Nell lay, feeling for a book and finding only a purse, a poor cloth thing. When I emptied it into my palm, I came up with three pennies, two farthings and a small but beautiful brooch in the shape of a red rose.

"I gave her that," Bedwalters said. I put it into his hand. "Last year, on her birthday. She used to wear it when we were together." He stared down at the small thing on his palm, then closed his fist around it.

"Look," Hugh said. "There's no difficulty about this. In three days or so, Nell's spirit will disembody and she'll be able to tell us what happened. She'll tell us all about the book and who her customer was."

He was right, of course. The spirit, once it disembodies, always lingers in its place of death; poor Nell would be confined to this house for eighty or a hundred years before her spirit's final dissolution. And it's a rare murder victim who won't accuse its killer. But Nell's murderer must surely have taken that into account.

"He may not have given her his real name," I said.

Silence.

"Right," Mrs McDonald said. "So I can shut up the room and get on with business, till she comes back to us, can I? About time."

"I'm staying here," Bedwalters said.

For a moment he sounded remarkably like his old self, calm, confident, a man of business and standing in the community. He looked haggard still, but I felt a sudden hope that after all he'd be all right, that he'd come through this tragedy and build up the pieces of his life again.

"I won't leave her," he said firmly. "Someone must keep her company."

"The undertaker," Hugh murmured.

"I'll deal with her," Bedwalters said. "Mrs McDonald and I will lay her out decently, and deal with her body and spirit." He caught my hand. "You catch him, Patterson."

"Of course," I said soothingly.

Hugh and I went out into the chill warmth of the August night, stood looking up and down the cobbled street. I felt like a traitor, assuring Bedwalters that I could achieve something I was already convinced was well-nigh impossible.

"The fellow will have left town," Hugh said. "Long since. Obvious thing to do."

"Yes."

"And given a false name to the girl, anyway."

"If he had any sense."

"There's not the slightest chance of catching him."

"The book, Hugh," I said. "What the devil was that all about?"

11

"God knows."

"But it's at the heart of the matter. It must be! Why else should he kill her? For want of something better to do?"

"The girl'll tell us in three days' time."

"I'll be in the country entertaining lords and ladies who don't even know people like Nell exist."

Hugh gave a bark of laughter. "I bet the gentlemen do!" He slapped me on the shoulder. "You can come back, Charles. Long End's only an hour out of town on a tolerably fast horse. Don't worry about this one – this isn't going to puzzle you for long."

We parted in Amen Corner by St Nicholas's church, Hugh to go to his lodgings on Westgate and I to cross town by the High Bridge to reach my rooms in All Hallows parish. I needed sleep if I was to be fit to flatter the ladies and gentlemen tomorrow. *Today.* The streets were dark and I walked in a brooding silence, haunted by thoughts of the dead girl, by the memory of Bedwalters's face, by a longing to be able to turn back the clock and prevent this dreadful thing happening.

And killed for such a small cause too. How could a book be so valuable that it was worth a life?

I heard an owl moan and glanced up to see it swooping low across the dark street in front of me, rising up again towards the tower of All Hallows church –

Towards the rosy glow of dawn…

I held my breath, stepped cautiously forward. A moment's shiver of cold and I was standing in morning sunlight.

There is a world that runs alongside our own, as near as two pages in a closed book. The other world looks much the same as our own; there is no difference between All Hallows church and its counterpart in the other world, no difference in many of the houses, the streets, the trees and gardens. We living men have our counterparts there too, sometimes uncannily like ourselves, sometimes unnervingly different. My own self lives there – a much wealthier man than I; Hugh's counterpart is twenty years older. There seem to be, as far as I have been able to tell, two main differences between the worlds: there are no spirits there; and time does not run at quite the same pace. Sometimes, as now, it is night in our own world, day in the other. Sometimes the seasons seem to change at a different rate.

Worlds like pages in a book. Separate, self-sufficient. But at times it's possible to step from one world into the other. Not everyone can do so but I seem to have that ability. I have been to that world a number of times now, knowing my *stepping through* from one world to the other by a faint sensation of cold.

And I have learnt that it is only at times of crisis that the passageway between the worlds opens up. Principally, when I am searching for answers to a death.

I walked down the street in that other world. I heard a servant talking, a distant fiddler strike up a tune. The gate to All Hallows churchyard stood invitingly open. I put my hand on it, intending to go in, to walk among the sunlit graves, to look for whatever had brought me here...

But the owl swooped down again, bringing darkness back with it. I shivered, stood in the darkness of my own world, a hand on the closed gate of the graveyard.

3

**There are few fine country homes in this region;
the gentry here are much decayed.**
[*A Frenchman's guide to England*, Retif de Vincennes
(Paris; published for the author, 1734)]

The residents of the entire street turned out when Claudius Heron's travelling coach drew up at my door. As my patron and, I strongly suspected, the man who'd put my name forward for the houseparty, Heron had not unnaturally offered to transport me. I'd expected to be travelling in his servants' coach but it was Heron's own equipage that stopped up at my door, drawn by glossy black horses, the bodywork of the carriage polished to shining perfection, and notable by the lack of a coat of arms on the door, though Heron was perfectly entitled to bear one.

I was watching for him from the window of my room and hurried down with my bags, battling through crowds of children to the carriage. One footman took the bags from me, another flung open the door and let down the steps; I went up them in a hurry and the carriage was in motion almost as soon as I was in it. I jolted back in my seat and caught a glimpse of the cheesemonger's disapproving face as the carriage passed.

Heron, in the opposite seat, was dressed in his usual pale colours, and the noon sunshine glinted on his fair hair. A man in his early forties, he considers himself immune to fashion but even his practical travelling clothes were several degrees smarter than my best coat. I saw his gaze flicker over me with a gleam of amusement.

"New clothes, Patterson?"

"I felt nothing else would do."

The amusement turned a little sour. "Yes, I hear our host is always well turned out."

I'd never met the gentleman whose house I was about to

visit but I did know that Edward Edmund Alyson was barely twenty-three, four years younger than myself – I'd just passed my twenty-seventh birthday. He had very recently inherited his uncle's estates and was celebrating his good fortune with a summer houseparty for his friends. My part in providing the entertainment would earn me fifteen guineas – about as much as I got for an entire year's playing as deputy organist of All Hallows church.

"Am I to thank you for a recommendation to Mr Alyson?" I asked Heron.

He shook his head. "Lawyer Armstrong has arranged it all. Alyson apparently wrote to him from London asking him to hire new servants and draw up a guest list."

I stared. "Does that mean Alyson knows none of his guests?"

"Apparently not. But he is eager to make a place for himself and his wife in Newcastle society and wants to meet all the local notables. And of course few people are going to turn down the chance to eat and drink at someone else's expense for an entire month."

Heron's cynicism is familiar to me; I nodded and reserved judgement.

"His uncle and I had part shares in three ships," he went on. "I have been deputed by my fellow shareholders to ascertain Alyson's views on the management of the vessels. And he has inherited at least two mines – there is the question of how he intends to transport the coal."

"Did you know his uncle well?"

Heron nodded. "A very decent man. Very strict – he would not tolerate the least dishonesty, or immoral behaviour."

In my experience, that usually means maids turned off the moment they're seen to be with child.

"He was sadly reduced at the end," Heron said. "Not entirely sure what was going on around him. The nephew I don't know at all. His parents lived in London and on the continent in his early years. I fancy they were not on particularly good terms with the old man."

We looked out at the passing streets. Heron nodded to one or two acquaintances, made light conversation, commented on the pleasures of travelling in such good weather. But as we moved north, into the countryside around Barras Bridge, I could not drag my thoughts away from Nell. She'd been a mere girl, but in Bedwalters she'd found a man who would protect and care for her, and whom she could respect. And he'd found a refuge from a shrewish wife and the burden of everyday cares. What would he do now?

"You're thinking of the constable," Heron said quietly.

Startled, I said: "You've heard what happened?"

"The servants were all talking of it this morning." He looked out into the warm sunshine, on haystacks and shorn fields. "Is there any hint who did it?"

"A customer. Of medium height and build, medium dark. We're hoping Nell's spirit will be able to identify him."

He hesitated then said, "If there's any difficulty in finding him, I could offer a reward. Five guineas, do you think?"

I stared at him astounded. The last time he'd met Bedwalters, he'd bullied him mercilessly, with the hauteur of a gentleman born and bred, in order to get what he wanted. A mere constable – even one as resolute as Bedwalters – cannot hold out against a determined gentleman. As Heron's actions had saved me from a charge of murder, I'd been in no position to object, but I hadn't liked it. Was Heron feeling just the slightest twinge of remorse?

Somehow I doubted it.

"I think that might not be wise," I said reluctantly. "I suspect a reward will simply attract a whole host of undesirables ready to spin you whatever tale they think you want to hear."

He nodded. "So I suspected. But the offer stands."

I thanked him, stared out at a boy and a dog shepherding five sheep. "There was a book," I said absently. "Nell was keeping it for this man."

Heron raised an eyebrow. "Stolen, do you think?"

"Almost certainly. But who would kill for a book?"

Heron's lean, handsome face was cynical. "Last winter, a traveller on the Carlisle road was killed for his cravat."

"It had lace on it," I said tartly. "Worth a fortune, they say."

Heron's own cravat was plain. He smiled.

We travelled for perhaps an hour or two. Alyson's house, Long End, stands seven miles north of Newcastle; our way lay along narrow lanes not entirely suitable for carriages and our progress was at times slow. Fields gave way to woods then to fields again. We clattered through hamlets, scattering hens and geese; a dozen dogs leapt out of hedges to bark at us. The countryside hereabouts is not particularly fertile; the gently rolling hills verge on bleakness and the living is poor. The few people we saw tended to give our expensive retinue sour looks.

But the village we came to eventually, around the end of the afternoon, was well-kept, the houses all of the same type and apparently all built at the same time. An estate village. Beyond the church, a stone bridge curved over a fast-flowing river; we turned sharp left and plunged through pillars topped with extravagant lions, into a drive that led deep into a wood.

The drive was atrociously potholed. An attempt to fill in the holes had met with singular lack of success. The coachman slowed the horses. Heron swore as we bounced along, and held on to the strap beside the door. "Damned place has been neglected for years."

I craned from the window to catch a first sight of the house; naïve and callow of me, I know, but I've not so far moved in the sort of circles where country houses are a commonplace. I looked at it for a full three minutes before realising what it was; it was so small, I thought at first it must be a dower house or even a lodge. It was Jacobean, an old-fashioned building of red brick, with a tower at each corner and more gable ends than any house should ever have. The formal gardens that surrounded it were bedraggled and weed-choked.

Heron was smiling in faint amusement again. "Disappointed, Patterson?"

I sat back, resigned. "Beyond all measure."

"Well," he said, "the Alysons suffer the fate of all nowadays."

"No money?"

"Precisely. Not," he added with extra dryness, "that they don't have extensive rebuilding plans. Or so Armstrong tells me. They're planning something in a much more modern style and have an architect working on it even now."

"Does he know they can't afford it?"

"I suspect all architects expect a fight over money."

Whatever their financial situation, the Alysons were not short of servants. As we drew up in front of the house, footmen leapt forward to open the coach door, a butler waited in dignified disdain, maids hovered in the shadows.

Heron climbed down and was respectfully ushered in. The butler, however, took one look at my new coat, patently decided I must be Heron's secretary or valet and wanted to banish me to the back door. Heron turned his weary gaze on him. The butler reddened and stood back to let me past. I felt a reluctant sympathy for him; technically, of course, he was right – I was as much a paid employee as he was.

The butler himself escorted Heron into some elegant recess of the house; I was relinquished to the care of a maid who couldn't have been more than fourteen years old. She swept me off with ferocious dignity, across a dark wood-panelled hallway of miniscule proportions, to an ancient stair. The steps were of so dark a wood that they seemed black; they were canted at uneasy angles, first leaning into the wall then away from it. The banister was worn to a glossy smoothness by a century or more of handling and was truly beautiful. Morose ancestors in ancient fashions hung on every side.

At the first landing, the maid seemed to lose her way. She hesitated, turned left then turned back, found a narrower stair in a dark corner. She'd apparently decided I was of no consequence; she said insolently, "Honestly, they seem to think we can work miracles. When you get here in the evening and have to welcome the master and mistress next morning and their guests in the afternoon, well, you can't have everything sorted, can you? Let alone find your way round."

"You only got here yesterday?" I said startled.

"And the old servants had let everything go," she said scornfully. "Eighty if they were a day! Lucky for us, of course. This is the best place I ever had." She sounded thirty years old, not fourteen. "Pay's worse than a joke, mind, and I never could stand living in the country, but give me a couple of months and I'll be in their London house. They must have a London house, don't you think?"

"No doubt," I said. She reminded me of the girl in Mrs McDonald's house, trying to be much older and more sophisticated than she was.

She found her way again and turned for a yet narrower stair; we were definitely headed to the attics, I thought. A voice floated distinctly from one of the bedrooms to my right.

"...damnably pretty. Poor thing. But these girls know what might happen when they choose to take up that kind of life."

An indistinct murmur from someone else in the room. A woman.

"No one condones murder, of course," said the first speaker, a gentleman and young by the sound of it. "But a girl of the streets! Could she honestly have expected to live a long life?"

I stood stock still. Could they be talking about Nell? Surely not.

The gentleman cackled with laughter. "And would you believe it? The constable was one of her customers! The constable!"

The maid caught hold of my arm as I started towards the room. "You can't go along there!" she said primly. "That's for the ladies and gentlemen." And she gave me a look of such insolence that it took my breath away.

I gave her back Heron's stare.

Her superior expression faltered. She hesitated, then withdrew her hand. I waited a moment longer. "I beg your pardon," she said in a low tone. I thought I heard anger in it. I waited still longer. "Sir," she added.

"Thank you," I said.

It was a small victory and, I reflected, could easily be unwise – it's not a good idea to get on the wrong side of servants. It would be sensible to offer an olive branch – I abandoned my expedition in search of the voice and gestured to the maid to carry on. She started up the new stair in outraged silence.

I turned to follow, but through the open door of the room from which the conversation emanated I caught a glimpse of a woman. She was young – perhaps twenty or twenty-two – and astonishingly beautiful, preening her dark ringlets and smoothing her fingers across her cheek. She was wearing only a shift. I never saw a woman more obviously a mistress. I wondered what kind of a houseparty this was to be.

The maid addressed not a word to me as we progressed up to another floor. She flung a door open so violently it banged back against the wall. "Your luggage'll be up," she said, sneering and adding with a flounce, "sir."

Her insolence didn't prevent her putting out a hand for her vail and staring me out until I put a coin on her palm. She turned up her nose at the penny and started downstairs at once.

I stood in the doorway, looking into a room with an inordinate number of windows on two sides – the room must be in one of the little turrets. It was sparsely furnished; a bed was covered with a plain white quilt, two chairs had green cane seats, an old armchair far too big for the room had wings so large as to severely restrict any occupant's view. A small square table with heavy scratches across its surface stood next to the bed. But it looked comfortable enough and I was pleasantly surprised to find the water in the jug on the washstand was piping hot.

I sauntered across to take in the view from the windows. On the left, they looked down on a wide expanse of grass and trees; on the right, they showed a terrace and the formal gardens, and even a hint of a canal beyond.

A servant struggled in with my bags. He put them down and stood, smiling blandly, with hand extended. He didn't seem to think the penny I gave him was adequate either, and muttered

20

his way out.

I unpacked – no servant to do that for me, unlike Heron who would of course have his valet with him. I washed, put on the best of my new shirts and brushed down my best coat before putting it back on. Regarding myself in the mirror, I thought I looked exactly what I was.

A tradesman.

Dinner was apparently according to town hours rather than country and was therefore late. I waited for a while, wondering if I'd be called, then thought it best to start down the endless succession of stairs.

The house was remarkably resonant; I could hear the voices of the ladies and gentlemen conversing in the hall and drawing room long before I reached the bottom of the stairs. The small rooms were crowded – there must be at least twenty people here, perhaps more. I glimpsed finely-dressed ladies in huge hooped skirts gossiping in the drawing room, the backs and shoulders of gentlemen in superfine coats. The servants were resplendent in gold and scarlet. I hesitated on the bottom step. It was all very well for Heron to tell me, as he had, that I was to dine with the guests, but my host had not indicated anything of the sort and nothing would get me off to a worse start than appearing presumptuous.

Heron was beckoning to me from the side of the hall; he was conversing with a boy whose back was turned: a boy of much my own height, build and colouring, dressed in a coat of particularly bright blue. When he turned, however, I saw he was older than I'd thought, not a boy but a young man.

"Patterson," Heron said. "I don't believe you've met our host. Alyson, Patterson here is in the way of becoming very notable in the world of music. Have you heard his Scotch dances? Hamilton of Edinburgh printed them last year."

"No, I don't believe I have heard them." The man smiled at me and I almost revised my view of his age again, so boyish was his grin. But I was too taken aback by my recognition of his voice.

He was the man I'd heard talking about Nell and Bedwalters.

4

They are inordinately fond of their history, and think
no other country half so distinguished.
[*A Frenchman's guide to England*, Retif de Vincennes
(Paris; published for the author, 1734)]

Edward Edmund Alyson was a charming man; he welcomed me as if I was the most honoured of guests. He asked me if my compositions were arousing much comment in the papers, if they had been acclaimed by any of the most knowledgeable judges of music. He trusted I knew his good friend, Dr Hayes of Oxford. Etc. Etc. And not one mention of such a sordid subject as money. In short, he treated me as a gentleman.

His other guests were not as generous: I saw sour looks cast my way as Alyson led Heron and me into the crowded drawing room. It was a small room, dark with wood panelling, and the curtains were drawn to shut out damaging sunlight. In a slight lull in the conversation I heard one man say, "… that musician fellow who solves mysteries."

Alyson looked interested but Heron was making compliments about the beauty of the wood panelling.

"Lord, yes," Alyson said. "But dreadfully old-fashioned. It'll all come out. Unless we just decide to tear the whole place down and rebuild, of course."

Someone said, "Females of that sort get what they deserve."

"But you can't have ruffians running about!" protested a plump gentleman with a tiny wig perched on a bald head. "They might get someone decent next time!"

"Allow me to introduce you to my wife," Alyson said. "Margaret, my dear, this is Mr Cuthbert Heron."

Heron looked annoyed at the mangling of his name but bowed over the lady's hand with punctilious politeness. I hardly glanced at her. I'd just seen the lady who sat two or three seats away. A lady in the palest of green gowns, with a ridiculous lace cap on her blonde hair, lace lappets dangling from the back of it down her elegant neck. Grey eyes regarded me icily.

Esther Jerdoun, the woman I loved. And had hopelessly argued with. Little more than a month ago, Mrs Jerdoun – an unmarried and damnably wealthy woman of thirty-nine – had steeled herself to proposition me, a poverty-stricken musician of twenty-seven. I'd turned her down. For her own sake. Society would ostracise her if she formed a liaison with me; they would think me a fortune hunter and Esther a fool. But inevitably, she'd been mortally offended.

I'd known that I must of course meet her again, but I'd hoped it would not be in so public a situation. And this houseparty was to last at least a month! I couldn't afford to make an exit, dignified or otherwise; not only did I need the money Alyson had promised me, but I might, if I were fortunate, find two or three new pupils among these ladies and gentlemen. So we were both trapped here, unless Esther chose to 'recall' a pressing engagement that demanded her attention elsewhere. I didn't know whether to be sorry or glad. It was painful to see her, but there was a great deal of pleasure mixed in with the pain.

Heron was trying to converse with Mrs Alyson; I looked at her for the first time and had my second shock of the evening. For she was the woman I had glimpsed through the open door of the bedroom. Not Alyson's mistress but his wife! Thank God I'd made no comment on the matter.

Alyson touched my arm. "You solve mysteries?" he said, with a boyish gleam of delight in his eyes. "How exciting! Are you trying to find the fellow who killed this girl?"

I didn't want to treat Nell and Bedwalters as a subject for gossip; I said, "Alas, I think the fellow's probably halfway to London by now."

Alyson looked as if he was about to say more but at that moment dinner was announced. He said impishly: "We will talk more later. Ladies and gentlemen…"

And he moved off to organise his guests as if he'd known

them all his life. Esther walked coolly past me, on the arm of a severe-looking man of fifty, who was paying her far too close attention.

We made our way into dinner; a host of servants pulled out chairs for the ladies, then went to stand at the sides of the room and look impressive. In the new fashion, Alyson arranged his guests alternately male and female, rather than men at the top of the table, women at the bottom. But there was a surplus of men, I noticed; even had I not been there, there were two men too many. As a result, I found myself with an elderly deaf lady on one side and a tall, rather gaunt man of middle age on the other; most of the guests were rather old, I thought.

Esther was near the head of the table on my own side; I couldn't see her, which was probably fortunate. I did hear Alyson call her 'Mrs Johnson', however. Heron was in the middle of the opposite side of the table, already looking bored with the chit chat of a plump woman on his left. I noticed that Alyson had put one of the few younger people next to himself – an attractive woman with red hair and a flirtatious manner; there was a man opposite me who kept straining to see what she was doing – a husband, no doubt.

I heard a snatch of a question from Alyson and fancied he was questioning Esther about me; I was already imagining censure in every gaze. Having tradesmen at dinner is not normal practice; I suspected that Heron and lawyer Armstrong had both intervened on my behalf. Perhaps they'd mentioned I was an organist – that usually conveys a little extra respectability.

The courses came and went with the efficient servants. Soup first, then fish, then some sort of jugged animal, hare no doubt. A huge chicken, together with virtually a whole side of beef, with some sickly-looking potatoes and cabbage cooked too long. Quails' eggs. A whole round of cheese. Then a flurry of tiny desserts in ornamental dishes, all heavily dosed in cream and wine.

And such a time it took. Conscious I was not used to such rich fare, I ate sparingly and inevitably finished quickly but many guests interspersed a bite or two with an anecdote or six and took an astonishingly long time to eat even a slice of beef. Heron, on the other side of the table, picked listlessly at his food and shot me wearied looks.

"Your friend doesn't look enamoured of the company," the gaunt middle-aged gentleman on my left said.

Startled, I glanced at him and saw a quiet smile that leavened the harshness in his face. He wore a rather old-fashioned wig, and his complexion suggested he was used to working outdoors. He had a distinctly odd accent.

"You're American, sir," I said.

A wider smile. "Philadelphia, sir. A city full of Quakers and tanneries. And I am more associated with the latter than the former. Though tanneries stink worse than Quakers usually do. Casper Fischer, sir, of German descent and proud of it."

I grinned back at him. "Charles Patterson. Newcastle born and bred. Are you visiting friends in England?"

"Family, sir. In search of a legacy owing to me. A sword and a book – are you well, sir?"

I'd spilled my wine in my surprise. The mention of a book had reminded me of Nell and Bedwalters – I felt guilty that I'd so easily forgotten them. "Just tiredness, sir. You have family in England *and* Germany?" Belatedly, I made the right connections. "Then your family must have come from Germany to Shotley Bridge. They're sword makers?"

He nodded. "Since time immemorial. In the town of Solingen in Germany. But some years ago, my grandfather decided to search for pastures new and came across with some other men to set up sword making at this – Shotley Bridge." He pronounced the name carefully. "Is that far from here?"

"A little way to the south of Newcastle. A day's ride – perhaps slightly more. But how did you end up in Philadelphia?"

He needed little prompting to expound his family's history. "There were three sons of which my father was the eldest. When my grandfather decided to come to England, my father seized the opportunity to strike out on his own, and headed for the Colonies, for a newer world. I was born a mere six months after my parents landed in Pennsylvania."

"A sword maker travelling to a Quaker city?" I asked, puzzled. "I know a few Quakers and they won't lift a finger to defend themselves even if they're attacked. Wasn't your father's decision a little – uncommercial?"

He laughed. "You've hit on a sore point, sir! Some Quakers in Pennsylvania indeed stuck to their principles but others decided pretty quickly that non-violence is not a good long-term policy when the natives are coming at you with bows and arrows. The two sides have not made up the argument yet. But it didn't matter to my father – he was a mediocre sword maker at best, though a very good businessman. He took to the tannery business and therefore so have I."

"And your legacy? The book and the sword?"

"Left to my father in *his* father's will and never sent to him. I took a fancy to reclaim the inheritance, and to see my cousins."

A woman's voice drifted up the table towards us, sharp and angry. "Clumsy fool! Crompton, get this idiot out of here."

The butler hurried forward; an errant servant was pushed from the room. Through the heads turned to the foot of the table, I saw Mrs Alyson, beautiful and pale, wiping her mouth with a napkin and lifting a glass of wine to her lips.

The meal wound to its interminable end; the ladies rose and departed, the men shifted to the host's end of the table and brandy was brought out. Two gentlemen wandered out on to the terrace to piss. Talk turned to horses and sport. Fischer dragged his chair closer to mine.

"Do you know this Shotley Bridge, sir? Is it a big place?"

It was years since I'd been near the town; my father had a pupil there once and I used to accompany him from time to time. But that was before I was twelve years old and the memories were hazy. Heron shifted nearer and offered a few observations – he had a cousin out that way himself, apparently.

"The book?" I asked, trying to sound normal. "Of what kind is it?"

"A book of tunes, sir."

"Then Patterson's your man," Heron said with a faint smile.

"Traditional tunes?"

"Church tunes. For the psalms. My grandfather was a keen amateur musician. When he came to England he was fascinated by the tunes sung here in church, and collected as many as he could find." Fischer sipped at his brandy, frowned down into it. I'd already discovered that it was not of the first quality; Heron has many times offered me his own brandy, which is excellent, and I've come to recognise inferior stuff. "The book has sentimental value – I have little that was my grandfather's. But in addition, Mr Patterson, we have great need of such books in America for our churches. And good singing teachers for that matter." He cast me a sideways look. "You wouldn't fancy a new life yourself, would you?"

"Patterson's no expert on singing," Heron said sourly.

I had to admit the truth of this although I wished he'd phrased it more diplomatically. "You need to visit Durham Cathedral, sir, there are excellent singers and teachers there. You may tempt one of them to travel."

The talk at the top of the table had turned to politics. In time of war, such talk is inevitable and we are on the verge of war. I was silent for a moment, trying to calm myself. If I started every time someone mentioned a book, I'd have a hard time of it. I was tired; I told myself a good night's sleep would make a great deal of difference.

"Don't blame all the trouble on the French!" Alyson said, laughing, to the severe-faced man who'd escorted Esther in to dinner. "I'm French myself, you know." He chuckled at the horrified faces around him. "Well, technically, at least – I was born in Calais. My parents married and lived there for some years. My father sold out of the army when he married and took to the wine trade."

I looked into the brandy again, thinking that father had not passed his expertise on to son. I glanced up and caught Heron's sarcastic glance, which nearly made me burst out laughing.

"The French!" the plump gentleman said. I fancied I'd seen him in Newcastle once or twice but didn't know his name. "Never mind the French, sir! It's the Americans to blame…"

A silence fell. Gazes drifted and settled on Fischer. He held up a hand humorously. "Don't look at me, gentlemen. It's the Georgians you need to question. I'm a law-abiding Pennsylvania man."

Alyson called for more brandy. Heron pushed away his glass, said, "I have a letter to write," and walked from the room. I glanced at Fischer. "Do you care to join the ladies, sir?"

"Indeed," he said, abandoning the brandy almost untouched. "And I think I might have another attempt at persuading you to join us in Philadelphia."

"I believe – "

"No, no," he said in good-humour. "Don't give me an answer now. Later."

I searched for a diplomatic answer. And heard myself saying: "I'd be interested to know more about this book…"

5

Marriage here is a flexible institution; as long as the
partners in any *affaire d'amour* are married, no one
cares much if they are not married to each other.
[Letter from Retif de Vincennes, to his brother Georges,
10 August 1736]

The ladies are always said to be eager to see the gentlemen after
dinner. The ladies were not pleased to see Fischer and myself. Mrs
Alyson was standing by the fireplace, straightening ornaments on
the mantelshelf – she gave us a cold hard stare. Another lady was
slouched back in her armchair, rubbing her distended stomach;
she sat up suddenly with a grimace and assumed a look of polite
boredom. An elderly dowager dozed over a book of drawings; two
middle-aged ladies were laughing over an anecdote.

"Patterson," Mrs Alyson said, as if I was a servant. "Play some
music." She jerked her head towards the harpsichord in the far
corner of the room.

A dozen gazes turned to me. Well, this was what I was here for,
after all; time to start earning my money. I excused myself to
Fischer and went to open the harpsichord.

The room was so small there was hardly space enough to edge
round the instrument; the stool was hard up against the wall and
I suspected I'd bang my elbow every time I played the lowest notes.
I knew too, by the dust when I lifted the lid, that the instrument
would be out of tune. Nor was there any light to read music by;
only one candle burned on the end of the mantelshelf and was
worse than useless, casting my shadow across the black keys.

Fortunately, any musician worth the name knows a hatful of
tunes by heart. I launched into a minuet, wincing at the out-of-
tune notes. Playing by heart did at least give me leisure to
look about. I spotted Esther at once, seated behind the two
gossiping ladies. She was staring at me expressionlessly. When she

met my gaze, she coolly returned her attention to her book.

What in heaven's name brought these people here, I wondered. Only the two middle-aged ladies were gaining any pleasure from the gathering – and Fischer, who was browsing along the pictures on the wall. The hostess was making no effort to entertain her guests – Mrs Alyson was restlessly moving backwards and forwards, glancing into the glass of pictures as she passed, putting up a hand to push a stray strand of hair back into place.

The gentlemen came in at last, and crowded us out, jolting the harpsichord as they pushed past. I carried on playing, though I was sure not a note could be heard in the hubbub. Close by, Alyson accosted Fischer at the corner of the mantelpiece.

"A sword and a book," I heard Alyson say, smiling.

"Alas," Fischer said. "A sword only. The book seems to have been sold."

I played a wrong note, and saw Esther glance at me sharply. No one else appeared to notice.

"It was in the family's possession ten years since," Fischer mused. "But two or three years back, a correspondent of mine came across it in a bookshop in Newcastle. A shop owned by a man called – Chartwell?"

"Charnley?" Alyson asked, smiling. He could apparently get names right when he chose.

"Indeed," Fischer said. "My friend asked the shopboy to put the book aside until he could write me about it. But the boy forgot and it was sold."

"You don't know the purchaser's name?"

"No one seems to know! I can't imagine why anyone should want it. My friend said it was in a very bad condition – the spine was evidently broken."

"But you're in no doubt it was your book?"

"It is distinctive," Fischer said, nodding. "A black binding, an inscription inside in German, and my grandfather's signature dated 1722 – the year before his death. I was asking Mr Patterson if he knew of it."

Alyson's gaze settled on me; he raised an enquiring eyebrow. I stopped playing. "I've not seen it but I do have friends who might be worth asking."

"Then you'll oblige me by asking," Alyson said. "You don't know our Mr Pattinson well yet, Mr Fischer, but he has quite a reputation for solving mysteries. Now, do come and meet my friend, Ridley."

He bore Fischer off across the room. 'Our Mr Pattinson' indeed. You'd think Alyson had lived in the area all his life!

His wife swept by again. "Play, Mr Patterson," she said. "That's what you're here for."

I played, while the ladies gossiped and the gentlemen talked about hunting. The severe-faced man plumped himself down beside Esther; she closed her book and greeted him with a look of cool politeness. I played on, until I spotted Heron making his way through the party with an assurance that cleared his path without his needing to ask. He presented me with a folded note.

"A letter for you, Patterson. Sent by messenger from Newcastle." He turned away, took two dishes of tea from a passing gentleman and handed one to me before sipping at the other himself. An heroic gesture; Heron loathes tea.

The note was warm from Heron's hand and was addressed to me in Hugh's writing. I broke open the seal.

There's the very devil to pay here, Hugh had written without preamble. *Bedwalters is refusing to leave Nell's room. Mrs McDonald wants to turn him out and install another girl in the room but he's bringing down all the force on the law on her and saying nothing can be done until Nell's spirit disembodies. And Mrs Bedwalters has descended on the house not once but twice to tell her husband to come home but he's adamant he will not. He's saying he will never go home, that he will live there, with Nell, permanently – he's even offered Mrs McDonald rent. (Which she is inclined to accept.) I can't keep going down there to stop the arguments, Charles! What will it do to my reputation to be seen in a place like that? For God's sake, come back. Or at least write to Bedwalters and persuade him to go home.*

Yr Obed^t Servt

Hugh Demsey

Hugh didn't care to be seen in such a house but he didn't seem bothered about *my* reputation. He wasn't thinking sensibly – how could I leave here within hours of arriving? Especially when I wanted permission to go back to town when Nell's spirit disembodied. I could write to Bedwalters, certainly, but I hardly thought a note from me would persuade him.

"Trouble?" Heron asked. I gave him the note. He read it, considered, gave it back. "The man has more courage than I gave him credit for."

That made me pause. He was right; Bedwalters's behaviour *was* courageous – I'd not seen it in that light before. To throw away respectability, home, reputation for the sake of love – I'd not realised I was staring at Esther until I met her gaze. Still icy.

My situation with Esther was entirely different, I told myself. Poor Nell had had no reputation to lose; she could not have been damaged by Bedwalters's devotion. Esther stood to lose a great deal by any selfishness on my part.

"What will you do?" Heron asked.

I went upstairs to write a letter, not sure if that last question of Heron's had been about Bedwalters or Esther.

Of course, there was no notepaper or ink in my room, so I went downstairs again to find the library, where considerate hosts usually keep such things. I got lost, inevitably, and was on the verge of calling out for a servant, when I glimpsed bookshelves through an open door and went in to find a room shrouded in twilight; a single candle burned on a large central table. A few books were scattered on the table; I turned one over idly and found it to be music in a strange old notation. Written by a man called Dowland, evidently. How quickly composers are forgotten, I thought – maybe one day my own music would suffer the same fate.

Pen, paper and sealing wax were on a small shelf in one corner and I took them to the table, where I could have the benefit of the candlelight. I'd hardly sat down when a voice said: "Good day, my son."

A faint brightness slid across the tarnished wood of the table-top; its feebleness suggested the spirit must be very old, eighty or more, which meant the living man must have died around 1666. He must have lived through Cromwell's Commonwealth and King Charles's days.

"I am Monsignor Collins," the spirit said with great dignity, lingering at the foot of the candlestick. "Pray do continue. Do not let me disturb you."

"Monsignor?" I echoed, startled.

"You're not prejudiced against the church, I hope, my son."

"No, no, not at all." I hesitated. "You mean, the Church of Rome."

"Oh, indeed." The spirit was positively cheerful about it. "I'm the black sheep of the family. Everyone else has followed the Protestant faith since Good King Henry brought it to England." He sounded rueful. "I've always been one for being different. But don't let me stop you writing your letter."

"It's a private matter."

"And you're afraid I'll read it and pass the details on? Never fear, sir – I never learnt to read!"

A churchman who couldn't read? I began to think the spirit had been less a churchman and more a rogue.

"It's very cheering to have so many people in the house," the spirit murmured as I hunted for a knife to sharpen the quill. "The old master liked his solitude. And his money."

I plainly wasn't going to be rid of him and I've found, through painful experiment, that it's wise to be friendly with spirits. "A miser, was he?"

"Careful. Didn't like spendthrifts. Turned his nephew down more than once when he came applying for a loan."

"He's got everything now," I pointed out.

"Everything comes to he who waits," said the spirit sententiously.

The door opened; the spirit was gone in an instant. Edward Alyson hesitated on the threshold. His bright blue coat was rumpled, his face red, and he walked unsteadily. But he talked sensibly enough.

"This business with the girl," he said, with good humour. He supported himself on the edge of the table as he eased into the chair opposite me. "Surely it's not worth pursuing? The girl was a whore."

It was unlikely he – or any man of his class – could be brought to regard Nell as a human being, rather than a mere convenience for gentlemen's worst urges, so I merely said: "As your guest suggested, a man who kills once may kill again and next time he may choose someone of – " I chose my words carefully " – more standing in the community."

Alyson lounged back in his chair, grinning. "I'll not persuade you, I see. You're a man who finishes what he starts."

"Always," I agreed.

He jumped up, wandered round the room, trailing his fingers across the spines of books. "I'm told you've dealt with three or four matters of this kind."

"Three."

"It must be devilishly exciting!"

I contemplated the past. "A little frightening at times. But satisfying to bring someone to justice."

His hand settled on a book's spine, hesitated. He hooked his finger over the top; I winced as I heard the binding tear.

"I thought it must be here somewhere," he said in delight, and brought the volume across to show me. It was a large Bible, of the sort most commonly seen on lecterns in churches, and when he lifted the heavy front cover, I saw a long list of names hand-written on the fly leaf. Browning ink recorded the names of children as far back as 1649. The last entry read:

Jany 13, 1713. Maria married this day in Calais to Richard Edward Alyson. The tastes of women are ever mysterious.

"He didn't approve," Alyson said unnecessarily and with great glee. He tapped the page. "You note he didn't add my birth!"

He grinned. "I was born in August, sir. Care to work out the implications?"

I made a show of calculating the dates, wondering why he felt obliged to wash his dirty linen in front of me. "You were born seven months after the marriage."

He grinned again. "The impetuosity of love! The passion that cannot bear to wait for a piece of paper!"

I said nothing. Passion that cannot bear to wait for a piece of paper often never gets the paper at all. Maria could so easily have been left unmarried with an infant son, ostracised by both family and society.

"Are you married, Pattinson?"

"No," I said, gritting my teeth against the urge to correct him.

"It was the best day of my life when Margaret said she'd be mine," he said. "Is she not beautiful, Pattinson?"

"Very." What else did he expect me to say?

He was off on a rambling discourse, speaking of his wife in an obviously besotted way, extolling her many virtues. And, as if on cue, the door opened once more; Mrs Alyson stood on the threshold, her hair and dress perfectly in order, her jewels sparkling at throat and ears. I'd thought her beautiful but cold; now, as her gaze lighted on her husband, I saw a brightness in her eyes and a gleam of gladness.

Alyson went to her and slid his arm round her waist. As I was about to avert my eyes, he turned her round and led her into the hall. The next moment, I glimpsed them slowly climbing the stairs; his lips were on the nape of her neck, she was laughing.

"What is the world coming to?" the spirit said, sliding on to the table again. "I was all for the pleasures of the world, when I was alive, but a little decorum is necessary!"

"I think they must be newly married," I said. In truth, I felt more than a little envious.

Dear Hugh [I wrote].
If Bedwalters is as you've described him, I don't see what I can do. You know that once he sets his mind on something he'll not be

moved. You count his staying with Nell, even past death, as folly – well, I have a certain sympathy with that view, but it takes courage to do something of that sort. Let him stay.

In the meantime, you can put about town that he suspects the girl can give him her murderer's name and he stays for that reason. No one will believe you but it will safeguard his reputation. Besides, the first shock and determination will soon wear off; such intensity never lasts. Once he's spoken to the girl's spirit and laid his hands on the murderer, he'll start to pick up the threads of his life again. All you (and Mrs Bedwalters) require is a little patience.

I read over what I'd written and found it more than a little sanctimonious and full of hints to myself. *Such intensity never lasts.* Did I hope my feelings for Esther would wane, given no hope to feed on? And that remark about courage: Heron's comments had affected me more than I'd thought. Bedwalters had courage to stay with his love; I needed courage to stay away from mine.

I felt I owed Hugh a more courteous and friendly ending, so I scribbled:

I seem besieged by mysteries concerning books today. First there was the tome poor Nell was holding for her customer, now there's an American gentleman staying here hunting a book that's part of his inheritance.

I gave Hugh a description of the book and suggested that if he wanted a distraction, he might like to visit Charnley's bookshop, and see if he could find out what had happened to it.

I'd be pleased to do the American gentleman a favour, I wrote, *For apart from Alyson and Heron, he's the only one here who thinks a tradesman can be a human being too.*

And I added: *How odd to find two such puzzles on one day. And totally unconnected too.*

6

**The lower orders are kept so much in subjection
that there is no telling what they might do.**
[Letter from Retif de Vincennes, to his wife, Régine, 16 July 1736]

I added my signature, sealed the note and wrote Hugh's
direction on the front of the sheet, then went in search of a
servant. It was a surprisingly difficult task; the footmen had all
withdrawn, along with the dirty dishes, from the dining room,
where two or three gentlemen were pondering the possibilities
of a game of cards. Not a maid in sight, nor the butler. Finally, I
spotted a footman crossing the hall; eighteen years old at most
and a magnificent six feet tall. And whether because of his extra
height, or a consciousness of my ambivalent position, he looked
down on me with more than a touch of insolence.

He took the note from me between forefinger and thumb as if
it was dirty, assured me he'd find a messenger to send it off at
once and waited, with unending patience, until I took the hint
and dug in my pockets for a coin. His mouth twitched as he saw
the slightness of my offering. I'd been here half a day and I was
already aware I hadn't brought enough money with me. And
Heron had suggested the other guests had come here to *save*
money! I daresay he himself would adhere rigidly to his
customary policy of offering no vails to servants; his resultant
unpopularity would bother him not at all.

I went back, reluctantly, to the drawing room. It was plain
when I got there that no one was in the mood for music. Too
much had been drunk, and a great deal stronger than tea. Two
gentlemen were openly snoring; the plump gentleman was
wooing the red-headed woman who'd caught Alyson's attention.
Even Casper Fischer was flirting outrageously with one of the
older ladies of the party. I wandered about the room aimlessly,
inspecting pictures without seeing them, glancing out into the

hall where the insolent footman was now conversing with Edward Alyson – our host had apparently decided after all that it was not polite to desert his guests.

Of Claudius Heron there was no sign. Nor of Esther.

I didn't imagine they were together; they don't particularly like each other. I wondered if either of them might be outside on the terrace. The windows in both drawing and dining rooms gave access on to the terrace; I pushed them open, and closed them quickly behind me as I saw one of the ladies shiver melodramatically.

The setting sun was laying down bands of pearl-pink and green across the sky; above dark hulks of trees, the evening star glittered brightly. I leant on the terrace railings; below, the formal garden stretched away to a hint of gleaming water, and thence to shadowy woods and meadows against the translucent sky.

Someone moved at the far end of the terrace. A blur of pale dress and paler hair. Esther Jerdoun.

I hesitated, then walked towards her. She was holding a glass of wine; a cobweb-thin scarf thrown over her arms and shoulders protected her against the chills of the evening. She waited, silent and still, watching me, intimidating me.

We stood, looking at each other. Then she moved suddenly, restlessly, looking away from me. "Mr Patterson." Her tone was flat, expressionless.

"Mrs Jerdoun." The title is, of course, purely honorary; the lady is not married. Although she has made clear, in a way no lady would usually contemplate, that she would like to be. And I'd refused her. No, I'd done worse than that; I'd pretended not to understand, in order to avoid a confrontation.

I'd been afraid I might lose the argument.

We stared out at the darkening sky.

"I have been talking with Claudius Heron," she said at last. "He tells me the constable's girl has been killed."

This was not the sort of subject any lady should know about. I should change the subject at once. I nodded. "She was killed by a customer."

"Women in her profession must run such risks almost daily," she said with a trace of anger.

"I don't think it's as bad as that," I said. "They get beatings and rough treatment, yes. But not many are killed. Relative to their numbers, I mean."

That was hardly the point, I thought; such considerations would mean nothing to Bedwalters. For that matter, they meant nothing to me.

We stood on the elegant terrace of the elegant, if old-fashioned, house, a woman of high social standing and wealth, and a young man of neither, contemplating the sunset. I was trying to think of an unexceptional topic of conversation and thought Esther must be doing the same. I should have known better. After a moment, she said, expressionlessly: "I take it you have not changed your mind."

I grimaced inwardly. But I knew I'd done the right thing; all I had to do now was stand by my decision. "No," I said, and stared out into the darkness, realising that once again, despite my last rebuff, she'd summoned the courage to approach me and that, once again, I'd rejected her. Damn, damn, damn.

She said nothing more. I heard her steady, even breathing in the silence of the twilight. From the drawing room behind us came the sudden splutter of laughter.

"You must know why I think the way I do," I said, despite myself. "You must know it's impossible for us to – "

"I had not marked you down for a coward, Mr Patterson," she said.

I caught my breath. She knew, *must* know, how that accusation would rankle with any man. She was trying to provoke me. "I am not a rascal who'd destroy a lady's reputation," I retorted.

"My reputation is *my* affair," she said coldly.

Another silence. A nightjar called; someone in the dining room dropped a glass with a crash.

"There appears to be nothing more to be said," Esther said.

"No."

She did not move.

Belatedly, I realised she expected me to go and leave her to her solitude. Despite everything, I did not wish to go, to move from her presence, to lose that tiny regular intake of breath, that delicate scent she wore, the rustle of her dress as she shifted slightly.

I pushed myself away from the railing. "I – I do believe I shall go for a walk in the gardens," I said as if we had been having the most innocuous of conversations. "Such a lovely night."

"Indeed," she said emotionlessly, and stood aside to let me go down the steps to the garden below.

The last light was sufficient to show me my way down the gravel walk. I strolled along, making a show of inspecting the bedraggled, overgrown flowerbeds, exhibiting my careless nonchalance should anyone be watching from the house. As I reached the middle of the garden, I cut across to the fountain sitting in the very centre and inspected its dry basin full of dead leaves. As I did so, I risked a glance back at the house. The drawing room was ablaze with light; I saw the multi-coloured backs of the ladies. Candles still burned in the windows of the dining room where the gentleman had settled down to their cards. Alyson was laughing with them as he dealt. Upstairs, two or three rooms seeped light from behind curtains.

The terrace was empty.

I walked on. Beyond the garden was a stretch of lawn, then an ornamental canal, gleaming brightly in the last of the daylight. The canal had once had stone walls but many of the stones had crumbled into the water and the banks looked slippery and dangerous. One or two patches of mud lingered, presumably from the last rains. A gentle slope led up to a stone bridge; I leant on the wide parapet and looked down into stagnant, weed-filled water. It stank.

Beyond the bridge, a path led into a small wood. I pottered along it, through the gloomy trees, along a path broad and pale, brooding about Bedwalters and Nell and the murderer who had struck so coolly, so brutally. That glimpse I'd had of the world that ran alongside our own worried me – it always portended danger. But the murderer – the apprentice – must be miles from town by now – the chances were we would never know who he was.

I came to the kitchen garden wall and a path that led towards the house on one side and the village road on the other; I stood and kicked at the earth of the path. This was no good. For all I knew the ladies were demanding to know where I was; I had a living to earn and had better go and earn it. I strode back through the wood.

As I crossed the bridge over the canal, I realised more time had passed than I'd anticipated. The drawing room looked empty, and gloomy, most of the candles snuffed out; I saw a female servant cross the window gathering up tea dishes. The dining room was well-lit still but apparently empty.

I would not sleep. I knew that already. A strange bed is never particularly comfortable and there were too many mysteries to worry over, too much concern for Bedwalters and Nell. And as for Esther…

I'd just put my foot to the bottom step up to the terrace when the last candle in the drawing room was blown out. I stood in sudden darkness for a moment, cursing – the dining room candles further along cast no light here. If I didn't hurry, I was likely to find the servants had locked me out. I groped for the stone balustrade at the side of the steps –

And felt warm flesh beneath my hand.

The world slipped away from me in a burst of pain.

**And the servants are insolent! I'd not have a
single one of them in my house.**
[Letter from Retif de Vincennes, to his sister, Agnés, 18 June 1736]

Voices eddied around me like water, an indistinct ebb and flow of words. Someone said in annoyance, "… but I wanted to talk about the woodland." I tried to protest: *no, I'd walked through the wood safely – I was attacked on the steps.* A soothing voice murmured; a warm hand was heavy on my shoulder. Alyson said, "No, no, my dear Ridley. Poachers are much more exciting!" My head was briefly full of midnight skies and stars in another world.

The hand pressed down on my shoulder. I prised open my eyes, winced at bright light and squeezed them shut again. Someone said: "He's awake."

Candle flames flickered when I opened my eyes again. Blotches of darkness resolved themselves into gentlemen: the plump gentleman – he was the one who'd mentioned the woodland; the red-faced man who'd been too friendly with Esther; Claudius Heron, in shirt sleeves and waistcoat, looking at me with the oddest expression, a mixture of resignation and concern. His was the hand urging me to be still.

Edward Alyson bent over me with a glass of brandy in his hand. "Drink this, Pattinson. It'll make you feel better."

I doubted that. I doubted anything could take away the head-ache pounding behind my eyes. I struggled to sit up, clutching the pale back of the couch on which I lay. Leaving, I saw with horror, a vivid smear of blood.

I felt for my head. My hand encountered a ridiculously large bandage wound round my temples.

"You fell," Alyson said, like a man encouraging a child to remember. "You misjudged the steps in the dark and tumbled down."

"They were slippery," the plump gentleman – Ridley – grumbled. "We've had far too much rain recently."

I had not stumbled or slipped. I remembered putting my hand on top of someone else's on the balustrade. I remembered a blow to my head. I started to say exactly that, but Heron intervened. "It was nothing of the sort," he said curtly. "I know what I saw." He glanced at me. "I heard a noise outside, looked out of my bedroom window and saw someone standing behind you. Not that I could tell who it was – it was too damned dark."

He overrode a faint suggestion of *servant* from Ridley. "Do servants generally go around hitting guests over the head?" He nodded at me. "I shouted to warn you but I was too late. Nevertheless, the fellow must have heard me – he took fright and ran. So I hurried down to rescue you."

That was embarrassing, I thought: to have to be *rescued* on my first night at a gentleman's house. But Alyson was in high spirits, explaining to the others how he'd met Heron in the hall, as he came back from the library, and hurried out with him to help me. Belatedly, I saw a little pile of books on the table beside the sofa; Alyson must have been looking for bedtime reading, although, given his obvious affectionate relations with his wife, I was surprised he had time to read.

"A pity it didn't happen earlier," Ridley said, as if I'd been inconsiderate. He rubbed his plump stomach. "If we'd still been playing cards in here, we'd have seen it all."

"Poachers!" Alyson said, with more gaiety than I appreciated. "They were hunting for my rabbits, saw Pattinson here, thought he might have a guinea or two in his pocket and went after him instead!" He grinned, like a little boy given a longed-for present. "This is exciting – London has nothing on this! Poachers, my God!"

"So near the house?" Ridley said horrified.

"Men like these are always daring," Alyson said.

"They didn't dare in my day."

It was hot in the room. I lay back, sipping Alyson's dreadful brandy, and let them argue. I could tell by Heron's expression that the idea of thieving poachers didn't convince him, but the only other possible reason for the attack was that it had some connection with Nell's death. And that was no better than the poacher theory; what fool would travel seven miles out of Newcastle to attack me, particularly when it must be obvious I'd not the slightest idea who'd killed Nell?

Unless… I toyed with the idea of one of the servants being the killer. They'd only arrived the day before Alyson, the day of the murder. Perhaps one of them was the villain? He'd killed Nell, hurried off to take up his new post, then been horrified to see me among the guests; he'd panicked, tried to get rid of me…

It didn't sound convincing. If I'd been a servant in that situation, I would simply have run.

I surfaced from my thoughts to find that Heron, as usual, was taking charge. "Patterson will be a great deal better off in his room."

"Of course." Alyson ushered his other guests out; they went grumbling. Heron took the brandy glass from my hand. He slung my arm around his shoulders, heaved me up. The room tilted alarmingly then steadied.

"I'll see Patterson to his room," Heron said. "Don't feel obliged to stay up, Alyson."

Alyson flushed. "I don't neglect my guests!"

I looked on as they stared each other out, and was tempted to grin. Alyson was very affable, and conscientious in his wish to be the complete host, but he didn't have the casual assurance and confidence of Heron. Of course the latter was around forty years old, Alyson's senior by nigh on twenty years, and it was inevitable he had greater authority, but it was clear that Alyson didn't much like his ruthless display of it, or appreciate being dismissed in his own house.

"If you're recovered, Patterson," Heron said. Not a question, an order. I smiled at Alyson, thanked him for his assistance, apologised for making so much trouble. At my side, Heron muttered with impatience. I thought him unfair – Alyson clearly meant well. I rather liked him.

I submitted to Heron's guidance; he took a firm grip on my elbow and steered me out of the room, picking up a nightlight from a table at the foot of the stairs. My head was clearing and I navigated the uneven steps and creaking landings without too much difficulty. All the same, I was glad to see my bed.

Heron pushed me down on to it, looking about him with disdain in the faint candlelight. "I wouldn't house a dog in a room this small."

I'd thought the room spacious; it was twice the size of my own lodgings and ten times more luxurious.

"What happened?" Heron demanded. He set the candle on the bedside table, pushed it safely away from the edge.

I eased myself against the pillows, outlined what little I could remember. "I think you probably saw more than I did. Didn't you see his face at all?"

He shook his head. "By the time I'd thrown up my window and called out, he was off. You were merely two blurs."

"But you recognised me."

"By your walk. And I knew you were in the gardens – I saw you strolling down towards the canal earlier."

"Poachers?" I asked meditatively.

"Nonsense," Heron said. "Not unless there is a particularly stupid breed of them in these parts. Poachers avoid all human contact on their expeditions."

"Then it must surely be someone connected with Nell and Bedwalters."

He strolled across to the nearest window, peered out. "That seems extremely unlikely."

"The servants are all new. Who knows what they might have got up to in Newcastle?"

"Lawyer Armstrong hired them – he is a cautious man and would not accept anyone in the least dubious."

I was so tired I could have fallen asleep sitting up. "There's one man no one knows – the American, Casper Fischer."

Heron let the curtain drop, leant against the wall. "Why should he kill a streetgirl? And he's too old, surely. You told me the other girl saw an apprentice. Fischer is much too old to be mistaken for an apprentice."

"Then I've no ideas left," I said in exasperation. My head was starting to thump again; the respite had been brief. "It must have been poachers after all – or a wandering vagabond intent on stealing what trifles he could find."

"Perhaps," Heron said.

He stood impassive and silent in the half-shadows of the room; I said awkwardly. "I haven't thanked you properly for – *rescuing* me."

He pushed himself upright. "Perhaps, like Alyson, I feel starved of a little excitement."

I'd noticed before that he didn't accept gratitude well. He added, "You will of course note that I have long ceased to urge you not to get involved in these matters."

I winced.

"Exactly so," he said. "I recognise futility when I encounter it. But I still think you should be careful, until we have at least some idea of what is going on here."

I stared into the candlelight. "I still think Nell's murderer is long gone from the area. London, at least."

He nodded. "I'm inclined to agree."

He offered to help me undress and climb into bed properly but I was too tired to budge and declined. I was asleep almost before he was out of the door.

I slept fitfully, plagued by the headache and hampered by the bandage round my head which prevented me from getting comfortable. At one point, I thought I heard the arrival of a carriage, the rattle of wheels on gravel, the muted greetings of servants. But sleep overwhelmed me again and when I woke, heavy and unrefreshed, I was inclined to think I'd been dreaming.

The sun was high across the floor of the room, shining through gaps in the curtains. I staggered up, suddenly feeling ravenous. The mirror showed me a wild-eyed apparition. The bandage had been inexpertly applied; blood darkened the left side of my face. My shirt was crumpled from being slept in and my new breeches were streaked with mud.

I heard a scratch on the door a second before it opened. Fowler, Heron's manservant, came in bearing shaving gear, grinning as he took me in. "Getting yourself in trouble again, Patterson? And leaving the rest of us to pick up the pieces?" He stepped back to admire my clothes. "They'll need a good bit of cleaning. Sit down and let me have a look at that cut. One of these days you'll be calling on me to get you out of trouble again."

He pushed me down into one of the cane chairs and started to unwind the bandage around my head. Fowler is not one of those servants who believes in being deferential, except to his employer. Or perhaps he regards me as a servant too. He certainly seems to think I've been severely restricted in my experience of the world and in urgent need of education. He's helped me before; not so long ago, he was sniping at murderers on rooftops in my company – and a fine shot he is too. I'd not want to get in front of him. Heron picked him up years ago in London, rescued him from transportation and made him respectable.

Allegedly. I never saw anyone less respectable in my life. A lean, deceptively strong man, with no loyalty to anyone but himself and Heron.

He grinned at me in the mirror. I winced as his fingers brushed the wound on the back of my head; he set about washing it and unmatting the hair with capable hands. "Nothing much," he said dismissively. "Hardly worth a headache, even."

"You've had much worse?"

"Of course. I told his Lordship as much but he would insist I take a look at it. He's gone down to the village to enquire after poachers. Want to hear what I think happened?"

"No."

"It was Mr Alyson."

"Alyson?" I started, and gasped as my hair pulled in his grasp.

"Why the devil should he attack me?"

"Flat broke." Fowler leant forward to whisper in my ear. "Spends what he doesn't have. Always did."

I sat up straighter. He dipped the cloth he was using into my washing water, leaving it alarmingly pink. "*Always did*? You know him?"

"Not *know*, exactly," Fowler said, giving me a meaningful look in the mirror. "Not in the biblical sense."

I sighed. "I didn't mean that way!" Fowler's tastes have apparently never run to women, a fact that I consider none of my business, and a secret I rather wish had never come my way. A dangerous secret for Fowler. "Did you come across him in London?"

"Five or six years back, before I was lucky enough to take a potshot at Heron. A baby sheep ready for fleecing."

"Six years ago he'd have been seventeen."

"And looked younger. He couldn't game for love nor money but thought it was just a matter of time *until his luck turned*."

"Where did he get his money?"

Fowler finished his minstrations, combed my hair down and regarded me critically in the mirror. "It'll do. Sit back so I can shave you. He kept disappearing – he'd lose a fortune he didn't have, get out of town, come back a month or two later with his pockets full, pay off his creditors and start the whole process again. Trustees, he said."

"Trustees gave him money?" I echoed. "Then they're not like any trustees I've ever known."

"Well," Fowler said, draping a cloth round my shoulders. "Doesn't matter now, does it? Now he has his hands on this estate. He can indulge his tastes in cards and wine and women."

"He was probably borrowing from moneylenders," I said, "against the expectation of his inheritance. And talking of women…"

"No," Fowler said firmly. "They're not. I'd stake my life on it. Not married."

"I thought not," I said. "But she's not a typical mistress – I'd lay odds she was respectably reared."

"She'll want what women always want – money."

I sighed and changed the subject. "Did someone arrive late last night?"

"Old man, young wife. Just back from their bridal trip."

"Do these people have names?"

"It's your friend," Fowler said, with a devilish gleam in his eye. "Ord."

He was about to lather my cheeks; I stared at him. "Philip Ord? Good Lord." Ord and I had crossed paths several times in the past, most notably just before his marriage; he did not regard me with any favour. "I used to teach his wife, Lizzie Saint as was. Daughter of the printer in Newcastle."

"Married into trade, did he? Must have been hard up."

I closed my eyes, submitted to Fowler's swift and competent work – it was strangely soothing. Well, at least there'd be one person who'd listen to my playing; Lizzie was a keen harpsichordist herself. I wondered how she and Philip Ord were dealing together; she'd been head over heels in love with him, like the innocent girl she was, and he'd had a great desire for her father's dowry, like the ruthless businessman he was. And twenty years difference in age between them…

"There was something else," Fowler said, pausing in drawing the razor down my left cheek.

Dozy again and trying to keep at bay that nagging ache that kept prodding at the back of my head, I said lazily, "What?"

His eyes met mine in the mirror; light winked off the razor's edge. "Don't get Heron involved in anything dangerous."

Yes, I thought, staring into his reflected gaze, there was still a considerable portion of the ruffian lurking beneath Fowler's bland exterior. "I can't govern what Heron does," I pointed out.

His mouth twisted wryly. "No one can. I know that better than anyone. But you don't need to encourage him."

I knew that wasn't a request. It was a warning.

8

There is no culture here. They have a fetish for some composer of German origin, who writes Italian operas. I long to introduce them to *true* opera, the French operas of M. Rameau.
[Letter from Retif de Vincennes, to his brother, Georges, 6 May 1736]

On my way down to breakfast, I heard low furious voices coming from one of the bedrooms. It took me a moment to work out that the room in question was the Alysons'. Husband and wife, if that was what they truly were, were having a bitter argument. I couldn't quite hear what was being said; I hurried on, before I could be tempted to eavesdrop.

The breakfast room was a small chamber in the corner of one of the turrets; a long table and a longer sideboard loaded with serving dishes were pretty much the only furniture. I couldn't understand why anyone should have a room especially for breakfast when they already had a perfectly good dining room.

There were only two occupants. The severe gentleman who had been eying Esther yesterday was reading one of the London newspapers over a massive plate of eggs and devilled kidneys; on the other side of the table, Casper Fischer was just rising from his chair. He looked far too alert for a man who'd not been long out of his bed.

"My dear sir, are you well?" He greeted me with enthusiasm. "I hear one of the local villains had a go at you last night."

I gave him an abbreviated version of what had happened; Fischer sympathised wholeheartedly. His tone was just right, conveying sufficient sympathy to make me feel he was genuinely concerned for my well-being, but not lingering on the matter so long as to embarrass me.

"You need some fresh air," he said at last. "Marvellous for clearing a bruised head. I was just about to go for a walk. Nothing too long – only four or five miles. Why don't you come with me?"

"I'll probably have to play for one of the ladies," I said, trying to sound regretful.

"Of course," he said immediately, without rancour. "Work must always come first."

Now that was a sentiment I'd never expected to hear in a gentleman's house.

The severe gentleman cleared his throat, obviously annoyed at our talking; Fischer went off for his walk and I helped myself to coffee and a plate of bread and cheese. Sitting under that fierce glare would probably curdle the milk, so I retired to the library. But it was already occupied by Heron, writing letters at the large table in the middle of the room. He had a dish of coffee and a slice of toast to one side, and was dressed in sombre brown, clothes more suitable for a day's work on his estates than for a houseparty. He glanced up as I came in, finished his sentence and put down his pen.

"I've been to the village," he said.

"Fowler said you had," I admitted. "My thanks for lending me his assistance, sir."

He waved away my gratitude. "I have spoken to the local justice. There are no poachers in this area."

I laughed, and took the chair he nodded to. "Don't all countrymen say that?"

"In this case it appears to be true," he said dryly. "The local justice was annoyed by half his deer disappearing and undertook to wage war on the villains. Three weeks ago, he sentenced seven men to transportation and cleared the country of poachers at one fell swoop. They are all now in Newcastle, awaiting a ship."

"Can we be sure he caught them all?"

"Naturally not, but the strong possibility is that he did. The matter is more complicated than that, however." Heron broke his dry toast into two pieces. "Six of the men left families that are of course now destitute, and at least two of those families have male children of an age to take to poaching themselves. They

51

may have to," he added, "if they don't want their siblings to starve."

"And you think one of these boys was out on a poaching expedition, saw me and thought I was an easy target."

Heron broke the toast into smaller pieces. "Possibly."

"Forgive me, sir," I said, "but you don't sound convinced."

He sighed. "It is plain you were hit by someone much the same height as yourself. The oldest boy is twelve years old. He may of course be unnaturally tall but it seems unlikely."

I contemplated the view from the window; Fischer was striding down the formal gardens, two spaniels bounding joyously at his heels. Heron put down the fragments of toast uneaten, and sipped at his coffee.

"If I was not the victim of a poacher," I said, "then there's an inevitable conclusion to be drawn."

"Indeed," Heron said.

"Either it was one of the servants trying to rob me…"

Heron shook his head. "Why risk attacking you in person when they could slip into your room when you were not there and take what they want?"

"… or it was one of our fellow guests."

Heron set the coffee dish down very precisely. "Interesting, do you not think?"

"No," I retorted. "Believe me, sir, I have offended no one here, disadvantaged no one, cheated no one. Indeed, until yesterday, I knew no one, except for yourself and Mrs Jerdoun."

"I suggest you think a little more deeply," Heron recommended. He went on, "Did you see Mr and Mrs Ord have arrived, fresh from their wedding trip?"

Heron has a low opinion of marriage; his own was apparently merely tolerable, and its end, with the death of his wife, a great relief. His cynicism showed in his voice. I recognised he'd drawn a line under the previous part of the conversation.

I nodded. "I heard their carriage. They arrived remarkably late."

"A broken wheel, I understand." He picked up his pen again.

"Do you think Mrs Ord looks well?"

"I haven't seen her yet."

"I fancy Ord did not much like your influence with her before the marriage."

"Lizzie Saint was my pupil," I said, "and a keen musician. Nothing more."

"I never thought otherwise." He picked up his pen again, returned his attention to his letter. "I will let you know if I hear anything more about the poachers, Patterson."

Unmistakeably dismissed, I picked up my breakfast and went into the hall. Unlike Heron, I knew Ord's objection to me was nothing to do with his wife. I'd recovered some letters that would almost certainly have ruined any chance of his marriage taking place; worse, I knew exactly what the letters contained.

But the thought of Philip Ord riding over in darkness on the off-chance of having an opportunity to dispose of me? Preposterous.

I was hesitating in the hall when the breakfast room door opened and the plump gentleman – what was his name? Ridley, William Ridley – came out, followed closely by a scarlet-and-gold-clad servant.

"My lawyer? At long last, what the devil's kept the fellow? Where have you put him? Very well, I'll go and talk to him. Tell your master he's here."

The servant bowed and they took themselves off in different directions. It looked, I thought, as if Alyson was about to discover the legal complications of running a large estate. And I thought of Esther and her estates in Norfolk and Northumberland – the estates that must inevitably pass, if she married, to her husband. That was yet another reason – if one more was needed – why I could not marry her. What experience did I have in such matters? I'd probably ruin her inheritance in months.

I heard my name called and looked up the stairs to see the two lively middle-aged ladies of the previous evening waving down at me.

"Mr Patterson!" one called. "We were saying how delightful it would be to have a few songs. Will you play for us?"

I said I would. The ladies disappeared upstairs to 'fetch the music'; I suspected this would occupy half an hour at least and took my bread and cheese out to the terrace to the steps where I had been attacked.

There was little to see. The gravel path at the foot of the steps was scuffed; a faint trace of blood on the bottom step was dried to a dull brown. I looked up at the windows of the house above. One must be Heron's. I'd been lucky; if he'd been given one of the rooms at the back, it might be all over for me.

One thing was clear – the attack could not have been pre-meditated. No one could have guessed I'd decide to walk in the gardens. Someone must have seen me from the house, seized a weapon, come out to attack me –

But why?

I heard voices from the rose garden to my right. At least one of the musical ladies was there; they'd probably already forgotten the idea of singing. And a glimpse of part of the drive showed me Alyson riding off on a spirited black horse, accompanied by Ridley and a cheerful young man in sombre clothing – the visiting lawyer, perhaps. It appeared that the various members of the party were entertaining themselves very well without my help. This could be the easiest – if most tedious – fifteen guineas I'd ever earnt. Although it allowed me much too much time to think about Nell and Bedwalters.

I went to my room for the key to tune the harpsichord. A couple of disgruntled servants helped me move the instrument into a better light and I set to with some considerable pleasure. It was an hour or more later before one of the musical ladies came hurrying into the room, her arms full of music.

"Oh, pray, do forgive us, Mr Patterson!" The second lady came in behind her. "But you know how it is. You see someone you haven't seen for years and find you have six cousins in common you never knew about – "

"And then," said the older lady with a mischievous smile, "they insist upon telling you all about them from cradle to grave, in the utmost detail."

"Particularly their illnesses," said the first lady with a groan. "And they *won't* listen when you say you have an appointment – Oh!"

She broke off in surprise as movement in the doorway caught her attention. It was Esther, in the palest of yellow gowns, a book in her hand. She looked at me for a moment, with her coolest gaze.

"Dear Mrs Jerdoun," said the younger lady. "Do join us. We are about to sing a few airs."

Esther shook her head. The lappets on her cap rippled against her neck. Why was she wearing so ridiculous a thing? She'd never cared for such conventional trifles. And it didn't suit her.

I reddened as her cool, ironic gaze lingered on me.

"No, thank you," she said. "I was merely looking for a place to read – I thought the room was empty." And she withdrew, the long fall of her gown swishing against the open door.

The ladies surprised me, both by their excellent voices and the serious manner in which they approached the Art. They were critical of their own performances where appropriate and insisted on rehearsing several parts to get them just right. Even more surprisingly, they complimented me on my playing. An hour or more passed very pleasantly.

We attracted some attention. One or two other ladies wandered in and out, then Mrs Alyson came in alone. She was a remarkably beautiful woman, still with the freshness of youth but with an edge of weariness. Her dress was of the finest material, with intricate embroidery and lace that must have been worth a fortune. Jewels glittered in her ears and round her throat.

She was restless, sitting down, standing up again, picking up a book, glancing inside, putting it down again, careful to line it up with the edge of the table. She walked to the fireplace, glanced down at the huge bowl of flowers set in the grate, bent to finger one of them. She seemed tense, unapproachable. I thought that the position of mistress must be damnably insecure – she must know how the ladies and gentlemen would react if they knew her real relationship with Alyson.

But he seemed so in love with her – why the devil did he not just marry her? Of course, Hugh often said the same of myself and Esther. How could I know the imperatives that governed their lives? I felt a surge of sympathy.

It lasted only a moment. "Mr Patterson," Mrs Alyson said loudly.

I'd been about to play the first chord of a new song, and caught myself just in time. "Madam?"

"I heard there was an unpleasant incident last night."

I had of course risen to address her; I bowed. "Indeed."

"I trust such a thing will not happen again."

This seemed in the nature of an order, as if I was to blame for the whole affair. She was staring at the huge portrait that hung over the fireplace, a picture of a slightly amused elderly gentleman. "I am aware you have 'low' connections, Mr Patterson. Perhaps that is hardly surprising. I made it perfectly clear to Alyson that I wanted no tradesmen here but he chose otherwise. Very well, I submit to his judgement. But you will oblige me by not bringing your cronies or their affairs into this house. Do you understand me, sir?"

I was speechless.

"I trust I make myself clear," she said, and walked out.

Just before dinner, while I was still fuming over Mrs Alyson's rudeness (and her curt dismissal of my friends), I received another letter from Hugh.

Things go from bad to worse, he had written. *Bedwalters still refuses to budge and is now saying he intends to live there permanently. He's offered Mrs McDonald twice the rent she asked, so she merely shrugs her shoulders and says: Why not? She says it will be useful to her to have a man living on the premises – he can deal with any customers who make trouble. But Mrs Bedwalters has gone to the parish officers to demand they dismiss her husband from his post as constable. The chaplain went down to talk to him and is now saying he's mad. They've done nothing yet, but I fear he'll be dismissed the moment they can have a meeting. For God's sake, Charles why have you not replied to my first letter? Come back and talk some sense into everyone!*

I stared at this missive in bewilderment. Why did he say I'd not replied? He should have got my letter hours ago – late last night.

I went in search of the servant to whom I'd entrusted my letter to Hugh. He was nowhere to be seen. The footman on duty in the hall was six and a half feet tall, as handsome as any girl could wish, and remarkably simple. After explaining my problem to him three times, I began to suspect his simplicity might be deliberate.

Fortunately, just as I was having difficulty containing my annoyance, the butler arrived. He dismissed the footman with a nod and enquired with extreme politeness how he might help me. I would have been more mollified if I hadn't seen the footman go off with a huge grin.

I gritted my teeth in an effort to be civil. "Crompton, is it not?"

He was a few inches taller than myself, a man in his late forties, with a well-muscled body under the fine cloth of his livery. His wig was neat and well-kept. "Indeed, sir."

"I gave a servant a note to send off for me yesterday and it doesn't appear to have arrived."

I expected him to give me some emollient platitudes but I saw something unexpected in his eyes – a sudden stillness. "To whom did you entrust the note, sir?"

I described the footman. I saw his jaw set hard. "I will – " the slightest of hesitations – "*deal* with the matter, sir. I suggest that if you wish to send another letter you give it directly to myself."

The footman, I thought, would regret his decision to pocket my money and ignore my orders.

"Thank you."

"And – "

I was turning away but hesitated. "Yes?"

"I apologise, sir," he said, "for the misunderstanding when you arrived."

I didn't know what to say to that. The butler went silently out of the hall and I was left wondering why on earth he should voluntarily have raised a matter so embarrassing to himself.

Before dinner, in the drawing room, Alyson was in high good spirits, extolling the virtues of horse-riding in fine country. William Ridley was telling everyone who'd listen to him, and everyone who didn't want to, about the iniquities of a neighbouring landowner who insisted on claiming woodland that belonged to other people. Heron came in as quietly as usual; Esther, I noted, seemed tired and worn. I accidentally caught her eye; she looked away.

I didn't meet the Ords until we sat round the dinner table, and then I was shocked at the change I saw in Lizzie. I'd not seen her since the day before her marriage, when she'd prettily thanked me for all my teaching and presented me with a hand-made pair of slippers. She'd been a girl then, sixteen years old, with artfully naïve dark ringlets and a fresh open look about her.

The woman who sat opposite me seemed ten years older. Her hair was dressed too elaborately for one so young; her cheeks were rouged too heavily. Her dress aged her too; it was very fine and expensive no doubt, but the low neckline showed off her immature breasts too cruelly, and the heavy fall of material at the back seemed to drag her down.

She looked dully at me, as if she hardly recognised me.

Her husband did not look at me at all.

Casper Fischer, beside me, was as full of his family history as ever and glad of a new audience. Lizzie Saint, now Lizzie Ord, picked at her food listlessly without comment but Philip Ord was bored by the talk of sword makers and tanneries and not afraid to show it – he was barely polite. A man of thirty-three or so, he plainly wanted to be talking politics with a gentleman across the table; Fischer, catching on quickly, was happy to join in but his Colonial view of the matter was not welcome, and he wanted a deeper discussion than the languid complaints about government and trade that the other two gentleman favoured.

"My view, sir," he said, with incautious directness, "is that Mr Walpole is going about the matter in an entirely incorrect fashion – "

"What the devil do you mean by that!" Ord demanded, red with anger.

One of the singing ladies said loudly, "Mr Patterson, I hear Mr Handel has a new opera. Have you heard it?"

"Handel always has a new opera," Heron said dryly, "and all the plots are equally nonsensical."

"But some of the music is extremely beautiful," the lady protested.

I launched into an explanation of the first opera that came to mind and the singing ladies laughed and joked over the antics of Handel's leading actresses, and retailed the latest scandals. A few sly remarks were made about castrati singers, and their attributes, or lack of them. Under cover of the merrymaking, I leant towards Fischer. "I'm afraid you hit on a sore topic."

He regarded me wryly. "Is that a tactful way of suggesting I should not talk politics, Mr Patterson? Shall I talk about my book after all?"

"A book?" said the musical lady. "I like a good book."

Fischer, casting me a humorous look as if to say he was doing his best to be unexceptional, obliged with a description of his inheritance, explaining about the psalm tunes his grandfather had collected. This led to much condemnation of the tunes currently in use – too slow, too old-fashioned. "Why should church music be so dull?" one of the ladies asked.

"I think I've seen the book," Lizzie Ord said.

9

I have to say there are some pleasant buildings. The bridges are
particularly fine – there is one over the Tyne which
pleases me greatly, with houses and shops on it.
[Letter from Retif de Vincennes, to his wife, Régine, 16 June 1736]

All eyes turned to Lizzie. She flushed. It was the first time she'd
spoken and I fancied I saw a mixture of fear and determination in
her eyes. She was the youngest here by far and must feel very out
of place, particularly as she'd not been brought up in this world.
Lizzie Ord was the daughter of a printer, and her father's money
was even now sustaining the finances of her gentlemanly, but
cash-strapped, husband.

"It had a black cloth cover," Lizzie said. "Very dilapidated and
worn – the spine had almost come away and was hanging by a
thread. The sewing of the folios was giving way too."

I tried to catch her eye. Lizzie, if she was not careful, was about
to show she knew more than a lady should about trade.

"There was an inscription in German on the flypaper," she
said. "At least, Papa said it was in German. He read it out to
me though I'm afraid I've forgotten it. But I do remember it
mentioned Shotley Bridge because I at once thought of the
German swordmakers there."

"And when was this?" Fischer asked.

Lizzie was sounding more confident now; she even managed a
little smile. "About two years ago. Someone brought it in to show
Papa. He said he wanted it rebound and he even asked if Papa
would print it. But when Papa told him how much it would cost,
he said it was much too expensive. Music printing is, you know –
it's all the copper and the engraving –"

I broke in quickly to avoid unladylike talk of money. "Did you
recognise any of the tunes? Were they all English or had some
been brought over from Germany?"

"I hardly think anyone is interested in such matters," Philip Ord said in a bored voice.

A silence. Ord's reaction was hardly grateful, considering I'd been intent on rescuing his wife from a social error. At the other end of the table, Esther said, "I have long thought that more attention should be paid to the history of music. After all, we embrace the lessons of ancient Rome and Greece when it comes to architecture and art – why should we so neglect the history of music?"

"Indeed," Heron agreed urbanely. "I am told there was much excellent church music composed even as long as two centuries ago."

"But it must sound so old-fashioned!" declared one of the musical ladies. And so the awkward moment was smoothed over; conversation picked up again in a lively manner, with William Ridley grumbling that he'd no taste for Romish music, and Alyson musing on the likelihood that it had been sung in foreign languages.

I retreated to the drawing room almost as soon as dinner was finished. Fischer had been ready for a cosy chat but I could not endure Ord's cold stare any longer. Besides, I hoped for a conversation with Lizzie, partly to wish her well, partly to ask for more details about the book.

The ladies were apathetic when I arrived in the drawing room. Lizzie Ord was sitting dully beside her silent hostess and a sleepy elderly matron; there was plainly no prospect of talking to her at present. I retreated to the harpsichord. My mind reverted inevitably to Nell and Bedwalters who would have been so out of place in this company. Why should Philip Ord's own loveless marriage be considered acceptable, and Nell and Bedwalters's relationship contemptible?

Someone moved close to me. I knew at once who it was by the faint scent of roses. Esther. She held two dishes of tea, put one directly into my hands, and shook her head as I attempted to rise politely. My heart was beating ridiculously quickly. She said loudly, "Do you have any Scarlatti, Mr Patterson?"

I have endless Scarlatti sonatas off by heart but I pretended to look among the music piled on the top of the harpsichord. Esther idled around the instrument until she stood with her back to the rest of the company. "Ord has not forgiven you yet, I see," she said.

I met her cool gaze. She knows all about my previous encounter with Ord; I told her about it when we were in good charity with each other. The best of charity. When I was still entertaining foolish romantic notions.

I nodded. "He's not a man who likes being obliged to others."

"He was not here last night, however," she mused. "I cannot conceive he would carry enmity so far as to attack you."

"You heard – " I stopped, remembering her brief visit to the drawing room that morning. Had that been to make sure I was unharmed? No, I must not let my imagination stray too far…

"Of course I heard," she said acerbically. "The entire servants' hall knew within minutes. My maid Catherine told me about it when I woke."

"The general opinion is that it was poachers," I murmured.

"Nonsense!"

I sipped tea. Esther pretended to leaf through the music on top of the harpsichord. We both tried not to look at each other.

"You were not badly injured?" she said after a moment.

"It was little more than a scratch."

"Do you think he meant to kill you?" Her tone was carefully casual.

I shook my head. "He could have put a knife in my back and I'd never have had a chance."

She seemed to grip the tea dish more tightly. "Then he wanted to frighten you."

"Apparently."

"He believes you endanger him." She cast a glance at the other ladies, picked up a piece of music at random and handed it to me. It was a Corelli violin sonata. "Are you investigating anything other than this matter of the constable's girl?"

"No. And I know nothing much of that!"

I covertly studied Esther as I pretended to look at the music. I could hardly believe that, given the acrimony of our last meeting, she had again voluntarily approached me, that we were talking in so civilised a manner. Could it mean that she'd at last given up hopes of persuading me to marry her and accepted the inevitable? Or perhaps it was the opposite; she still hoped to convert me to her way of thinking...

Absurd how happy I felt at the thought that I'd not alienated her irrevocably. Any alliance between us was unthinkable. I had to make that clear.

My voice stuck in my throat. Our gazes met...

The drawing room door opened and Edward Alyson sauntered in with the other gentlemen, full of drink and good humour. I saw his gaze go straight to his wife, sitting by the unlit fire. A smile curved his lips, she sat up, eyes shining...

"She is a clergyman's daughter," Esther said dryly. "An unequal marriage. Like the Ords." She didn't trouble to lower her voice; I glanced round uneasily to see if anyone was listening. "But apparently it is acceptable when it is the *lady* who is elevated by the alliance."

One of the gentlemen started telling a long and involved story about a carriage accident, which had the entire room in gusts of laughter, engrossed in the tale. Esther leant forward.

"Take care, Charles," she said urgently. "The man was thwarted in his last attack – he may decide to try again. And I could not bear it if anything happened to you."

Before I could gather my wits to reply, she walked away.

Alyson was all excitement when I asked him if I could return to town the following day.

"To see the girl's spirit? To ask who killed her?" His eyes lit up with pleasure. "You might catch the fellow. Catch a murderer! How exciting!"

"He's probably left town already," I said. We were standing in the hall, out of the way of the noisy party who had taken to trying to better each other with accounts of perils suffered; there were tales of shipwreck, highwaymen and pirates. Most of the tales were fuelled by drink and Alyson had been encouraging the worst excesses of exaggeration. But now he'd been captured by something more exciting. His enthusiasm made him seem like a boy – I felt abruptly a decade older than him, rather than a mere three years.

"A man with that kind of audacity will never run!" Alyson said. "He'll brazen it out. He's probably going about his everyday business with no one the wiser. And the spirit will give you his name!"

"I doubt it," I said.

"Or at least tell you what he looks like!"

"I really don't think – "

"I've half a mind to come with you!" he said. His face lit up. "Damn it, I will."

I was desperately searching for a way to dissuade him when Ridley came out of the drawing room. "Go, Alyson? Go where?"

"To Newcastle." Alyson grinned. "Hunting for a murderer."

"Tomorrow? You can't."

Alyson's face darkened. He was plainly not accustomed to being told what he could or could not do.

Ridley didn't seem to notice. "Lawyer's coming back, remember? So we can sort out the details of the court case."

Alyson grimaced. "We'll put him off a day or two."

"Can't," Ridley said. "He goes back to London on Saturday."

He went off in the best of good humour, leaving Alyson mouthing silent oaths. I hovered awkwardly; I didn't yet have Alyson's explicit permission to be absent the next day. He gave me a sour look.

"You're not put off by last night's attack?"

"No," I said. "And I owe my friends my attendance at this sad time."

"Of course, of course." He sighed. "If you must."

I hesitated. "I may be back rather late. Nell's spirit will probably not disembody until the evening."

"As long as you're here the following morning. He gave a faint smile. "And I shall look forward to hearing all about your trip. Damn it, I wish I could come!"

I rode into Newcastle on an overcast day seeping a warm drizzle, astride a borrowed horse that Edward Alyson's grooms had assured me was well-trained and placid. I gathered Alyson had told them my riding ability was limited; it was not, and the gelding, thank goodness, had more energy than the grooms had suggested.

I'd set off before any of the other guests were up, so I could spend as much of the day as possible in town — there were several things I wanted to do in addition to talking to Bedwalters, and to Nell's spirit. It was an unexpectedly pleasant trip: a well-bred expensive horse under me, a greatcoat protecting me against the worst of the drizzle and no need to go anything beyond a steady canter. The farming people were all up, and looked as if they'd been working for hours.

I came to Barras Bridge at last and turned down Northumberland Street, past the stylish houses and gardens of the wealthy. Past Heron's house, one of the oldest on the street. Cutting across town, I reached the stables on Westgate, paid the men there to look after the horse for a day and walked down to Hugh's dancing school.

We met on the stairs to his attic room as I went up and he came down; he stared at me then came clattering down in a rush.

"Where the devil have you been? Why didn't you reply to me?"

"I did," I said wearily.

"The devil you did!"

"One of the servants pocketed my money and didn't bother to send the letter."

Hugh glared. "The fellow ought to be turned off!"

"I fancy that's the fate the butler has in store for him."

Hugh squinted at me. He grabbed my arm and dragged me towards the street door where the light was better.

"I thought so," he said. "You've been getting yourself in trouble again. What's happened?"

I explained my contretemps with the unknown assailant. Hugh crossquestioned me on every detail before finally exploding. "But it's appalling, Charles! Who the devil would attack you out there?"

"Poachers?" I offered, without much hope of being agreed with.

"Nonsense! When did you hear of poachers doing anything but creep away with their ill-gotten gains!"

"It's either that or believe Nell's murderer took the trouble to travel seven miles north on the off-chance I might know something or that he might get a chance to attack me!" I watched as he subsided into disgruntled silence. "I know it doesn't make sense, Hugh. Now tell me, how is Bedwalters?"

He sighed, peered out into the drizzle. I saw how weary he looked. "Won't budge. And Mrs McDonald just takes his rent and says how useful it is to have a man in the house!"

"Having a resident constable isn't exactly going to help business."

"He isn't a constable any longer. The vestry of All Hallows have dismissed him."

"Then the vestry of All Hallows are hypocrites," I said. Suddenly everything about this matter annoyed me. Particularly the plight of Bedwalters. "Everyone knew about the girl," I said. "She used to go everywhere with him if he was called out at night. That's how I first met her. And everyone pretended they didn't know. When it suited them."

"That's the point though, isn't it?" Hugh said. "You can do anything as long as you keep it quiet."

"You're beginning to sound like Claudius Heron."

We went out into the drizzle and walked to All Hallows parish and the shabby streets where Nell had lived and died. Women were already out looking for potential customers; on one corner, workmen repairing a dilapidated roof were enjoying their attentions. One or two more respectable women hurried past with hard stares.

Maggie was lounging against the door of Mrs McDonald's house; she smelt of gin. She grinned, displaying a gap in her teeth, jerked her head. "He's still here."

"We've got to get him home!" Hugh said exasperated.

She put out a hand to block our way. "Leave the poor bugger alone. He was sweet on her and kept her from harm more than once. And he's always been polite to the rest of us. If it makes him happy to stay here, leave him be." She turned to glare at the workmen. "Makes a change to have a decent man in this house."

Inside, I heard a woman shrieking with laughter. A mangy cat shot out of a room and bolted for the street. A man upstairs shouted for a chamberpot.

We hesitated on the threshold of what had once been Nell's room. The door was wide open. Bedwalters had shifted the table into the middle of the room and was standing over it. Head down over a slate, scratching away, was a girl, no more than twelve years old, with a ludicrously elaborate hairstyle falling out of its pins. Bedwalters was nodding encouragingly. "That's right, Adele. Now, what comes after the 'd'?"

Laboriously she wrote another letter.

"Excellent. And next?"

In his distress, Bedwalters had returned to his chief occupation, that of writing master.

He glanced round, saw us, smilingly dismissed the girl. She started up with a glowing face and dashed off into the back of the house where she could be heard calling out excitedly: "I can write! Look, I can write!" Bedwalters regarded me with a steady gaze.

"It's good of you to come, Mr Patterson. I'm sorry you've been inconvenienced."

"It's nothing. I was glad to get away, if truth be told."

He stood his ground in the centre of the room, like a man who owned it. Or at least like a man who was up-to-date with his rent. "I know what you intend to say, Mr Patterson. You hope to persuade me to go back home. I will not."

67

There was no arguing with that quiet tone of voice; he'd made his mind up and would not be moved. As always with Bedwalters, I was tempted to apologise for questioning him.

"What will you do?" I asked.

"Teach. As always." He noticed that I'd involuntarily glanced at the empty bed. "We buried her last night."

I nodded. It's not a good idea to allow a spirit to see the body that once housed it. "I'm sorry to have missed the funeral."

"Mr Demsey was there," he said, inclining his head to Hugh. "For which I was very grateful."

He offered us wine but we declined. We arranged a time to return and parted at the door of the house. Hugh had a trip to London to arrange and I wanted a few questions answered. The matter of the books troubled me. It must surely be a coincidence that Nell had been killed over a book and that Fischer had lost one but, as I had the time, it seemed sensible to find out what I could. If I could find Fischer's book, I could show it to the spirit and discover once and for all if it was the one she'd kept for her killer. If not – well, I could restore it to its rightful owner.

I walked down Pilgrim Street, heading for the Key. But as I came up to the end of Silver Street, I took it into my head to go to All Hallows church and say a prayer over Nell's grave. The town was still relatively quiet and I passed only two or three labourers and one of the organist's children, sitting on the doorstep, stroking the family cat.

The gate to the churchyard squeaked open; I hesitated, remembering the last time I'd been here and had had a view of the world that runs alongside our own. But on this occasion, nothing happened as I pushed open the gate.

Nell's grave was easy to find for the earth was still raw; a simple wooden cross with her name painted on it stood at the head of the grave, but I suspected that Bedwalters would somehow find the money for something more prominent. I found myself offering not a prayer, but an apology. For not keeping her safe, for not intervening to make her life easier, for being part of a society that condemned her to the life she had led. She was a woman who had deserved more.

I shivered and pulled my greatcoat tighter, belatedly realising what the shiver meant. I looked up. The graveyard lay around me, silent and ghostly in bright moonlight. A frost lay whitely over the grass, stiffening it. I looked down at the grave. It was grassed over, the blades stiff and brittle. At its head stood a sturdy gravestone. *Nell Ross*, it read. *Shamefully snatched away in the 18th year of her age. She was loving and beloved.* And then the appropriate dates.

It was like intruding on Bedwalters's grief. I took a step backwards. The frost dissolved, the night lightened and shifted back into day, into thick cloud. Rain dampened my coat.

10

The coffee in the drinking houses is passable.
[Letter from Retif de Vincennes, to his sister, Agnés, 18 July 1736]

Thomas Saint's printing office stands at the end of the Key. The day being Friday, the office was crowded with men shifting bundles of the latest edition of the *Newcastle Courant* to be sent out to all the local towns; Saint himself was distractedly ticking off items on a long list. I hesitated to interrupt him but he glanced up and saw me, and his face brightened at once.

"Mr Patterson! I thought you were out at Mr Alyson's house."

"I've just come back for a day. On business."

"Did you by any chance – " His face glowed, transforming him from a rather plain middle-aged man in a respectable wig, to a warm and loving father. "Did you by any chance see Lizzie? She's supposed to be staying there."

"She is indeed," I said reluctantly. "They came yesterday."

"And she's well and happy?"

I was careful with my words. "She looked very fine indeed."

"*Mrs Ord*," he said with a satisfied chuckle. "Well, I admit, I was wrong. When she first told me she admired Mr Philip Ord, I thought she'd end up disappointed. But he took after her and she got her way. A fairy tale, is it not, Mr Patterson?"

Ord had been courting a play actress at the same time as betrothing himself to his bride, and I knew of at least two widows who'd been his mistresses at various times. I didn't think Lizzie had much chance of stilling his wandering eye. Although he might be more discreet about it to avoid offending his wealthy father-in-law.

"Dreams do sometimes come true," I said, trying not to sound sanctimonious. "Mr Saint, I'm trying to trace a book – "

"Another of your mysteries, Mr Patterson?" he asked with good-humoured indulgence.

"Lizzie – I mean Mrs Ord – recollected being shown it two or three years ago."

He excused himself to deal with a boy who was picking up the wrong parcels. When I described the book to him he remembered it well.

"It was Mr Hodgson brought it in."

"Mr William Hodgson?"

"That's right. Less than two weeks before he died. He said he'd bought the book from a house sale. Someone out in the country who'd gone bankrupt. He wanted it rebound."

"It was in a bad state?"

"Very. It had been mistreated at some stage." Saint wandered off into technicalities which confused me. "I said I'd do the work for him, of course. Wouldn't have been much trouble."

"Lizzie said he wanted it printed."

"He was thinking about it. Wondered if anyone would be interested in buying a copy. I told him straight, Mr Patterson, no market for it."

"I thought psalm books sold almost as well as the Bible."

"Better!" Saint nodded at a shelf full of books for sale. "You can always bring out a new edition – small enough for a pocket, or big enough for a lectern, smart enough for a lady to hold, dignified enough for a gentleman to feel comfortable with. But words only, Mr Patterson. Saving your presence, no one wants tunes. Everyone knows them already."

That was true enough – I knew that from my experience as deputy church organist. But only if you stick to four or five old favourites. Anything unfamiliar is greeted with stony silence and *we've never sung that one before* meaning *and we don't want to now.*

"In any case," Saint said, "you know yourself how expensive music printing can be, Mr Patterson. All that engraving takes time. And that means you have to set the price of the book high."

"What did Mr Hodgson say to that?"

"Oh, he was philosophical about it. Said it had only been half an idea."

"Did you rebind the book for him?"

"Never got a chance." Saint looked regretful. "We were about to negotiate terms when an old friend of his came by and he said he'd be back later to deal with it. Then of course he died."

"And you don't know what happened to the book?"

Saint shook his head. "Sold with the rest of his library, I daresay. Charnley took the lot off the hands of his heirs at a knockdown price – they wanted quick money, I'm told. A pity – I wouldn't have minded a look at what he had. Some treasures there, I'll wager."

"You've not seen it since."

"Never."

Saint had a dozen questions to ask about Lizzie: what had she worn? What had she said? Had she kept warm on the boat from France? She'd not been seasick? And was there any sign... No, I said, reddening, I hadn't see any sign of Lizzie being with child. It was nearly midday before he let me go and my stomach was reminding me I'd had nothing to eat since a snatched breakfast of coffee and bread.

I walked back along the Key, detouring round the gangs loading ships, the barking dogs harassing them, the women eyeing the sailors, the respectable elderly gentlemen handing out tracts in the hope of saving souls. At the end of the Key is the Tyne Bridge, where Charnley's bookshop is situated. The bridge is venerable, so much so that cracks have zigzagged their way from one buttress to another and find their echoes in the houses and shops that stand against the parapets. A prison and a chapel cluster among the buildings and there are dozens of spirits, all of them eager to chat. I dodged a flock of sheep, hastily returned the greeting of a prim female spirit and ducked beneath a low door into Charnley's bookshop.

After the noise outside the shop was eerily quiet, a dim place where old books stood regimented on older bookcases, ordered by some mysterious system no outside observer could hope to fathom. Prints filled any spare space on the walls depicting religious subjects: the killing of the Innocents, the Crucifixion, the harrowing of hell. I wondered if anyone had ever engraved the more cheerful moments of scriptural history, like the wedding at Cana. If they had, Charnley didn't have them.

A spirit said, "Can I help you, sir?"

I don't generally patronise Charnley's shop; I looked around the gloomy interior for a moment or two before I saw the spirit gleaming on an inkpot.

"I was hoping to see Mr Charnley."

"I generally deal with customers, sir."

The elderly, rather fussy voice suggested the living man had once been Charnley's shopman, still performing his duties long after death. It must be invaluable to have all that expertise on call – not to mention the savings from not having to pay him.

"I'm trying to trace a book that was once in the library of Mr William Hodgson," I said. "A manuscript of psalm tunes."

"Ah," said the spirit, oozing unctuousness. "And you wish to purchase this book?"

"I'm acting as agent for a man who wishes to do so, yes."

The spirit shot away into the back of the shop.

After a few minutes, Charnley himself came out to talk to me, a bitter-looking man in his late forties, wearing a grey wig and black coat. Most of the religious tracts distributed on the Key come from his printing presses. He boasts there is nothing in his pamphlets to offend the most delicate of sensibilities.

He remembered the book but didn't think much of it. "The tunes were just the usual popular rubbish."

"My interest isn't musical," I said. "I believe it had a German inscription at the front?"

"To my beloved son, Luther," the spirit said. "Signed by Melchior Friedric Fischer, Shotley Bridge, 1722."

"It was bequeathed to a Philadelphian gentleman of my acquaintance," I said, "but it never reached him. I was wondering if you still had it."

There was a heavy pause. A thin smile curved Charnley's lips.

"Stolen. I had a shopboy who left it lying around instead of putting it aside for the gentleman who requested it. The book

73

was purloined. I dismissed the boy, of course."

"Young people nowadays are so lazy," the elderly spirit said.

"Disrespectful," Charnley said. "Caring only for the pleasures of the world."

"Indeed," said the spirit comfortably.

"Did you report the theft to the constable?"

Charnley's smile turned into a sneer. "You mean Bedwalters the writing master? The one who has abandoned his duties and responsibilities for a dead whore?"

The spirit tut-tutted.

"Well," I said, deciding to go before I lost my temper. "If you no longer have the book I want, I can keep my money in my pocket, can't I?"

And I turned on my heels and walked out, feeling self-righteous in my indignation.

Outside, I hesitated in the drizzle, wondering if it was time to meet Hugh – we'd arranged to meet in Nellie's coffee house before going back to Mrs McDonald's. The female spirit slid down the wall and settled on the corner of a shelf built on the front of the shop to house a dozen very old, very damaged books.

"I saw him," she said primly.

"Who?"

"The fellow who stole the book!"

I stared at the virulent gleam of spirit. "The book of tunes?"

"The lad put it outside on the shelf," she said. "This shelf. Charnley told him to. Said it wasn't worth waiting – the gentleman might never send to America at all. *Get a penny or two for it*, he said. *Put it with all the other rubbishy stuff.*"

The worst thing, I thought, was that Charnley had been happy to blame an innocent lad for his own misdeeds. "And someone stole it?"

"Young man, dark hair, dreadful clothes." She sniffed. "An apprentice, I warrant. Just came along whistling, glanced round, picked up the book and walked off with it. I did call out *thief*," she added, "But the street was busy and no one heard. And then

I decided not to call again. About time Charnley was on the wrong end of life, even in a small way."

"You didn't know the apprentice?"

"Never seen him before. Nothing more I can tell you."

"I'm very grateful."

She cackled with laughter. "Don't worry – you're doing me a favour. I've been waiting years to get my own back on Charnley and that shopman of his." And she whizzed back up towards the eaves, calling back, "He's a liar, sir. A sneaking snivelling liar!"

Around midday, I found Hugh in the coffee-house on the Sandhill, sitting in a corner with a newspaper open in front of him; he was chortling over the latest sensational London trial.

"Listen to this, Charles!" He waved me to a seat. "Lady Monro told the court that she had never been in company with the gentleman in question except with several other persons present. Mr Elder asked if she had not on one occasion sat her maid behind a screen while she and the gentleman engaged in intimate activities on a drawing room chair…"

"Hugh," I said, wearily. "Just at the moment, Lady Monro can go to the devil as far as I'm concerned. I've been talking to Charnley."

"The devil you have." He threw the paper aside. "Then you need something stronger than coffee!" He signalled to a serving girl to bring some ale. "Was he his usual dreadful self?"

"Why did you not warn me his shopman was a spirit?"

"Is he? Well, I'm not surprised. No living man would put up with him. Do you know, he stood outside the Assembly Rooms for every dancing assembly last year distributing tracts railing against *trivial amusements*? It's not trivial to me, I can tell you – it's my living he's trying to abolish. Did he have the book?"

"He had once." I told him the gist of what I had learnt. "What I don't know is where the book is now, what it has to do with poor Nell's death and even if there's any point in running after it!"

The girl brought the ale and Hugh waved away my offer to pay. We sat in silence for a minute or two, which Hugh occupied by folding the paper and neatly smoothing it out. I drank my ale. Around us, gentlemen debated Mr Walpole's misdeeds, or the price of coal, or the advantages of investing in government stock.

"Ready?" Hugh asked eventually.

Just at that moment I wanted to be anywhere but in Mrs McDonald's house, waiting for the spirit of a murdered girl to disembody, facing Bedwalters's grief.

I finished my ale. "As much as I'll ever be."

11

If I have one piece of advice for all visitors,
it is to leave the questions of politics and religion alone.
No good will come of discussing such things.
[*A Frenchman's guide to England*, Retif de Vincennes
(Paris; published for the author, 1734)]

The empty bed, with its linen freshly washed and folded, dominated the room. If I looked at it out of the corner of my eye, I half-thought I could see a body there still. But Bedwalters's razor was on the table now, and a copy of the latest *Courant*. The women's clothes had been put away; Bedwalters's second-best coat hung over the back of the chair. He brought a bottle of wine and three mismatched glasses from the kitchen; the wine was cheap but not unpalatable.

We sat for three hours, making desultory polite conversation. Beyond the closed door, we could hear the women coming and going, laughter, men's voices… We talked about the political situation, the weather, the cracks recently found in All Hallows church. We managed to work up some righteous indignation on this latter topic – the building has been known to be insecure for years and nothing has yet been done. I thought Walpole's latest doings would probably occupy a good few minutes but since we were unanimous in condemning the government entirely, that conversation petered out quicker than all the rest.

Our ingenuity failed us at last. We sat in embarrassed silence until, luckily, someone knocked on the door. Bedwalters opened it to reveal a middle-aged woman of respectable appearance, a letter in her hand. She looked from one to the other of us in nervous apprehension then her gaze settled on Bedwalters. "I've had a note from the landlord, sir, and I was wondering…"

"Of course I'll read it to you," Bedwalters said. "Do come in."

"I can pay, sir – "

"We'll get some food," Hugh said brightly and dragged me out of the house. Behind we heard the woman explaining how her husband was in the navy and she had four children; Bedwalters murmured in sympathetic understanding.

"It's the damnedest thing," Hugh said. "I could swear he's almost happy."

We had to go some distance before we could find a shop whose wares we felt happy eating. "All Hallows vestry have elected a new constable," Hugh said, as we rejected a dark hole of a house with a few loaves on a dusty table in the window. "Philips the shoemaker."

"His sons sing in church. Nice voices."

"His daughter's one of my pupils. One of those girls who always whine."

"Philips himself is decent enough." I squinted against the lowering afternoon sun. "A trifle strict, perhaps."

We found somewhere clean, bought a large bread pudding and a jug of ale and carried them back to Mrs McDonald's.

We'd hardly set foot in the house when we realised something had happened.

The door to Nell's room was shut. The entire population of the house stood in doorways, at the foot of the stairs, in the kitchen. All the women, young and old. A girl of sixteen or so was trying to stifle tears; Mrs McDonald was patting her on the back. We heard low voices from Nell's room.

"We'll come back," I said.

It was almost an hour before Bedwalters came out to us. We were sitting on the cobbles of the street sharing the ale and pudding when we heard footsteps and looked round to see him in the doorway.

"She would like to talk to you, Mr Patterson."

I scrambled up and shook the dirt from my coat skirts. When I went back into the house, the women were nowhere to be seen, clearly going about their business as usual. We ventured into Bedwalters's room in some trepidation. The spirit gleamed on the edge of a cheap print hung above the bed – an unsteady fluctuating brightness.

"Mr Patterson," the spirit said.

"I'm sorry to meet you again under such circumstances."

"No need to worry, sir," she said softly. "It was going to happen some day."

"It should *not* have happened," Bedwalters said, with sudden vehemence. "I should have protected you."

"I need to know as much as possible, Nell." I spoke soothingly more for Bedwalters's sake than the spirit's. "We need to know what happened."

She told us in a quiet voice so calm it was eerily out of place. Hugh, face set hard, sat down on the uneven chair, leaning his arms on his knees; I thrust my clenched fists in my pockets and hunched into my damp greatcoat. To hear such a terrible tale told in such a tranquil voice was almost more than I could bear. Only Bedwalters seemed composed, watching the gleam with steady dedication.

It had been like any other day, Nell said. She'd been working. She and two of the other girls enjoyed a gossip in a tavern then went out to ply their trade.

"Where did you go?" I asked.

"Down on the Keyside, sir, as usual. But it was very quiet. Hardly anyone about. Not many ships in. The tide was running out, you see, and most of them had set sail." The young voice sounded almost amused. "You wouldn't think there'd ever be a shortage of sailors, would you, sir? But when I went into the taverns they were all dead drunk, or already taken. So I went into the Old Man Inn."

"A very disreputable house," Bedwalters said. "The watch have to break up fights there almost every night."

"And I met the young gentleman there again."

"Again?" I said. "You'd met him before?"

"Four or five times, sir. Though not always in the Old Man."

"What's his name?"

"Jem, sir."

Hugh groaned. How many *Jems* were there in the world?

"Can you describe him?"

"A year or two younger than you," the spirit said. "About your height, but a bit darker."

"With his own hair?"

"Yes, sir. And a bit of a stutter, sir, except when he's excited – if you know what I mean."

I knew exactly what she meant. And anyone can feign a stutter. "Did he ever tell you what he does for a living?"

"I think he said he was an apprentice, sir."

"In what trade?"

"He didn't say."

"When did you first meet him?"

"A year or more ago, sir. Usually in the street. He kept a look-out for me, he said. But I only came across him now and again. I – " She hesitated.

"Yes?"

"I think maybe he wasn't from here. Maybe he was from Shields or Sunderland or some other place. If he lived in Newcastle, I think I'd have seen him more often."

Hugh swore. But I was heartened by the news. If the apprentice lived in some other local town, he might think himself safe there. He might not have run off to London after all.

"Did he ever threaten you?"

"Never," the spirit said firmly. "I never imagined he might. He was always so full of himself, never thought of anyone else." A hint of amusement. "Thought no woman could resist him. Thought he was a heaven-sent lover. But he was nothing of the sort. No better than any of the men. No better, no worse." Her voice softened. "Not the kind *I* like."

Hugh shuffled his feet in embarrassment; Bedwalters kept his steadfast gaze on the spirit of his lover.

"So what was different this time?" I said. "What made him violent towards you?"

"The book," she said simply. "It was the book. And I don't know why, sir. Why should anyone kill for a book? And it wasn't an expensive book, neither. Nothing but a book of old tunes."

12

It goes without saying that one should never travel by night.
[*A Frenchman's guide to England*, Retif de Vincennes
(Paris; published for the author, 1734)]

My voice sounded distant and oddly matter-of-fact. "What did this book look like?"

"Old," the spirit said. "And black. And the covers were loose and coming away."

"Was there writing in the front?"

"It was all written," she said. "None of it printed. But some of it wasn't in English – I couldn't read it. And I *can* read."

"Of course you can," Bedwalters said fondly. His expression was astonishing, a mixture of grief, and love, and pride.

"And there was music too?"

"On every page."

Fischer's book. Casper Fischer's inheritance, that Lizzie Ord had seen in her father's printing shop a year or two back. How in heaven's name did all this come together? And how was I to tell Fischer that his book had caused a girl's death?

"Did *Jem* say where he'd got the book?"

"No, sir."

"So you met him at the Old Man and he had the book with him. When was this?"

"A week ago, sir."

"A week before you – " I couldn't say the word.

"Died, sir," she said composedly. "It was the Saturday. A little over a week before. I brought him back here and after we were finished, he asked if I'd keep the book for him for a week or two. He said it was a gift for his father and he didn't want to keep it at home in case his father saw it."

"A gift? In such a bad condition?"

"He said he was going to get it repaired, sir. He said he'd give me sixpence if I kept it safe."

"And then you met him again on Tuesday?"

"Outside the chandlers, sir, on the Key. He recognised me at once and said straight away he'd get his book off me, and use my services at the same time."

"So you came back here, you – er – " I foundered, casting a panicked look at Bedwalters, but he was perfectly calm. "Afterwards, he wanted the book."

"Not afterwards, sir," she said. "He asked me for it as soon as we got here. I got it for him and he thanked me and gave me my sixpence. And then – " She faltered for the first time; she fell briefly silent, then said more firmly: "I never saw him do it. I was lying on my face for – " Another hesitation. "That's the way some gentlemen like to do it. And afterwards, he leant over me and whispered in my ear. And I'd just realised he'd said *goodbye* when I felt a great burning in my back and – and – "

"Hush, hush," Bedwalters whispered. "I'm here. You're safe now. I'm here."

Hugh, still hunched over his knees, shifted violently.

"And he never told you his surname?" I asked.

"No, sir."

"Is there anything else you can tell me? Anything odd he said? Any jewellery he wore?"

"No jewellery, sir," she said straightaway. A pause. "I don't remember anything."

"Well," I said. "If you do, will you tell Mr Bedwalters?"

"Indeed, sir."

"I'll be here," Bedwalters said.

I had no doubt of that.

He accompanied us to the door. The fine drizzle had eased; the sky was clearing. We stood for a while in silence. An elderly man plodded morosely by, bowed under the weight of half a tree trunk. I said, "I must go back to Long End tonight. Can you enquire about any missing apprentices?"

Bedwalters's face lightened. "Indeed, I would be glad of something practical to do. I can send to the towns round about too, to see if anything is known there."

"We could send a notice to the London papers," Hugh said. "Raise the hue and cry."

Bedwalters shook his head. "We don't know enough, sir. A young man, dark-haired, about Mr Patterson's height? How many men would fit that description?" He looked at me with a direct challenge in his eyes. "Can we catch him, Mr Patterson?"

I would not lie to him. "I'll try."

He nodded, as if it was exactly as he'd expected. He looked up and down the road as if the passers-by interested him greatly. "Westgate was busier," he said, "but there are not so many carts and carriages here, which is a great blessing. There is much less noise."

We walked away in silence. Only when we reached the end of the street did Hugh say bitterly, "He's reconciled himself to the change in his station. He already looks on this place as home. *This place.*" He threw out a hand to melodramatically demonstrate the dilapidated street. "Of all the people who deserve better, Bedwalters and that girl must be foremost." He took a deep breath. "When do you have to be back at Long End?"

"As soon as possible. Hugh, can you enquire at the Old Man and some of the other taverns along the Key? Ask if anyone saw Nell with someone of the right description. Someone might know him."

Hugh regarded me dryly. "That's a long shot."

"Everything in this matter is a long shot," I said bitterly. "Hugh, you know as well as I do we've little chance of success. But we must try!"

Hugh wanted me to linger over a drink with him but we had spent longer than I'd anticipated talking to the spirit and it was later than I'd hoped. I didn't fancy riding the seven miles to Long End at night, so I decided to set out at once. I was riding up Northumberland Street on my way to Barras Bridge when I heard my name called. A horseman in a yellow-green riding coat came clattering up behind me, causing pedestrians to scatter.

I looked at the dark lively face with astonishment and doffed my hat. "Mr Alyson."

He urged his horse alongside mine; the animals might be from the same stable but his was undoubtedly better bred and more highly strung – a glossy black horse that seemed to take fright at every scrap of paper or flash of colour. Alyson controlled it effortlessly and I felt lumpen by his side.

He was grinning broadly, like a boy playing truant. "See! I made it after all. Am I too late? Is the excitement all over? You have the fellow?"

"Not yet."

"But the spirit has disembodied?"

"Indeed."

"And she gave you a good description of the villain?"

"An excellent one," I said dryly. "Young, dark-haired, about my height – oh, and he wore a gaudy waistcoat."

Alyson laughed. "So detailed! Does he have a name?"

"Jem."

"In short," he said, apparently finding it all exquisitely humorous, "she knew nothing."

"Nothing of any use," I admitted. "Except – "

He curbed his horse's interest in a passing dog, raised an eyebrow. "She didn't think he was from Newcastle. He didn't have a local accent. And she only saw him occasionally, as if he came to town only now and again."

"A hint," Alyson said, thoughtfully. "But hardly of great help. You can hardly go around questioning every man not native to the town."

"Every *young* man," I said.

"Even so – there must be hundreds." He cast me a sympathetic look. "Your trip seems to have been disappointing, Pattinson. You think he will escape unscathed?"

I wondered if there was anything I could do to persuade him to use my correct name. "Not if I have anything to do with it," I retorted. "I'm not finished yet." I was tempted to tell him about the book but thought better of it; I owed Fischer that information first.

We turned to ride over Barras Bridge; a wagon coming the other way narrowed the space so Alyson and I had to ride single file. He, of course, went first. He waited until we could again ride side by side. "Have you seen the constable?"

"Bedwalters? He's been dismissed from the post."

"One has sympathy of course," Alyson said, in an unsympathetic tone. "But he can hardly be surprised. Associating with someone of that girl's kind is bad enough, but to throw caution to the winds and sacrifice everything to her, is simply preposterous! And she is in any case dead! How can such a whimsical gesture profit him?"

I bit back anger. "It can be very difficult to divine other people's motives."

Alyson laughed. "I think that's an understatement!"

He urged his horse into a trot and I was forced to do likewise to keep up with him. We rode out into the country. The sun at times peered through gaps in the cloud layer – it was so low that it dazzled us as the road twisted and turned. We saw a few locals: two or three labourers in the fields; a clergyman in a smart carriage; an elderly woman picking berries in a hedge. Alyson began to whistle through his teeth.

"Did your business go well, sir?"

"Business? Oh, the matter of the woodland. I warn you, Pattinson – never inherit an estate. You start out thinking it will be wonderful to have such wealth and then you suddenly find you've also inherited a score of disputes with neighbours, half of which are just about to go to court. I've tried to talk Ridley out of it, but he insists on going ahead. Are you enjoying yourself at Long End, Patterson?"

Startled, I stared at him. He was my employer, paying me to do a job for him. What did he expect me to say? *No, your friends are rude and patronizing. No, the conditions are dreadful.* "The house is very comfortable," I said. "And your guests are interesting people."

"Lawyer Armstrong picked them very well," he agreed. "They are good people, very good people. Of course, some are rather *idiosyncratic*, shall we say? Heron, for one. Have you ever got a word out of the fellow?"

"He is naturally reserved," I said.

"And that Colonial, always talking about his inheritance." Alyson was looking about him as if he thought he'd caught a glimpse of something unexpected. We were on a lonely stretch of the road with no one about, and a hump of woodland loomed up ahead. I fancied he didn't like the look of it – all gloomy and shadowed – and neither did I.

"Have you been looking for this book today?"

I tried to sound indifferent. "With singular lack of success, I'm afraid. I spoke to Charnley but he didn't know what had happened to it. It appears to have been stolen from his shop."

The sun hid behind a cloud again as we entered the first stretch of woodland following the pale road in the gloom, I began to think I'd been unwise to set out so late. And my early start was catching up with me; I was tired, and it had been a long day. I began to be desperate for sleep.

"Stolen?" Alyson mused. "Then it must be valuable. Perhaps it's bound in gold!"

"Perhaps there's a family tree drawn on the flyleaf – valuable evidence in an inheritance dispute."

Alyson chuckled. "Perhaps there's a bequest described in verse and set to music." And he raised his voice – a remarkably pleasant tenor – in a mocking rendition of that popular psalm tune, Old Hundredth, with only a mild distortion of the rhythm.

"And to my aunt I now bequeath
All that I die possess'd and own'd,
On one condition only made
That o'er my death she doth not grieve."

He had hardly sung the last note when a shot rang out.

13

The system of justice is rudimentary. Villains are rarely caught,
and only when they threaten the great and the good.
And often not even then.
[*A Frenchman's guide to England*, Retif de Vincennes
(Paris; published for the author, 1734)]

My horse started, danced. I hauled back on the reins. Alyson's
highly-strung animal screamed and reared and the reins flew
out of Alyson's hands. He crashed to the ground. I tried to grab
the animal as it bolted past but it jerked out of my reach. My
own horse almost took fright again.

By the time I had control once more, I knew we were safe. Any
robber would already have taken advantage of our confusion to
hold us up. I swung my horse round, and glimpsed two men
running across a distant field.

They were already too far away to catch. I clambered down
from my horse and hurried to Alyson. He lay face down on the
rough track, but was stirring as I reached him. I touched his
shoulder. His arm shot out in angry rebuff; he pushed himself
over on to his back, swearing viciously.

There was a graze along his forehead as if the shot had just
caught him; his hands were bloodied and crusted with earth.
Mud smeared his smart riding coat. "Get my horse, damn it."

The animal had bolted two or three hundred yards along the
track. I tossed the reins of my own horse over a low-hanging
branch and went after it. It was sweating whitely, dancing about
with rolling eyes. I muttered soothing nothings. Then I heard
unmistakable sounds and glanced back to see Alyson astride *my*
horse, cantering towards me.

He didn't even slow down. As he cantered past, he called out;
"Use my mount," and spurred on. By the time he came up with
his own horse, he was at the full gallop and spooked the animal

into another nervous frenzy.

And when I got to it, the damn animal was lame.

There were, I estimated, two or three miles still to go to Long End, and the only option was to walk, and not quickly either, with a lame frightened horse tugging on its reins at almost every step. In lanes where the setting sun penetrated less with every minute, where the fields on either side were shrouded in gloom, every rustle of leaves made me think the attackers were returning to finish me off.

Two attackers. And not simple highway robbers – no one had actually tried to steal anything. So, a deliberate attack. But *two* men? The apprentice had an accomplice? That suggested the matter was a great deal more complicated than I'd thought.

I passed two cottages deep in the wood and wondered whether to take shelter there. Better to continue, I thought. How could I be certain that neither of my attackers originated from these hovels or were sheltering there themselves? I would have made better progress if I'd turned the horse loose in the first field I came to, but ten to one someone would steal it and Alyson, I suspected, would probably insist I paid him the animal's full value.

I'd covered less than a mile and was in open country when I saw a horseman cantering towards me. A neat slight figure wearing a large concealing greatcoat, and a tricorne jammed down hard. There was nothing I could do but stand and wait for his approach. Swearing under my breath, I vowed to spend some of my few savings on a pistol.

The chestnut horse reined in beside me. I looked up at Esther Jerdoun.

Under that greatcoat, she was dressed in breeches. A cravat was knotted carelessly around her throat; a waistcoat of embroidered burgundy gaped at her breast showing the gathers of a white shirt beneath. She looked utterly beautiful and I was furious with her. Riding out alone! At night!

"What the hell are you doing here?!"

"Not looking for thanks at any rate," she said coolly.

I took a breath, unclenched my jaw. "My apologies, madam. I've had a very trying day."

"Was that before or after the attacker shot at you?"

I stared at her, then laughed unwillingly. "Oh – both! And how do you know about the attacker?"

"I chased him off," she said.

As I gaped at her, she swung down from her horse and began rummaging in her saddlebags. "Do sit down, Charles, before you fall down. There is a tree stump over there in the hedge. I have some wine and cheese. Thank goodness the night is warm."

"You shouldn't be out riding alone," I said, unable to hide my anxiety. "Not at this time of night!"

She gave me a cool look. "You are not my husband yet, Charles."

Nor ever will be, I thought, and lowered myself wearily on to the tree stump. My feet were aching; I'd walked around all day and never imagined I'd end by traipsing several miles along country lanes.

"You are right," Esther said. She pulled a bottle of wine from the saddlebag and two cloth-wrapped parcels, and came to sit down beside me. "I ought to be more circumspect. Scandalising people by riding around in breeches is not wise."

I was disconcerted. I'd never heard Esther give a fig for the opinions of other people. Besides, I disapproved of her riding alone, not riding in breeches. I rather liked Esther's breeches. And her independence of mind. Her cool head and her mischievous smile –

This would not do. I concentrated on the parcels she was unwrapping. One held two wine glasses – she held them up to the light to make sure they were still clean. The other contained white bread, cheese and two large apples. She filled the glasses, offered me cheese. It was all so genteel and civilised I felt a hysterical urge to laugh.

"We can't just sit here. There's a man out there with a pistol who might come back to finish us off!"

"No," Esther said firmly. "He is entirely gone, I promise you. Now, will you let me tell you the story without interruption, Charles? It will take much less time, I assure you."

Wine and cheese and the woman I loved. And she was plainly enjoying herself. In the breeches and waistcoat and greatcoat, she even began to behave like a man, putting one foot up on a stone and lounging back against a fence.

"You seem to attract these situations, Charles," she said.

"They attract me," I said, punning.

"I do know *something* about the habits of poachers. My stepfather suffered badly from them when I was a child. They decidedly do not go close to the big house, and they do not attack anyone unless they themselves are in danger of arrest. An injury – or worse – to another person would simply change a transportation offence into a hanging offence, which clearly would not be desirable. So you were not attacked by a poacher the other day."

I nodded. "I agree." I was surprised by how thirsty I was, drank down the wine, poured another glassful.

"Which means that the first attack was in all likelihood a personal matter. So, when you decided to go into town this morning, I thought the threat of another attack had to be taken seriously." She reached for her wineglass which she'd propped in the cleft of a root. "I followed you into town this morning."

"What! I didn't see you."

"I know you didn't," she said. "You were in one of those abstracted moods you fall into when a mystery absorbs you. You would not have seen a mad bull charging at you until its breath was hot on your neck, and even then you would probably have thought it was just a warm breeze getting up."

"I can look after myself," I said mildly, half-annoyed at being chided, half-pleased she was so concerned. "Did you follow me around town?"

"I did not. I went home and did some business for a few hours. Then I went back to Barras Bridge to wait for you returning. Whatever possessed you to start out so late, Charles?"

"The spirit disembodied late."

She was silent for a moment. "Did she tell you anything useful?"

"Not much." I waved her on. "And then?"

"I followed you back, at what I thought was a safe distance. Not far out of town, I became aware somebody else was following too. I did not want to be seen so I turned off into a little village and cut across country; I got myself on a low ridge, where I could see the pair of you riding along the road. But I could not see your follower. I was just worrying over this when I spotted him on foot in the wood. Before I could do anything about it, he had taken a pot shot at you. Or at Alyson."

That startled me. I stared at her over a mouthful of apple. "You think Alyson could have been the target? But I was the one who was attacked at Long End."

"Charles," she said, patiently. "You are tall and dark and young. So is Edward Alyson. Close to, there is only the most superficial of resemblances between you, but at a distance and particularly from behind – "

"Even the most inept attacker must be able to distinguish the difference in the quality of our clothes," I protested.

"It was dark in that wood," she said. "And you were both wearing greatcoats. From a distance, the difference was not obvious at all. And it was even darker in the garden at Long End." The gloom was gathering, blurring the lines of her face. She gestured with her wine glass. "It is a possibility that must be considered, Charles!"

"But is it then mere coincidence that the attacks come while I'm trying to find out who killed Nell?"

"You admit yourself there is little hope of finding the girl's murderer. What is more likely? That an apprentice is scared you will find out his identity even though there is no evidence against him, or that a wealthy man like Alyson might offend some villains? Or a husband or two? Or be involved in some dispute over property?"

I thought of the woodland. And wondered if 'Mrs. Alyson'

had a husband elsewhere.

"What happened after the villain fired the shot?"

"I saw Alyson fall. The man must have thought he had hit his target. He ran off. Across the fields. I set the horse after him and he must have seen or heard me – he veered off in another direction. Then my horse balked at a high gate and I thought it quicker to go after him on foot."

The men I'd seen running across the field, I realised, had not been two men at all, but a man and a woman: the attacker pursued by Esther. So – only one attacker then, as I had previously thought.

"He was rather faster on his feet than I am," Esther said ruefully. "I might have caught up with him in time but another man emerged from a hedgeline riding one horse and leading another. They rode off together and I had to give up the chase."

I was bewildered. Two attackers after all?

"In what direction did they go?"

"West," she said, "into the setting sun. He will not be back tonight, Charles. Even if he knows he failed to kill whichever of you was his intended victim, he knows too that he was seen. He will not come back and risk capture – best to be patient and try again another time."

"What did this second man look like?"

"Burly, middle-aged perhaps. I could see nothing more than that. Oh, and he was poorly dressed like a servant." She began to wrap up what was left of the food and the glasses, held out the wine bottle to me. "I think we should make our way back."

"To Long End?" I stood up, exasperated. "I'm tempted just to have done with it all and go back to town."

"Nonsense," she said. "You could no more give up on a mystery than fly. Besides, you have a living to earn. And I am here, because you are here." She smiled at my surprise. "Oh, really, Charles! Someone has to keep an eye on you!"

"You sound like Hugh," I said uneasily.

She was very close, a pale wraith in the gathering gloom, very still. Her perfume drifted to me like a night-scented flower.

A tiny smile touched her lips. "Charles, have you any idea how boring town is in summer?"

"Ah, I see," I said. "My company is better than yawning over a piece of needlework."

She leant closer. Her lips almost touched mine – I jerked back. She smiled again. "It is plain to me, Charles," she said, "that you will get that poor girl's murderer. I have every faith in you. And it is equally plain that *I* will get *you*."

She packed the remains of the meal, with the glasses and the wine bottle, in her saddle bag, swung herself up on to her horse, using the tree stump as a mounting block. "Time to start walking, Charles!"

Half a mile from the house, Esther spurred her horse on so we would not arrive at the same time. The sun had set completely and stars peeped through the rents in the dissipating clouds. As I trudged up the drive, the house loomed up ahead against the sky, an indistinct hulk sparkling with flickering candlelights.

I made the stable yard safely despite starting at every shadow. The grooms were waiting impatiently, probably warned of my imminent arrival by Alyson. One snatched the reins from my hands and started to coo over the dishevelled horse, another lifted its lame foot anxiously. No one cooed over me. No one addressed even one sentence to me – a far more effective display of contempt than any words could have been.

I crossed the yard to the back door leading into the scullery. A shadow detached itself from the darkness by the horse trough. A tall man, jerking his head to urge me back into the shadows; I retreated with him, looking in resignation at the lean marked face of Fowler.

"All right," he said, grinning wolfishly. "What's all the excitement? How did his high and mightiness Mr Alyson get to look like he'd fallen into a midden?"

"Someone fired at us on the road," I said wearily. "Fowler, I need sleep."

"And I need something to tell his lordship."

"Heron sent you?" I said startled.

"Likes to keep up with what's going on," he said. "And so do I. Come on, Patterson," he wheedled. "If there's excitement, let me in on it! You know how dull life is when all you've got to worry about is whether a coat is pressed and cravats bleached!"

"You should have kept to your old life then."

"I'd be hanged by now," he said, his grin widening.

"Then settle for a quiet life." I turned for the scullery door. "I'm going to bed before I fall asleep standing up."

Fowler laughed softly. "You know your problem? You attract trouble."

"You're not the first to say so."

"Nor the last, I warrant." He followed me into the dark scullery. A stub of candle burned on a table just inside the door; he took it up, gestured to me to precede him. "Thing is," he said. "There's only so many times you can get yourself out of trouble. Take my word for it. It always catches up with you in the end."

"You seem hale and hearty enough."

"I got out," he said. "Settled for the boredom of shirts and coats. *You* just get yourself in deeper, month after month." We started up the narrow servants' stair. "And I don't much fancy being the one who has to tell Heron you've got yourself killed."

"It won't come to that," I said.

He shook his head. "Always does."

14

I incautiously mentioned the Colonies last night to my host
and was treated to a diatribe of near four hours on the ingratitude
of the inhabitants there. Really, I should have known better!
[Letter from Retif de Vincennes, to his brother Georges, 11 July 1736]

He was at my door next morning before I was properly awake.

"Don't worry," he said. "You're not the last up. There's not a lady out of bed except Mrs Jerdoun and she's gone for a ride."

I rubbed sleep out of my eyes, wondering if Esther had ridden out to look at the wood to look for signs of our attackers.

"And only a handful of the gentlemen up too," Fowler said. He broke off, then started again in quite a different tone. "Would you like me to shave you, sir?"

Instinctively, I looked to the door. Heron walked in; his footsteps were soft but obviously not soft enough to escape Fowler's notice. He cast an assessing look over me. "No damage, I see."

"Alyson was the one who fell from his horse."

"Mr Alyson is in the breakfast room, sir," Fowler murmured and indicated deferentially that I should sit down to be shaved. "I believe he has suffered no ill effects from his adventure last night."

"He seems positively to have enjoyed the incident," Heron said dryly. "He is telling everyone about his narrow escape. You did not feature a great deal. I believe he frightened the fellow off himself. A great burly brute, I understand."

I sighed. "We never saw him. He never got within a hundred yards of us. Did Alyson – Mr Alyson – suggest a reason for the attack?"

"Highwaymen," Heron said, straight-faced.

I laughed. "On a country lane? They wouldn't find very rich pickings. And no one attempted to hold us up."

"If you have no clue as to who killed the girl," Heron said,

95

going straight for the heart of the matter, "why should anyone attack you? Unless there is some musician who wishes to take over your teaching practice?"

"They'd find it sadly unprofitable," I said, submitting to Fowler's ministrations. "I was wondering if the real target was not Alyson. There's some business about a woodland?"

Heron knew all about it, as I'd suspected he would – he'd evidently listened to William Ridley's rambling diatribes, and elaborated in detail as Fowler shaved me. There were ten acres of woodland, apparently, split into two by a stream; the woodland lay at the point where three estates joined. Ridley owned one of the estates, Alyson had just inherited the second; they claimed half of the woodland each. But the owner of the third estate claimed the entire wood was within *his* land, as the result of a marriage settlement a century ago.

"It's all the fault of bad maps, of course," Heron said. "If the parties concerned had employed a professional to draw up the map with the marriage settlement, there could be no dispute. Instead, some lawyer's clerk who had never seen the land did a rough sketch, put the stream in the wrong place, misnamed a field, and as a result has caused fifty years of wrangling."

"Is there any possibility," I pondered, as Fowler paused to sharpen his razor, "that this third landowner might have some reason to remove Alyson?"

"But it is Ridley who is the prime mover of the court case, and therefore the more likely target," Heron pointed out. "And I am certain that if he also had been attacked, we would have heard of it. Several times."

"If I may interject – "

We looked at Fowler, who was standing beside me with the slightest of deferential stoops. Heron nodded.

"I understand," Fowler said, "that the third landowner died last year. The claimants on that side are two ten-year-old girls. I was wondering if a more likely motive for the attack on Mr Alyson would be a jealous husband?"

Heron said, "I doubt Alyson is looking at any woman other

than his wife at this moment. He is a newly-married man."

Fowler looked at me. I said nothing. There was no *proof*, after all, that the Alysons were not married. And Heron was strait-laced; if he suspected some irregularity, he would not feel able to keep silent. Would he even stay in the house? It was ignoble, and dispiriting, but some part of my mind was thinking that if the houseparty broke up, I'd never get paid the fifteen guineas I'd been promised.

"I don't think this is about philandering. There's that damn book. I swear the book Nell kept for her murderer is the same one Fischer's looking for."

I related my researches of the previous day while Fowler silently finished shaving me and Heron leant against the door jamb with a neutral expression.

"You must tell Fischer about the book and the part it played in the girl's murder," he said finally. "The book is his – he has a right to know. Moreover, he may have information he has not yet thought to tell us, that might throw light on the book's significance."

I contemplated this idea. I'd been very dogmatic with Alyson yesterday – of course I would solve the crime, nothing would stop me – but that had been mere bravado. I'd known all along that my chances of locating Nell's murderer were slight; despite my reluctance to distress Fischer, I couldn't afford to neglect any possible source of information.

Where, I wondered, had the Philadelphian been on the night of Nell's death? The book was *his*, after all.

"If you are ready," Heron said as Fowler packed up his shaving gear. "We may find Fischer in the breakfast room."

Fowler gave me an amused look. There's no stopping Heron once he's decided to take a hand in something.

Fischer was indeed in the breakfast room, sipping coffee and eating eggs, ham and kidneys, while perusing Daniel Defoe's book describing his tour of England some ten years ago. He's an author I'm partial to myself; he has some complimentary things to say about Newcastle. I helped myself to eggs while Heron poured coffee, waving away the services of the magnificent butler. A footman came in and out replenishing the food and drink. I would have preferred to wait for privacy before speaking to Fischer but Heron, with casual indifference, behaved exactly as if we were alone and plunged straight in.

"With regard to your inheritance, Mr Fischer."

"Ah yes." Fischer set the book aside, pushed his empty plate away. "I've been investigating the possibility of visiting my cousins at Shotley Bridge. It's rather further than I anticipated."

"The sword and the book," Heron said. "Patterson was asking after them for you in town yesterday."

Fischer looked at me eagerly. "Indeed – and did you hear any news?"

I was not pleased that Heron left me to deliver the bad tidings. I outlined what I'd discovered. Fischer was amused to hear that an antiquarian had liked his inheritance so much as to want to print it but had balked at the expense; Charnley's behaviour reminded him of a cordwainer at home in Philadelphia. He was bewildered, however, by the behaviour of the young man who'd stolen the book.

"But why?" he demanded. "What is so important about a book of psalm tunes? I understand from Mrs Ord that the book is much damaged. Why should anyone steal such a poor specimen?"

"I don't know," I admitted. "I'd hoped you might throw some light on the matter."

He shook his head. His old-fashioned wig bobbed. "I've never seen the book, only had it described to me. There's nothing valuable about it, except to a musician."

Not even to a musician, I thought. I took a deep breath and told him about its presumed connection to Nell's death.

He was distressed, as of course he was bound to be. He kept repeating, "Killed for it. Dear God, killed for it."

"We don't know that for certain," I said, trying to soften the blow. "She had it in keeping for her murderer, certainly, but whether he killed her for it is not so clear. I've spoken to her spirit – she says there was no conversation between them, no threats, no explanation. The murderous attack came entirely without warning."

"If it had been the sword," Fischer said, still distracted. "Now that I could understand. But the book!"

"Has the sword disappeared too?" Heron asked.

Fischer thought on this. "I believe not. The terms in which my cousins have written suggest they still have it." He sighed. "There is an element of revenge in this, I regret to say. My father prospered in Pennsylvania and my cousins, I understand, are struggling. That's why I believe they disposed of the book – petty revenge, but it satisfies some people."

"But would they not have sold the sword too?" Heron asked. "For the money it would raise?"

Fischer shook his head. "By no means. The sword was my grandfather's masterpiece, made to show his skill – it is a kind of advertisement, sir, a demonstration of the work the family produces. And there is some considerable pride in it."

"So," I said, "was there anything in the description you were given of the book which suggests anything unusual about it?"

He fingered his coffee dish absently. "It's evidently a black book, longer than it is tall, with hand-drawn staves for the music and the words written in an immaculate hand. There is an inscription on the fly leaf at the front and an index of tunes at the back."

"It is probably in the river Tyne by now," Heron said. "The murderer would surely want to get rid of anything that tied him to the girl's death."

I shook my head. "He asked Nell to keep it safe for him – he valued it and thought it might get lost or stolen. Why kill a girl for the book then throw it away?"

"He killed her to prevent her talking about it?" Fischer asked. "But how can you keep a spirit silent?"

"You can't," I said, comprehension dawning. "That's not why he killed her. He killed her so she would not be able *to identify him* as being in possession of the book. She can describe the murderer to us but the description could fit a hundred men, and otherwise she cannot identify him unless she sees him. And, as a spirit, she cannot move from the place of her death. All he has to do is avoid that house and he's safe."

"Besides," Heron pointed out, "the testimony of a spirit cannot be accepted in a court of law."

The footman came in, lifted a few lids on the sideboard and took an empty dish out to be refilled. The butler stood stoically in a window embrasure. I was startled to catch his eye; he'd been watching me, I realised. Was it something I'd said?

The footman came back and I gave myself up to wondering how the devil I could question Fischer about his movements on the night of Nell's death without giving offence.

"All this must give you a very bad view of Newcastle," I said at last.

"It's a city," Fischer said heavily, "and all cities, alas, have their bad parts."

Newcastle is merely a town but there was no point in correcting him. "And to think you must have been in the town at exactly the same time as your book."

Fischer was startled. "Indeed, I haven't seen the place. My ship docked at Whitehaven and I rode to Carlisle and thence across country. And a worse road I have never seen!"

"There is no road between Carlisle and Newcastle," Heron said dismissively. "It is nothing more than a cart track. After two days' rain, moreover, it becomes a stream."

Fischer's thoughts, inevitably, had gone back to Nell and the book.

"Devil take it! That a man should kill for my book! Do you think it would help if I offered a reward? Damn it, yes, a reward. I cannot let this matter drop."

He required a great deal more persuasion than Heron to abandon the idea. And only, eventually, at the cost of my assuring him I could catch the villain without the aid of a reward.

A promise I regretted the moment it was out of my mouth.

As I left the dining room, I was accosted by the musical ladies who wanted to practise their songs. So we repaired to the cramped harpsichord, and the ladies spent some time arranging their music while I ran through a few scales. The harpsichord, thankfully, had remained more or less in tune – one advantage of the corner was that it was not in the direct line of sunshine through the window.

It became borne in on me that the ladies had something on their minds. They looked at each other over the top of the harpsichord; one – the elder – shook her head; the other looked mulish and obstinate.

"Is anything wrong?" I asked.

"No," said the elder. "Yes," said the younger at the same time. They stared each other out. The younger said, "It is no good, Amelia, I must speak." She turned to me with an air of kindly reproach.

"Mr Patterson. I understand that of course we do not move in the same social circles, that you do not have the – er – advantage of polite society, generally speaking. But this matter of the – " She struggled for the right words. "*Poor unfortunate*," she said after a moment. "My dear sir." She became animated. "One cannot pretend that such creatures do not exist, but really, one cannot extend sympathy to them. They do not deserve our consideration."

"She was God's creature," the elder lady said. "However fallen, she did not deserve to be killed."

"But to bring such sordid affairs into polite society, Amelia! It is simply not appropriate."

The other lady started, "Perhaps not – "

But at that moment, Mrs Alyson walked into the room. She was dressed magnificently, in a plum-red dress that defied all the fashionable conventions that ladies should dress in pale colours. Her jewellery sparkled at throat and ears and wrists; lace draped her sleeves and skirts and her low neckline. A fortune on her back and she proceeded, in a coldly efficient way, to demolish the character of a girl whose last sixpence, literally, had been taken from her along with her life. Like a true clergyman's daughter, she quoted portions of the sacred texts to me, designed to show how all decent God-fearing men and women should shun those whose morals are ruined beyond all retrieval. The younger musical lady nodded agreement at this, but the elder broke in sharply.

"It is my experience," she said cuttingly, "that more morals are ruined by poverty than by any other cause."

Mrs Alyson flushed but rallied. "My husband and I have been poor, Mrs Widdrington," she said. "I am not afraid to admit it. But *our* morals have not been ruined."

Given that I believed the Alysons to be unmarried, I thought this hypocrisy of the highest order.

"Moreover," Mrs Alyson said repressively. "Your investigations into this matter, Mr Patterson, have brought my husband into danger. He was grazed by a shot intended for you. I will not have this, Mr Patterson. This behaviour must stop." She brought her gaze to me; her eyes, the darkest of browns, flashed almost as much as her jewels. "If it does not, I will take steps to rectify the situation. In short, you will be dismissed. You will go back to Newcastle with your tail between your legs and you will never set eyes on that fifteen guineas you have been promised. And then, presumably, you may well find yourself in the same position as that whore!"

The younger lady murmured a horrified protest at Mrs Alyson's last word; the elder started to say something. They were both interrupted by Edward Alyson walking in with Lizzie Ord on his arm, saying to her, "Here you are, my dear. I told you we'd find music in the drawing room."

The change in Mrs Alyson was remarkable. All the anger slipped away; the woman that moved to her husband's side was lithe and eager, welcome lighting up her face. Alyson smiled down at her and, regardless of the company, drew a loving finger down her cheek.

In the middle of my anger, and humiliation, something else stirred. Nothing is more bitter than jealousy. To see others sharing what you can never hope for with the woman you love is galling. And when one of the happy parties is a woman whom you've just realised you despise – indeed, come close to hating… I could hardly stay in my seat.

The younger lady was welcoming Lizzie, asking her if she played or sang. The elder – Mrs Widdrington – leant over the harpsichord and spoke quickly and softly. "There are times, Mr Patterson, when it is impossible to close our eyes to the unpleasant things of this world. Do what you must."

And she turned to greet Lizzie, who was just admitting that she played the harpsichord.

I made my escape on to the terrace as Lizzie slipped on to the harpsichord stool to accompany the musical ladies. From the terrace into the formal garden. My cheeks were burning. The hypocrisy of the woman! To be unwed and yet condemn a street-girl – some of her guests would think there was precious little difference between Mrs Alyson and Nell.

I wondered if I'd be so anxious to solve the crime if it had been Margaret Alyson killed. I hoped I would have, but at this moment, I could not guarantee it.

One thing was for certain. Mrs Alyson could threaten as much as she liked. Whatever the difficulties, I would not let Nell's murderer go free.

15

There are areas of the countryside which are delightful,
in which one may know the sort of peace unequalled
anywhere since the Garden of Eden.
[Letter from Retif de Vincennes, to his sister, Agnés, 21 May 1736]

I walked down the steps on to the sunlit path. From the rose
garden hidden behind the hedge on the right, I heard women's
voices and the barking of a dog. I strode past the overgrown
flowerbeds and the neglected fountain, down to the grass border
that separated the garden from the ornamental canal. In daylight, I could see that the water in the canal was stagnant,
covered with a green mat of weed; the stone bridge with its wide
parapet was cracked and spotted with lichen.

Through the woods, to the kitchen garden, down to the drive
and the road to the village, trying to walk out the humiliation
and the annoyance. There was no point in being distressed at the
strictures of a woman who'd probably been shielded all her life
against the evils of the world. A clergyman's daughter from some
safe cathedral close. I wondered how she'd come to be Edward
Alyson's mistress. The two of them seemed deliriously in love –
was there some impediment to prevent their marriage? Had one
of them contracted an alliance before?

One thing I knew for certain: Edward Alyson would regard it
as a great game to pass off his mistress as his wife.

I found myself at the gate into the park, with the pompous
lions posing on top of its pillars. I could hear a horse's hooves
clip-clopping in the clear air, coming towards me along the
road though still hidden by a bend and the tall overblown
summer hedges. Then the horse came into view and I saw the
rider.

Esther. Sitting astride her horse, covering the immodest
breeches with the skirts of a large greatcoat. I was too pleased to

see her to be cautious. I smiled up at her. "Did you enjoy your ride?"

"Very much." She swung herself out of the saddle, shaking her head as I moved to help. Taking the horse's reins, she led him towards the park gates; I fell into step beside her.

"Did you go back to the wood?"

She nodded. "But I did not hope for a great revelation and indeed found none. There is a patch of mud roughly where I saw the two horsemen meet and a few hoofprints, but beyond that nothing. I went a mile or so in the direction they took but it is open country. I saw a few farmhouses but nothing of any significance. They could have gone anywhere."

I glanced up into the trees that overhung the drive as a greenfinch flitted across my view. "Including here?"

She frowned. "By a roundabout route, yes. Charles – do you suspect one of the guests?"

Could I imagine plump William Ridley wielding a cudgel and striking me down at the foot of the terrace steps? Or that severe fellow who was still paying too much attention to Esther?

"Not necessarily." I glanced around to make sure we were not overheard. "Our murderer may simply be lurking in the grounds, keeping an eye on my comings and goings. Esther – "

She gave me a smiling look. God, perhaps she thought I was going to propose here and now. Looking down at her slim figure, in those outrageously attractive breeches, at the hair that escaped the pins and hung about her pale neck – looking at her, I felt a sudden urge to do just that. To damn all the scandalised looks there'd be, all the gossip, all the insinuations –

But I remembered how I'd felt while Margaret Alyson was tearing me apart with her scorn and her unshakeable confidence in the way the world ought to be run. I would not subject Esther to that kind of experience.

"I don't think we should be seen together," I started awkwardly and saw her face darken at once.

And at that moment, William Ridley drove by in a carriage drawn by two of Alyson's best horses and driven by Alyson's

London coachman. Ridley was staring along the drive but his head turned slowly, irresistibly, as he caught sight of us standing side by side. I saw him register Esther's clothes and something else dawned in his eyes – a smile that started to curve his lips. Then he was past and Esther, to my amazement, was swearing.

"Damn – "

And she swung herself on to her horse and urged it into a trot. It – and she – were out of my sight round one of the curves in the drive, in seconds.

I walked across the park towards the canal so I could approach the house from a different direction from Esther. The encounter with Ridley was unfortunate but he had made my point for me. What a devil of a tangle it all was! What was there in the August air to produce this madness of unhappy couples? Nell and Bedwalters, Edward and Margaret Alyson, Philip and Lizzie Ord, Esther and myself... I itched to be back in town. Damn all this pretentious artificiality, all this idleness; what really mattered was to find Nell's killer, to bring at least some measure of comfort to Bedwalters. What could the Alysons know about that kind of pain? I certainly hoped Lizzie never came anywhere near such distress.

There was no sound of music from the drawing room as I climbed the steps to the terrace but I heard a confusion of eager voices discussing something. When I went in, Lizzie was seated at the harpsichord, looking nervously at a music book on the stand, and Edward Alyson was leaning over, pointing something out as if asking her to play. From what I could see it was an opera book, where the singer's melody has only a single bass line to accompany it and the harpsichordist must invent the chords from those notes.

Half the houseparty was in the room, it seemed – certainly all the ladies, chattering excitedly. Mrs Widdrington and the other musical lady were straining to see the music over Lizzie's shoulder. Mrs Alyson hovered behind her husband, looking bored. Beyond was Philip Ord, silent and hostile, as if he suspected Alyson was making an advance on his wife. Three or four of the other gentlemen (Heron not among them) were admiring the ladies.

What on earth was going on?

Alyson glanced up; Lizzie instinctively followed his example. Her face cleared. "Mr Patterson! Oh, pray do come and play. It is a figured bass and you know how difficult I find that."

She jumped up and made way for me. I took her place, and flicked to the front of the book to see what I was about to play. An opera. Or a *pastorale*, rather, like the one Dr Greene, master of the King's music, is allegedly writing at present.

Alyson was giving me advice on how to accompany a singer; it transpired his wife was to be the soloist. I glanced up at Mrs Alyson; her face was stony. There was one piece of advice of which Alyson did not need to remind me: if a mistake is made, the accompanist is always at fault, even if the singer has patently caused the problem.

I played the opening symphony. Mrs Alyson took an imperceptible breath and opened her voice and her throat, and let out into the warm sunny air of the drawing room tones of exquisite beauty and sweetness. Every onlooker was silent. She had a natural voice, totally without artifice, a voice that could touch high notes with the clarity of a bell and low notes with the warmth of sunshine. And, unlike most musical amateurs, she sang not only the notes, but the emotion behind them too.

Engaged in sight-reading the music and nodding to Lizzie when I needed the pages turned, and listening with great enjoyment to Mrs Alyson's beautiful rendition of the simple air, it was not until I struck the last chord and glanced up that I realised the effect the song had had on the others. The two musical ladies had sunk down on the couch in simple pleasure. Alyson was staring enraptured at his wife. Fischer was just inside the door, nodding in appreciation, and Heron – whose musical judgement is exacting – stood behind him with a distinct look of approval. I saw Esther come quietly in; she had changed into an elegant hooped gown of pale green and one of those absurd caps with lace lappets hanging down behind. Looking round, I saw only one person left unmoved; Philip Ord's gaze was fixed on his wife.

Lizzie was excited. "Oh, that was wonderful, wonderful!"

"My dear," Alyson said reverentially, taking his wife's hand and kissing it. "That was magnificent!"

In the murmur of agreement, the younger musical lady said wistfully, "Oh, I would love to hear you sing it *all*."

Alyson swung round. "Madam – so you shall," he cried exultantly. "We shall perform it all – the entire opera!"

There were cries of agreement, demands for a *proper* performance with costumes and props. Hurriedly, I glanced back to the beginning of the score. It was all very well to propose a performance but did we have sufficient singers? More importantly, did we have sufficient good singers?

It was already too late to protest. Alyson was explaining the plot: shepherd meets shepherdess, father locks shepherdess up until she agrees to marry his elderly crony, her friends lament. Shepherdess falls ill with heartbreak and shepherd threatens lifelong celibacy. Fortunately, the wise counsellor – usually the most infuriatingly sententious of characters – persuades the father to relent in the most unlikely fashion.

Alyson proceeded to allocate parts, making everyone laugh by giving them to the most unlikely people, then withdrawing the honour and passing it to someone else. We accumulated a hero and heroine: Alyson and his wife. Two friends of the heroine: the musical ladies of course. The heroine's irascible father: the tall gentleman with wandering eyes. I doubted he knew what a musical note was, but he certainly knew his character had at least two scenes in which he physically restrained his 'daughter' from flying to her lover. And – Alyson reached into the crowd and pulled out Lizzie Ord, with her too-perfect hair and her rouged cheeks. "And you, my dear, will be the pert young maid!"

That dreadful word: pert – with all its connotations of impropriety! I saw Lizzie's scared look fly at once to her husband's face. Ord looked furious.

I intervened before he could say anything. "I would appreciate Mrs Ord's help at the harpsichord. I'll need someone to turn the pages."

Alyson was straight on to the next matter – appointing a host of non-singing nymphs and shepherds to 'dress the scene'. With a face of thunder, Philip Ord gripped the back of his chair. Then he gave me the briefest of nods. It was more than I had expected.

Alyson was trying to press Heron into service, insisting, not entirely tactfully, that the scene required an older man in it. Heron was apparently not insulted; he merely said, "I have already decided my role I am to play the audience." Esther assured Alyson she was also very content to watch.

I let the hubbub rage, flicking through the pages of the score. There was nothing in the accompaniment to worry me; a little rehearsal would be all I needed. But one thing struck me at once and I anticipated what was about to happen – a fraction of a second before Alyson leant over the harpsichord, smiling.

"As for the parts – Mr Pattinson, how soon can you distribute them to the singers?"

I met his guileless gaze, the open boyish smile. Dear God, he didn't even understand what he was asking. We had only one score of the *pastorale*; Alyson wanted me to write out each character's part so they could take it away with them to practise, and he was probably expecting them all within an hour. Had he any idea how long it took to write out music?

"Is this the only copy?" I asked carelessly.

"Certainly. I picked it up only a few weeks ago in London. Shall we say we will have a little rehearsal tonight after dinner?"

Choruses of approval.

"Just the first act?" I said, hoping to limit the task.

"The entire opera!" said one of the ladies eagerly.

"Very well." Alyson clapped his hands. "Let's leave Pattinson to his own devices. Ladies, what are we to do about costumes?"

I gathered up the book. There was nothing to be done in this chaos. If I was to write anything at all I must retreat to my room. Writing out the entire opera before dinner was an impossible task – I must think of a way to satisfy Alyson without appearing uncooperative. And just when I needed to concentrate on the matter of Nell's murder!

As I went into the hall, the butler approached me with a note on a salver. I'd hardly taken the note when he bowed and retreated – I didn't even have the chance to thank him. I stared after him in surprise. A servant not waiting for a tip?

The note was from Bedwalters, brief and to the point. He'd questioned his contacts and there were no missing apprentices, either in Newcastle or in the towns immediately round about. I went upstairs thoughtfully; that suggested the murderer was staying close by, trying to brazen it out.

In my room, I leafed through the score to see the magnitude of the task Alyson had set me. Page after page of arias. The two musical ladies would happily share a part; Alyson and his wife would no doubt be pleased to sing their songs off the same part too. All the same – I threw the book down in disgust. The whole thing was beyond belief – I would not have time to write out half of it!

And there was the matter of paper and ink. I might be able to find sufficient ink in the household to complete the task, but I'd only brought a handful of the raven quills I usually use for writing music. And paper! I'd never anticipated writing out an entire opera – I'd brought only a few sheets.

I seized paper and pen, scribbled a desperate note to Hugh and went off to find the butler again. He was just coming out of the drawing room and took the note with a murmur and a bow. This time he even turned down the coin I offered him. I made a mental note to ask Fowler if he had managed to glean any information about him.

I took the stairs back to my room two at a time, pondering where to start. The Alysons' parts of course – I'd start with the hero and heroine.

Esther Jerdoun was waiting on the landing outside my room.

In the dimness, she was like a light; her pale skirts took up almost the entire width of the narrow landing; her fair hair

110

glowed. Those ridiculous lappets swung as she turned her head. I caught my breath.

"You need someone to draw the staves for you," she said.

"I buy ready-ruled manuscript paper," I said. Regretfully.

She laughed. "I've seen it advertised in the papers. Then I will copy out parts for you."

"No," I said.

She shook her head. "I will not be dissuaded, Charles." She stood back to let me unlock my door, walked forward as soon as I had it open. I instinctively stood back to let her go in first, then cursed. Surely she must see she couldn't enter a gentleman's room – a single woman and a single man in a bedroom alone. Dear God, what would people think!

She was already walking towards the window, looking about with some annoyance. "This is a ridiculously small room. And the curtains could do with a wash." She gave them a twitch and dust flew out.

I went to the table, busied myself unpacking the few sheets of ruled paper I'd brought with me. "I'm sorry, but I've very little time."

She held out a hand. "Give me a pen then."

I stared at her. A little smile curved her lips. "You will not finish in time if you have to do it all yourself, Charles, as you very well know."

"You cannot stay," I said forcibly. "In heaven's name, think what talk it would give rise to!"

"Let it," she said, still holding out her hand for the pen.

"I will not let you risk your reputation!"

There was a brief scratch and the door opened.

And there was Claudius Heron, a red-bound book under one arm, and his mouth already opening to say something. Then he saw Esther, and his mouth snapped shut like a steel trap.

16

Morals are lax here, but woe betide you if you are found out!
[Letter from Retif de Vincennes, to his brother Georges, 11 July 1736]

There was a storm of an argument. Heron shouted; Esther was icy in return. I tried to intervene, to explain; Heron snapped at me to be quiet. He called Esther a stupid female with all the intelligence of a cat. Esther lost her temper and screeched at him. I hurried across to close the door. Half the servants in the house were probably eavesdropping.

It all subsided in the end, of course. Heron stood red-faced and breathing heavily in the centre of the room; Esther had gripped the curtains in her rage and was as white as ice. I stood between them, looking from one to the other, desperately trying to think what to say.

Heron was not looking at either of us. "No one must hear of this."

"We were not anticipating advertising it," Esther said. "Not until you chose to shout loud enough for the whole village to hear!"

"No one can hear," I said, trying to soothe the troubled waters. "Everyone's downstairs."

"The servants are not," Heron snapped.

"If they heard anything, the blame is at your door," Esther said.

"No one will hear!" I said in desperation. "I know this looks bad but – "

"Damn it!" Heron said furiously. "If this comes to Alyson's ears, he'll throw you out of the house and the story will be round town in days. What gentleman will employ you?"

"Thank you for your concern about *my* reputation," Esther said in a friendly fashion so false as to be highly offensive – as it was clearly intended to be.

"If you cared so much for it," Heron snapped, "you wouldn't be up here. Leave this room at once."

"This is my room – " I began. "No," Esther said at the same time.

"Then there is only one thing for it." Heron took a deep breath. His mouth twisted in distaste. "You must – you must marry."

"Indeed," Esther said, brightening. "I would be delighted."

"Oh, God," I said.

17

Sunday is a day of rest and must not be defiled.
Or, at least, not visibly so.
[*A Frenchman's guide to England*, Retif de Vincennes
(Paris; published for the author, 1734)]

Four hours later, in mid-afternoon, I was furiously copying out music when I heard the clatter of footsteps on the stairs. The door flew open, banging against one of the cane chairs, and Hugh staggered in, laden with parcels and grinning broadly.

"An entire ream of ruled manuscript paper, a hundred ravens' quills and enough ink to float a coal barge. And – " He saw my face; the grin faded. "All right, Charles," he said, sighing. "What trouble are you in now?"

"I'm betrothed," I said hollowly.

Hugh burst out laughing.

"It's not funny!" I protested and told him what had happened. He dumped the parcels on the floor, dragged up the cane chair and sat grinning even more broadly.

"Esther was only here to help me copy out the music," I said. "And Heron had to find another copy of the damned opera in the library and come up with it."

"Well, there is one good thing about it, Charles," Hugh said, still grinning. "If there are two copies of the book, you won't have to copy out all the parts."

"Hugh…" I said warningly.

"And," he said. "You love her."

Silence. Outside someone called; a dog barked.

"What's done is done," Hugh offered at last. "All you can do is make the best of it."

He was right, though it didn't make the situation any more palatable.

"We're not telling anyone," I warned. "Heron tried to insist we marry at once but Esther would not be rushed – she said we'll marry when we get back to town. We all agreed it would be best to marry first then announce it."

Hugh nodded. "Avoid all the arguments. A good idea. But don't dare forget to invite me, Charles."

"I'm counting on you for moral support," I said gloomily.

Hugh slapped his hands together. "Well, I have some good news for you."

"Impossible. Hugh, I have still pages and pages of arias to copy out and not even time to eat!"

"We've got a description of Nell's murderer."

"What!" I sat up. "Are you sure? Who saw him?"

"A chapman. He'd been down to the Keyside to pay a few bills and was walking back home when this fellow came running out of Mrs McDonald's. He didn't think much of it at the time. He left town at dawn next day on a tour of the local villages and only got back last night. He heard about Nell and went looking for you – when he heard you were out of town, he came to me instead."

"He didn't go to Bedwalters?"

"You're the one with the reputation as a solver of mysteries, Charles."

"And he's sure this person was the murderer?"

"The time's about right. And the lad was carrying something under his arm. A brown-paper-wrapped parcel. Book-sized, the chapman said."

I took a deep breath. "What did he look like?"

"Young. Maybe twenty. But the chapman thought he might even be a year or two younger. Soft complexion, not a boy who'd been in the open air much."

I could imagine the chapman's complexion; it would be weatherbeaten from years of tramping through sun and wind.

"He had dark hair, tied back, and an open face." Hugh scowled. "Whatever that means. Untroubled, the chapman said."

I began to doubt this was our murderer. "Could anyone be *untroubled* after killing a girl?"

"The book, Charles," Hugh insisted. "He *must* be the murderer."

"Not necessarily. He could have been a thief wandering in off the street. He saw the book, picked it up to steal, saw Nell's body, and took off in fright – "

"In which case, he would have looked terrified," Hugh pointed out. "And no one could wander into Mrs McDonald's unseen! That woman would never let a potential customer get away."

"What clothes was this man wearing?"

"The sort you'd expect an apprentice to wear. Neat, clean, tidy, poor quality and gaudy. A brown coat, a waistcoat with too much embroidery – silver on puce evidently – white stockings under his breeches. The stockings were embroidered too – white clocks, badly done. The chapman has an eye for that sort of thing; it's his business after all. Puce-coloured shoes, with a fashionable heel and big buckles."

"Typical apprentice," I grumbled. "Aping his betters." I'd had an apprentice last year and it had not been a happy experience. "Height?"

"Medium."

"What the devil's that supposed to mean?"

"The chapman said about his own height. Which is a couple of inches shorter than me."

Hugh is around six feet tall, an inch or so taller than myself. Our apprentice was not a runt, then.

"Fat? Thin?"

"Slender. Well-nourished, the chapman said."

I contemplated all this. It was good to have a description, but did it get us any further forward? "He's sure the apprentice came out of Mrs McDonald's house?"

He nodded. "The chapman frequents the house himself so he wouldn't have made a mistake."

"And did he see where the lad went?"

"Down towards the Keyside."

I groaned. "Towards the centre of town. We'll never trace him."

Hugh nodded sympathetically. "I've paid the fellow a shilling to wander around the Keyside for an hour or two, to see if he can spot our man." He overrode my objection. "Don't worry, I've told him not to approach the lad. And I know it's another long shot, but what else is there to do?"

A servant appeared in the doorway, a young lad himself, looking embarrassed and reluctant. "Message from Mr Alyson, sir. He was wondering if you'd finished copying the music."

I gave Hugh a speaking look but curbed my temper. "Pray assure Mr Alyson it'll be ready for this evening."

The servant hesitated, looked as if he wanted to say something more, changed his mind. "Yes, sir." He withdrew.

Hugh grabbed his parcels from the floor. "All hands to the deck, Charles. Tell me what you want me to copy."

"But you'll need to get back to town before dark, surely?"

"Brought my bags with me and bespoke a room at the local inn." He leant closer and whispered, "The barmaid's a sight for weary eyes." He put sheets of ruled paper beside him, looked for a knife to sharpen a quill. "Come on, Charles. I can spare an hour or two to help a soon-to-be-married man."

We scribbled away, while I filled Hugh in on the attack on Alyson and myself in the wood. Hugh was of the opinion Alyson was probably the target. "And unmarried, you say?"

"In heaven's name, don't shout that abroad! There's no evidence."

"But?"

"But I'd lay odds on it. Fowler thinks the same."

"Then Alyson is the target – the attacker's a jealous husband."

"Then why not challenge Alyson to a duel? Or tell the guests the truth – that would ruin his reputation and be very satisfactory revenge. Why all the secret attacks?"

"Maybe he's trying to blackmail Alyson. *Pay what I want or your life is in danger.*"

"It's the book," I said morosely. "It's all about the book. I know it is."

Unbelievably, we got all the copying finished, though at the cost of scrawling some bars rather untidily towards the end. I planned to give the Alysons the second book that Heron had found, to sing the main parts from; I'd have the original at the harpsichord and everyone else would have their parts on paper.

My eyes were smarting and my wrist was painful but I got through dinner somehow. Heron was distant and did not so much as look at me; Esther smiled to herself occasionally, like a woman with a happy secret, and several times apologised to her neighbour for being distracted. William Ridley regaled everyone with the details of his court case; Fischer was preoccupied and twice asked if I was sure a reward for the arrest of Nell's murderer would do no good.

At the lower end of the table, Mrs Alyson was sour and silent for the most part. She spoke only once, when an unlucky lull in conversation meant that a harmless, naïve remark of Lizzie Ord's rang out to all the company. Mrs Alyson said loudly: "Oh, for heaven's sake, have you no sense at all?"

Philip Ord started up. Heron, sitting next to him, said something quietly. Ord sat down again. Casper Fischer intervened; he waved a hand at Lizzie's hairstyle. "I do admire the fashions over here. It makes our ladies in Philadelphia look sadly behind the times. Tell me, Mrs Ord, is there a special name for that colour ribbon?"

Lizzie, looking shaky, managed a reply. Fischer, who must certainly have a great deal of experience with young people, jollied her into a discussion of fashion.

I retired to the drawing room in company with Fischer, shortly after the ladies had repaired there. I'd left the copied parts, labelled clearly, on the tea table and the musical ladies, I saw, had seized upon theirs and were sitting in a window embrasure, humming through the tunes. I saw Mrs Widdrington look up sharply as Esther came up to me with a dish of tea and gave me a private smile.

"Do you know the reason for my presence in this select

gathering?" she asked. "According to lawyer Armstrong, I am the best person to instruct Mrs Alyson in the ways of the Newcastle ladies. I am beginning to think my task impossible."

"Her remark to Lizzie was unforgivable," I said. "That's not a matter of social conventions – it was bad manners and cruelty of spirit!"

I kept my voice low as I spoke and noticed that Mrs Widdrington was watching me even more closely. The last thing I wanted was gossip so I nodded at Esther and moved towards the harpsichord.

At which point, Mrs Alyson picked up one of the scores of the opera, and said very loudly, in a bored voice, "It really is impossible to get interested in such ridiculous trifles. I cannot be troubled to sing tonight."

The musical ladies were disconcerted. "Tomorrow, perhaps?" Mrs Widdrington said brightly.

"Tomorrow is Sunday," Mrs Alyson said. "It would not be devout."

"Of course," Mrs Widdrington said. "I had forgot. How silly of me."

The evening was very long and dull.

Sunday was equally tedious. We all went to church of course. Hugh was in the congregation too, sitting towards the back with a big bluff man, very red-faced, and a young woman in a very gaudy dress – the barmaid, no doubt. Hugh winked at me. The ladies yawned their way through the service, the gentlemen ogled the young women of the village. William Ridley snored his way through a sermon which was actually rather good.

The luncheon back at Long End was cold, as the servants were required to be at church too. That was followed by a very slow afternoon. Fischer looked over a book of architectural drawings of Italian ruins with Heron, who answered his many questions – Heron of course had seen all the ruins in the flesh, so to speak. Esther read what she said was a book of sermons, but the print looked not quite right for so serious a subject. Several of the gentlemen went to sleep; several more yawned constantly.

I wandered into the library to look for any music that had previously escaped our attention, hoping to find something of a sacred nature that would be unexceptional for Sunday performance. One of the library windows looked out the side of the house, and in the sunshine I saw Alyson chatting to his London coachman. Perhaps he was thinking of an expedition. A picnic would be nice, a lazy afternoon on a sunny bank with a bottle or two of wine and good friends... Would Esther worry over her complexion?

I returned to the drawing room, to find that Alyson had already returned and was leafing through a newspaper in a bored manner. The younger musical lady enquired whether I'd found any suitable music. I said I had not.

At the word *music,* Alyson's head snapped up. "Of course! We will rehearse the opera!"

All devout scruples went immediately out of the window in a scramble for parts.

I opened the opera book on the harpsichord music-stand, and Lizzie Ord came with anxious alacrity to sit by my side, ready to turn the pages. I smiled reassuringly at her. She looked hot. I was not the only one who thought so; a moment later, her husband brought her a fan. As he turned to go, he dropped a hand on her shoulder, gripped firmly. Lizzie seemed to relax, managed to smile at me. I flicked a glance at Ord, but he'd already turned away.

Behind Lizzie's head, I glimpsed Claudius Heron, moving to take an empty chair beside Esther. She looked startled, but nodded politely at something Heron said. More conversation. Esther smiled, and reached to offer Heron a dish of tea. He accepted politely. It looked as if they were making peace.

Alyson hung over the harpsichord, smiling with boyish charm. "Pattinson, what do you think we should do? Start at the beginning and work our way through – or play the big scene at the end of the first act? I think we should start at the big scene, don't you? Give us all a chance to warm up our voices."

"Of course," I agreed, turning pages. Given that Alyson had nothing to sing for at least ten minutes after the beginning of the opera, I was hardly surprised at his suggestion.

There was considerable confusion as the singers leafed through their parts looking for the right page. By the fireplace, Heron and Esther talked on, Esther nibbling at a small cake, Heron occasionally gesticulating, as if explaining a point. A servant came into the room, looked about, and squeezed through to me.

On a silver platter sat a note, showing signs of haste – it was badly folded. I was getting more correspondence in two days than I'd had all year. I nodded thanks at the servant, dropped a coin into his hand; he edged back out of the room. The letters and the servants were going to bankrupt me.

I snatched a look at the note while Alyson was still helping Ridley find his place. The note was in Hugh's handwriting; the red seal was of poor quality, already crumbling – all, presumably, that the inn could furnish. I unfolded the paper.

Charles, Hugh had written. *The chapman's sent me a message. Get here as soon as you can and come prepared for a ride into town. He's found the apprentice.*

18

A hunting expedition is generally greatly entertaining.
[*A Frenchman's guide to England*, Retif de Vincennes
(Paris; published for the author, 1734)]

That evening I sat through the longest rehearsal of my life. Alyson's enthusiasm was so infectious it looked likely to carry us on to the small hours of the morning. *Come as soon as you can*, Hugh had written but it was impossible to leave until everyone had gone to bed. And did he propose travelling at night? I'd had my fill of that!

Alyson's idea of a rehearsal was simply to sing through the music from beginning to end. If someone mangled a tune, he thought it a good laugh and carried on. When the younger musical lady asked if she could try a difficult passage again, he waved her away with a "You sound lovely, my dear". It was obvious that he and his wife had sung the piece many times before, and equally obvious that the whole evening had been designed to show off their talents. They performed magnificently and movingly. Lizzie, conscientiously turning pages for me, was lost in rapt wonder at the way their voices melted together, complimented each other effortlessly. I was looking at the way they unashamedly smiled at each other, even in public; they were certainly in love. I did not think that 'Mrs Alyson' would find herself cast off in the near future. Or perhaps at all.

After a while, enthusiasm inevitably waned among the rest of the company. Some of the gentlemen went off to the dining room, allegedly to talk, but in reality – to judge by the laughter and shouts that soon arose – to play cards, in defiance of Sunday conventions. Esther sat in a chair by the window and read; some of the other ladies retired early. After a while, Heron laid down the newspaper he'd been browsing through and nodded goodnight. All that were left were myself and Lizzie, the Alysons, and Esther, who was still reading. And Philip Ord, who'd turned a winged armchair so he could stare fixedly at us.

Lizzie started to fidget. Under cover of the music, I whispered, "Are you all right?"

She turned a gaze to me that verged on tears. "He – he is always watching me."

"Of course he is," I whispered back. "That's because he's so proud of you."

She stared at me bewildered, remembered just in time she had to turn the page, did so, and sat back down again. Her face lit up with hope. "Do you think so?"

"I'm sure of it," I said. It was a lie but I didn't regret it – she was at once much more at ease. She cast a glance back over her shoulder, with a shy smile for her husband. I saw Ord's lips twitch. Well, he was at least trying to smile.

And still the Alysons sang on.

It was gone midnight by the time the singing stopped; Esther had gone up to bed an hour or more before. Ord rescued us. He waited until an air had finished, got up briskly and said loudly: "Madam, it is late."

Lizzie was looking very tired. She got up at once with a fine assumption of surprise. "Heavens, is that the time? Yes, certainly I will come." I was left alone with the Alysons. Edward kissed his wife's hand. "Shall we, my dear?" Her face was glowing. In a moment, they too were gone.

Leaving me with dozens of sheets of music, scattered about the room.

I shut the harpsichord and locked it. I was weary, and the thought of a long ride into town was not appealing. Leaving the trip till morning would be wiser, but every hour lost was an hour in which the apprentice might escape. Alyson had already lost us too much time. And if we went now, and suffered no real delays, I might be back by midday tomorrow; the chances of anyone of the company being up before then were slight and my absence might go unnoticed.

As I bent to pick up the papers, the butler, Crompton, came in to secure the windows. "If you would care to leave that for the maid, sir?"

I met his gaze. He seemed about to say something, but clearly changed his mind.

"No, I'm fine," I said. "I need to put them in order."

He bowed.

In my room, I tossed the papers in an untidy heap on the table, scrambled into my oldest clothes and riding boots, seized my greatcoat and cautiously crept down the stairs into the hallway below. The front door was bolted and I balked at trying to unlock it without being heard. So I went swiftly past the dining room where the remaining gentlemen were still drinking and laughing over obscene jokes, to the servants' door. A narrow flight of stairs led down to a huge bare kitchen; three female servants were chattering over a pile of dirty dishes, their backs turned to me. I slipped through into the scullery.

The back door of the house was open. Across the stable yard, grooms were lounging on stone benches, drinking ale between weary yawns. They were not pleased when I demanded a horse.

"What for?" one said bluntly.

"I've urgent business in Newcastle."

Another laughed coarsely. "Plenty of 'em here." He jerked his thumb at the scullery door. "Don't need to go to town. Maids or mistresses, take your pick."

I was weary and short of time. I snapped at him. "Don't argue with me. Saddle the damn horse!"

The groom straightened instinctively at my tone of voice; he said uneasily, "I'll have to ask the master first, sir."

"That's all right, Hawdon," a voice said behind me. "I know all about it. Saddle up Mercy for Mr Pattinson and I'll have Black Boy."

Edward Alyson, grinning broadly, strolled across the yard. He was dressed almost entirely in black, except for a white cravat mostly hidden under his buttoned-up waistcoat. He waited until the grooms had bustled into the stables then whispered, "I'm coming with you. Can't miss the chance of laying my hands on a murderer!"

"Sir – "

"No, no." He was having great difficulty in containing his excitement. "Come on, Pattinson, don't deny that's where you're off to."

"Patterson."

"They've found him, haven't they?" Alyson slapped his gloves against his thigh. "Come on, Pattinson," he said, a wheedling note in his voice. "It's unfair to disappoint me! I haven't had so much excitement for years. You can't expect me to sit quietly at home while you dash about the country having fun!"

I gave up. There was plainly no chance of dissuading him. With a clatter of hooves, the grooms led out the horses. "How did you know what I was going to do?" I asked curiously.

He laughed. "You receive a note and then creep out of the house and ask for a horse? Well – certainly it could be an *affaire d'amour* but I very much doubt it." He made it sound as if he thought no woman would find me attractive.

The groom boosted him on to the back of his horse. He looked down at me. "I envy you, Pattinson," he said. "Envy you more than I thought I'd ever envy any man. Life can be so damn dull."

And he cantered for the gate.

Hugh was waiting impatiently outside the inn, absent-mindedly patting his horse, a placid pale grey. His expression when he saw Alyson would have been, in other circumstances, a pleasure to behold – I've never seen him so taken aback.

"Come on, man," Alyson said, leaning down from his horse and grinning. "Don't dawdle. We've work to do. Bringing a murderer to justice! That would be a good night's work, wouldn't it?"

Hugh looked at me; I remained impassive. Hugh sighed and swung himself up on to his horse.

"Now," Alyson said. "Tell me all about this murder! I've heard so many rumours and you know how unreliable the gossips are."

The moon was full, the first part of the road broad enough for two riders abreast but not three. I dropped back and let Hugh tell the tale, which he did, briefly and succinctly. By the time he came to the chapman, we were trotting through the first of the trees and the bright moonlight was only fitful; the horses picked their way carefully. I pushed my animal closer, so I could hear Hugh more clearly.

"You know the fellow, Charles. Lives up the top of Butcher Bank. Name of Carver."

"Yes, I know him. He usually travels the villages between Newcastle and Durham."

Hugh summarised what the chapman had seen for Alyson's benefit and his offer to ask around about the apprentice. "He didn't have much luck until he came to the chandler on the Key, James Williams."

Jas Williams was the father of my late apprentice, George – a severe man, but law-abiding and decent.

"Williams said he'd seen a lad like the one the chapman described and seen him with a book too," Hugh said. "He described it exactly as Lizzie Ord remembered – black, the spine hanging off. He said the lad had come into his shop a week or so ago, just pottered about. Williams was talking to a customer and by the time he'd a chance to see to the lad, he'd gone. As had a couple of candles, a tinder-box and various other things. And then he had the nerve to come back again for a hammer and saw! On the day of the murder that was, although he made sure Williams was not in the shop that time."

"A murderer *and* a thief," Alyson said with every sign of relish.

"Williams didn't get much of a look at the lad evidently – not enough to know him again. And much the same can be said of his customers. Three or four of them were there the first time but didn't really look at the fellow. But one of them was a mercer and he made a note of the dreadful waistcoat. Puce and silver, he said, and much too much embroidery. He reckoned he'd seen it before too. He thinks the lad has a room in a lodging house in one of the chares."

I groaned. I'd had some unhappy experiences in those

crowded, filthy chares.

"But no name?"

"Not that the chapman can find. He had a word with a spirit in the lodging house in question. The lad lives there all right but he's only there now and again. Apparently he was there earlier this week – Monday and Tuesday."

"So he's there now?" I asked.

"As far as I can tell."

Alyson was exultant. "Then we can lay hands on him!"

"I did think it important we move quickly," Hugh said, "before the fellow learns someone's been asking about him."

"Very wise," Alyson agreed. "We don't want him to run off."

We rode on in silence. Lodgings in the town, I thought. I'd convinced myself the apprentice was from Shields or Sunderland or some such place. He was presumably going about his daily business as usual, or Bedwalters would have found word of a missing apprentice. That was audacious – or foolhardy. I wondered why he was only in the lodgings 'now and again'.

Alyson stirred. "The last time I had such fun was years ago." He cast me a mischievous smile which was somehow half-ashamed. "I regret to say I had a very misspent youth." And he launched into a surprisingly honest account of his life as the younger son of a younger son who'd never anticipated he would inherit an estate with coal under its fields, and a couple of ships on the Tyne, and stocks and shares in the South Sea.

"I tell you frankly," he said as we came out of woodland on to a stretch of road that lay between moon-silvered open fields, "there have been episodes in my past of which I'm not proud. Gambling," he said. He grinned. "But I'm respectable now. Positively elderly and much more sensible. I shall remain so. But damn it all!" He gathered up his horse's reins. "It's damned dull and I'm glad to be getting some excitement at last!"

And he let his horse have free rein and galloped off ahead of us.

The town was almost silent as we rode down Northumberland Street towards the Key. It was just after two in the morning. We detoured to the Golden Fleece where we left the horses in the care of a yawning ostler and from there walked across the open expanse of the Sandhill, round the dark hulk of the Guildhall, and out on to the Key. On our right, the dark waters of the Tyne lapped – the tide was in. Across the river, lights glimmered on the bank around St Mary's church in Gateshead.

The long deserted stretch of the Key was dotted here and there with heaps of coal and coils of rope. Two keels were moored in darkness; one or two houses along the Key showed faint lights.

"The lodging house is down towards the Printing Office," Hugh said. "It's on the corner of the Key and the chare, evidently. The main door's on the Key but the chapman says access to the apprentice's lodgings is by a passage and stair from the chare."

We passed the chandler's shop, shuttered and dark, and the Old Man Inn.

"Here," Hugh whispered.

I paused to look down the narrow chare. Not a light, not a sign of movement.

"Do we go up?" Alyson asked.

"Which floor?"

"Third," Hugh said. We were all whispering.

"I hope to God he's not got wind of the chapman's enquiries."

"He might be lying in wait!" Alyson said, with delighted ghoulishness.

"It's so damned quiet!"

"Are we going to look or not?" Hugh said irritably. "Damn it, Charles, you can't come all this way just to say it's a bit too dark and you don't fancy it." He was searching in his pockets; he pulled out a candle stub and a tinder box. "Hold that."

I held the stub while he struck a spark and lit it.

"Someone should stay here on the Key," Alyson said. "In case the lad makes a run for it."

"Good idea," I said. I thought he was going to volunteer for the task, that he was having second thoughts about the expedition. Perhaps he was thinking that excitement could be carried too far.

But he said brightly, "Good. Dobson, you stay here. Come on, Pattinson, let's see if we can catch ourselves a murderer."

And he was halfway into the chare before I could stop him.

I caught Alyson up few yards down the chare – the alley was moonlit and not a soul moved in it.

"I don't think this is a good idea," I whispered. Meaning – leave it to Hugh and me.

Alyson was grinning.

"He could be dangerous."

"Oh, I certainly hope so," Alyson said. He plucked the candle stub from my fingers and strode on ahead.

A broken-down gate led into a yard next to the lodging house; beside it an open doorway gave access on to uneven stairs. Alyson started up with some energy but almost immediately had to grab at the wall as the slope of the stairs threw him sideways. A white dust sprinkled over the shoulder of his coat where he brushed against the lime mortar; fragments of it crumbled around his feet. The stairs creaked loudly; I cursed. The whole place looked as if it would fall down any minute.

I heard Alyson mutter but he went on, shielding the candle stub with his hand, climbing to a turn in the stairs. Once we were round that and out of sight of the door there was almost no light at all; there were no windows in the stair. This had probably been an outside stair, I thought, walled in at some point to keep out the worst of the weather. The work looked shoddy.

Alyson stopped. In the pitch blackness, I walked into him. "This must be the place," he whispered.

"Are you sure?" I couldn't see a damned thing.

The candle went out suddenly. Alyson yelled. A door crashed open and Alyson fell back against me. "Get him!"

I was blind. The extinguishing of the candle had made

the darkness more intense. Someone pushed past me. In the blackness, I grabbed out, caught hold of cloth. The skirts of that damned waistcoat no doubt. Then the cloth was snatched out of my hand and I was shoved back against the wall. Fragments of plaster pattered around me.

The stair disappeared from under my feet as I stumbled. I tried to grab something, anything. There was a burning in my side. Alyson was still yelling, "Stop him! Stop him!" as he clattered down the stairs.

I put my hand to my side, and felt stickiness and warmth.

I'd been stabbed.

19

The quality of lodging houses varies greatly.
[*A Frenchman's guide to England*, Retif de Vincennes
(Paris; published for the author, 1734)]

I clung on to the wall. Fragments of mortar crumbled under my fingers. Shouting from the chare below. Alyson. Was he fighting with the apprentice?

He might need my help. Cautiously, I felt for the next stair down with my foot, found it, slid on to it. The next step, keeping my hands against the wall. This was ridiculous. The fellow could kill Alyson before I got there. I abandoned caution, stumbled down the stair, missed a step, tripped, slammed into the opposite wall. Something creaked loudly.

I could see round the bend of the stairs now. The moonlight filtering in from the chare cast a dim light, over the lower stairs. I clattered down, wincing against the pain in my side. Out into the chare.

The gate of the yard next to the house was swinging. I pushed it open and saw Edward Alyson staggering back to me with the heavy breathing of a man winded. "He got away," he gasped, and waved his arm wildly in the general direction of the far side of the yard. "Over – over – there!"

Hugh raced up from the direction of the street. "What happened! I heard yelling… "

"It's my fault," I said, pressing my hand to my right side. "I should have remembered he'd have a knife."

Speechless for lack of breath, Alyson gestured. "Just a scratch," I said.

Hugh flew into an alarm and would not be pacified until he'd examined the cut just under my ribs. Reluctantly, he agreed it was a mere graze and gave me his handkerchief to dab at the blood.

We heard voices, froze in alarm.

"Residents?" Alyson whispered.

"I don't want to meet anyone who lives here," Hugh whispered back. "Let's get back on the Key."

But on the deserted Key we felt even more exposed in the bright moonlight.

"What now?" Hugh whispered.

"I don't want to stay here," Alyson said. "He might come back." He looked flushed, still out of breath, and somewhere between the exultation of excitement and the fear of new danger.

"He surely won't attack us again!" Hugh said. "His whole aim's to get away!"

My head throbbed with tiredness, my side burned.

"I need sleep," I said. "Tomorrow I want to see the chapman – no, better still, James Williams. He actually saw the lad – maybe he can remember more than he thinks."

"Good idea," Hugh said.

Tiredness, and the crossness that comes with it, suddenly took hold of Alyson. "Question a chandler? Devil take it, Pattinson, I'm not a lawyer!" He was breathing more easily. "I'm going back to that inn where we left our horses – what was it – the Golden Lion."

"Golden Fleece."

"They'll have a room. And then," he said decisively, "we're going back to Long End. What the devil's the time now? Very well, we'll set out at noon. If you're not at the Lion by then, Pattinson, you can consider your engagement at an end."

We watched him stalk off along the Key. "Gentry," Hugh said scornfully. "Always do the easy bits, and leave the dull stuff to others."

We went back to Hugh's lodgings which were a great deal closer than mine. But sleep was never going to come easily. I was too tired and Hugh snored too loudly. I lay awake most of the time, staring at the dimly visible cracks in Hugh's ceiling and trying to avoid the lumps in his mattress. As dawn crept into the room,

I staggered up, wincing at the stiffness in my side.

I pissed in Hugh's chamberpot, splashed the cold water in his jug over my face and crept down his attic stairs. The town was just beginning to wake; some early travellers were already out: women going to market, grimy-faced miners trudging back home. I cut across town to my lodgings, stuffed a few extra clothes into an old violin bag and retrieved some of my store of money from under the mattress. Alyson's servants were benefitting from this trip far more than I was.

My back prickled as I walked through town towards the Key. The apprentice would surely not be so foolish as to attack me in broad daylight but I couldn't rid myself of the suspicion that he was even now out and about, watching me.

At the Cale Cross, at the foot of Butcher Bank, I bought and ate some buttered barley, then went on to the chandler's shop. Jas Williams was outside his store, fingering some candles in a box as if exasperated with their quality. He looked up, saw me, grimaced. He gave his son into my care as an apprentice last year and the son died – and the fact that Williams disliked his son, despised him even, is neither here nor there. He was short with me, answering my questions as if he thought them an imposition.

"How often have you seen the apprentice in here?"

"The shop's always full of customers. How the devil can I keep my eyes on all of them?"

"What exactly did he steal?"

"Half a dozen things. I told that chapman."

"A hammer."

"Yes."

"A saw?"

"Yes."

"Nails?"

"No doubt."

"A tinderbox."

"Yes. Now if you don't mind – " He moved to go back in.

"Did you ever see the streetgirl?"

He snorted. "I don't allow her sort in my shop."

"But if you can't keep your eye on every customer," I said, moved by an ignoble annoyance to get my own back, "how can you be sure?"

He went back inside.

Well, that had been profitable.

I hesitated on the Key. There were several hours yet before I needed to be at the Golden Fleece. Alyson was probably still deep in untroubled slumber. I could talk to the chapman but what more could he tell me than he'd already told Hugh? And I was very close to the murderer's lodgings…

The chare was busier than it had been; a few ruffians leant against walls, smoking and conversing in a desultory fashion. A sailor stepped in from the Key to piss against a wall. I hesitated, wondering if anything I might find in the apprentice's lodgings would be worth the risk.

A spirit said: "You're the fellow was stabbed here last night."

I glanced up at the wall of the lodging house; a bright spark of light hovered on a window sill.

"This morning," I said. "Very early." I yawned. "Too early. Are you the spirit who talked to the chapman?"

"Never liked the fellow," the spirit said, sliding down the wall to my eye-level. "The lad, I mean."

I was suddenly more alert. Offended spirits often have a lot to say. "Nasty piece of work?" I suggested.

"Sharp tongue on him."

I tut-tutted.

"If you've got secrets you should live in an unspirited house." The gleam shifted. The voice had an edge of humour in it. "And if you live in a house with a friendly spirit, you ought to be friendly yourself."

"But he wasn't?"

"Banished me from his room. Said he wouldn't have me in there." The spirit had been a local man but he sounded as if he'd been respectable in life.

"That's what makes you suspect he has secrets?"

"I *know* he has secrets," the spirit said. "I was the landlord of the Old Man Inn in life and I listened to plenty of confidences in my time. I know the signs. They also say he's a murderer."

"He is," I said.

"Then I might be able to help you. Come up to his room and have a chat."

"I don't mind if I do," I returned cordially.

The spirit kept me company, sliding round the walls of the house as I went into the chare. Two ruffians looked at me sourly, but did not challenge me – perhaps they were wary of the spirit. I reached the side door to the house safely, went stiffly up the uneven steps, supporting myself against the walls. White lime mortar dusted my hands and sleeves.

I turned the bend in the stairs and saw the door to the apprentice's room standing open – I remembered it thudding back. I stood on the threshold, catching my breath, looked round at bare boards, a straw mattress thrown on the floor, a chamber pot in a corner and an empty shelf tilting against the wall. On the far side of the room, a blocked-up doorway had probably once given access to the rest of the house. The room looked barely lived in. But the apprentice had had it to himself, which is unusual in these chares, where two or three families can crowd into a single room.

"Did you see what happened here last night?"

"Alas, no," said the spirit, glimmering on the door jamb. "I was chatting to my old friend the carpenter. Front of house, ground floor right. He can't sleep and appreciates company in the small hours. I heard the shouting but I thought it was drunks. We get a lot of drunks round here."

"How long has the lad been lodging here?"

The spirit hummed and haahed a moment. "Three years at least, I'd say."

"And you knew him well – this apprentice?"

"Apprentice?" the spirit said scornfully. "You'll not find a master admitting to his ownership, sir. I daresay he was once.

But he doesn't do a stroke of work. He comes here for two or three days then goes away for a month or more. Where does he go then, eh? Nowhere respectable, for sure!"

Bedwalters hadn't been able to find a master admitting to ownership of the apprentice. Did we have any proof he actually *was* an apprentice? The women in Mrs McDonald's house thought he was; he'd told Nell he was – but anyone can lie. And as for his garish clothes, so typical of apprentices – well, anyone can wear clothes in bad taste.

"And noise!" the spirit said. "Last Tuesday, gone midnight, for instance, banging away."

I ventured into the room. It was clean, I noticed. No dust on the floor, and therefore no footprints. No dust on the shelf, therefore no hint of what might have stood on it. No piss in the chamberpot except for – yes, a tiny dried stain at the bottom. It had been used recently but not within the last few hours. Within a few days certainly. But we already knew he'd been here on Monday and Tuesday.

Clean and bare. Apart from a blanket thrown over the straw mattress, it was totally devoid of possessions. I'd come back for nothing.

"Anything wrong, sir?" asked the spirit.

It had remained in the doorway as if respectfully allowing me time and space to consider the room. I turned back to it – and heard a floorboard squeak under my foot.

"Everything creaks in here," said the spirit good-humouredly. "To be frank, sir, it's all ready to fall down. Old house, no money spent on it. Holes in the plaster, slates off the roof."

I stamped on the floorboard again; it squealed once more. I saw one end lift fractionally.

Hammer and saw, I thought. He'd stolen hammer and saw from Jas Williams's shop and possibly some nails as well. And then there'd been banging well after midnight. The night Nell was killed.

Kneeling sent a pain through my side that made me catch my breath. I grunted and scrabbled at the floorboard.

It did not give. I tried banging down on one end of it in the hope of seeing the other end jerk upwards. I tried to dig my fingers under the edge to prise it up, but I merely broke a nail. I sat back, flummoxed. Maybe it was just a loose board.

Then I caught a glimpse of something under the end of the straw mattress and tugged it out. A long nail with the end bent back. I looked at the nail, looked at the floorboard. I hooked the bent nail under the floorboard, slapped down on the end of it – and up popped the board, leaving the two nails that had appeared to secure it poking up out of the joist below.

"Very neat," I said, putting the bent nail back under the mattress.

The floorboard came out easily now – I laid it to one side. The spirit shot along the floor and hovered precariously on the edge of the hole. We both looked down on a brown-wrapped parcel, nestling between two dusty joists.

The spirit gave a rich sarcastic chortle. "Buried treasure! In truth, sir, I didn't think such a thing existed!"

"Nor did I," I agreed and picked up the parcel. Even through the paper, I knew what it was. I folded the paper back. And there it lay, black, battered and torn, rather thinner than I'd expected.

"Oh," said the spirit, clearly disappointed. "It's just a book."

20

An Englishman will defend his property to his assailant's last breath.
[*A Frenchman's guide to England*, Retif de Vincennes
(Paris; published for the author, 1734)]

I turned over the pages. Yes, here was the German inscription in a rather odd hand with characters I didn't recognise; I recognised the date, however: 1722. I turned over pages and found the tunes, written neatly on hand-ruled paper. Each tune was accompanied by a few verses of the appropriate psalm; the old version of the words I noticed, before Tate and Brady wrote their new version eliminating all the archaic words no one understands any longer. But this made the book all the more perplexing; there are churches who resolutely adhere to the old words, but most now use the new versions, which these tunes would probably not fit. No musician would want something so out of date.

The more I looked at it, the more puzzled I became and the more convinced the book had no musical value. But then what made it important enough to kill for?

"Wait!" the spirit said sharply. I looked up to see the gleam shift faster than lightning across the floor. A second later it was back.

"Trouble," it said. "Someone hanging around on the other side of the chare. Can't see who it is – he's all wrapped up in coat and hat. But I warrant you it's him. Best get out of here, sir. Take the book with you and look at it later."

I stared at the bright gleam. "I can't make off with it!"

"I know who you are, sir," the spirit said earnestly. "Charles Patterson, the music fellow. The one who solves mysteries. And I don't like mysteries, sir, not when they end in a young girl dying. And I'll like them even less if they end in your dying. Wrap that thing up and get out of here. I'll distract the fellow, get him round the front of the house so he doesn't see you. There's a gate, sir, just next the house."

"I saw it last night."

"It leads into a yard. You can get out the far side into an alley-way that leads up to Butcher Bank. Hurry, sir!"

The spirit shot out of the room again.

I bundled up the book, barely avoiding pulling the loose spine completely free. Hurriedly, I slotted the floorboard back into place, stamped down on the nails to secure it. If I could get out of here quickly enough, find the new constable or even a member of the watch, we might be able to get back in time to apprehend the murderer.

I stumbled down the steep, uneven stairs, the parcel under my arm. At the bottom, I hesitated, listening. But the clatter from the Key was too loud – I'd have to take my chance and hope the spirit could keep the apprentice occupied.

Darting out into the open, I flung myself against the gate. It was not fastened and I tumbled into a yard strewn with all kinds of rubbish: broken casks, lengths of timbers, shattered slates, a huge pile of rags.

My feet went out from under me.

I had time to register that I'd slipped on what looked like rotting potatoes. I grabbed at the nearest thing for support – a dilapidated ancient door poised against a pile of slates. I saved myself from falling, but the door shifted and the slates slid down with an earth-shattering din.

One of the slates nearly took my ankle off. I yelped, jumped backwards, almost slipping again on the black potatoes. And glimpsed something bright among the slates –

Fighting the stiffness in my side, I bent down. The shifting of the slates had revealed what had been pushed between them. A knife, dulled by brown stains.

Footsteps behind me. The spirit called: "It's the cat, sir. That mangy cat's always upsetting things – "

I snatched up the knife, thrust it among the folds of the paper round the book, leapt over the tumbled slates, climbed over a disintegrating pile of timbers. A narrow passageway cut between the heaps of rubbish – an alley, running flat for a yard or two before becoming a long steep flight of stone steps climbing the hill. I took the steps at a run, gritting my teeth against the pain in my side. Houses on either side were broken down, some deserted, some with rags at the windows suggesting occupation.

Behind me came a clatter of slates tumbling. I forced myself on up the steps, staggered out on to the street above. Butcher Bank stretched to right and left. A dozen people were tossing entrails into an open cart. A burly man gaped at me, bloody apron round his ample middle, cleaver in hand. I stared, he stared. He looked like a man accustomed to thinking slowly.

A shout from behind me. "Stop that thief!"

The butcher grabbed at my sleeve. The cleaver in his other hand dipped erratically towards my chest. I tore myself free and ran across the street.

"Thief!" the butcher roared. A middle-aged woman snatched at me. A dog barked furiously.

How had I got myself into this? I was running from a vicious murderer and yet I was the one they were trying to apprehend!

And I remembered with horror that I was the one who had the knife...

Why the devil hadn't I left it among the slates? Cursing, I swung into an alley. My legs seemed to belong to someone else, turning to water and barely able to support me. Half the butchers on the Bank seemed to be after me. There was only one way to be rid of them, I thought. If I could reach All Hallows church –

Had it come to this? I was looking for sanctuary! How the devil was I to persuade anyone I'd not killed Nell? I had the book and the murder weapon in my possession –

The tower of All Hallows loomed up ahead of me, with its ridiculous little spire perched on top. *Behind a row of houses*. I would have to go round the end of the street, turn left, run up Silver Street to the church door. Was there time? A dozen butchers were howling through the alley.

A woman's voice screeched: "This way, sir! This way!" A spirit gleamed on a lintel and a door swung open. I dived through it, stood in sudden darkness as it slammed shut behind me. "Straight through!" the spirit urged. "Quick!" The butchers were already battering on the door.

I staggered from room to room, thanking the spirit incoherently. Thank God for the spirits' message network that worked quicker than thought. The spirit in the lodging house must have alerted this one –

A back door flung itself open, dazzling me with the sunshine outside.

Behind the house was a yard, and a gate which the spirit threw open, and an alley, and a glimpse of All Hallows. I ran like the devil across Silver Street, into the churchyard, round the back of the church. I could still hear shouting, but it was more distant. Then something closer. The butchers must have broken through the house.

I stopped on the churchyard grass. Ahead of me was the raw earth of Nell's grave. I took a deep breath, winced as pain caught in my side.

There was only one place no one could follow me. The world that runs alongside our own.

But could I step through to it? I had more control over the process now than I'd ever had before, but it was still unpredictable. Chest heaving for breath, I walked forward, slowly, praying silently. A chill took me, the world blurred. The sun winked out. For a moment there was nothing. Then stars flickered overhead and I was walking along the same path towards Nell's headstone. Not a sound of pursuit.

I had escaped.

21

Inns are generally good, but their wine is appalling.
[*A Frenchman's guide to England*, Retif de Vincennes
(Paris; published for the author, 1734)]

I sank down on to the table tomb next to Nell's grave, put my hand to my aching side, waited until my heart stopped thumping and my breath settled. I slid round so that I could lie full length on the table tomb; I put my head back and stared up at the stars.

In the past year, I've seen many strange things, and I have ample cause to know the evil men can perpetrate on others. I've come to know that nothing is motiveless, no matter how pointless the violence might seem to others. I've learnt that men have endless ways to justify the unjustifiable to themselves. I've come close to danger, even to death.

But this felt different. I'd been attacked several times now, and I knew that must be because I was a threat. I'd found the place where the murderer lodged – he must believe I could go further and find him. But there was something more. The first time I'd been attacked was before I knew any of this. It was almost, I thought, as if the murderer was deliberately drawing attention to himself. As if he was daring me to find him.

I heard a sound, sat up in alarm. A young woman stood in the middle of the path, a pale dress wrapped around with a dark cloak. She stared at me in horror, shrieked and ran off.

God knows what she must have thought me! With grim amusement, I hauled myself off the stone. I could not stay here for ever. For one thing, time moved at different speeds in the two worlds; a few moments here might mean days in my own world. But the book – I flicked through it again, saw nothing I could think significant. I was completely at a loss as to why it was so important. I put the spine back in place, wrapped the book up again.

There was one thing I could do – I could safeguard the little I knew. The book was at the heart of the matter and needed to be examined in much greater detail. The knife too might give some clue as to the identity of the murderer, although it looked commonplace to me – no initials, no identifying features. But that would have to wait for later. For the time being, I simply needed to keep them both safe.

And where better than in another world entirely?

I walked down Silver Street, as sedately as I could, wondering if I looked presentable. St Nicholas's church clock struck the hour. In the long series of chimes that followed, I somehow lost count, wondered after the chimes fell silent, if the clock had struck eleven or twelve. It seemed I'd lost only two or three hours at most...

Alyson had threatened to set out for Long End at noon precisely.

I attracted curious gazes in my headlong rush along the Key towards the Golden Fleece. At least I saw no butchers, and since I'd never had an acquaintance among them, I hoped I'd gone unrecognised.

I paused outside the inn, hands on knees, gasping for breath, trying to look at least respectable before I went inside to enquire if Alyson had left. But as I straightened up, a young woman came out into the courtyard – a respectable servant in a good-quality but drab riding habit.

"Catherine!" I hurried forward. "What the devil are you doing here?"

Esther's maid gave me a mischievous look. "What you would expect, of course! I'm here to give my mistress respectability. She could hardly ride into town with a gentleman unchaperoned."

"Which gentleman?" I asked with foreboding.

"Mr Heron," she said primly, then, casting a look around, she leant closer. "Did you ever come across so severe a man?"

"Rarely," I agreed. "Are they inside?"

She nodded. "With Mr Alyson and Mr Demsey."

I breathed a sigh of relief. Alyson had not left yet. "What time is it?"

"The clock struck eleven a little while ago – "

I composed myself and walked into the inn. They were all in the passageway to the yard. Heron and Esther had their backs to me and I saw, with surprise and considerable regret, that Esther was wearing not her breeches but a dark riding habit whose long skirts she was holding up off the dusty floor. Hugh was looking sorely tried but was wisely keeping silent as Heron and Alyson, both greatcoated, argued some point or other. Alyson must have caught some hint of movement for his gaze slid over Heron's shoulder and settled on me.

I saw his eyes widen slightly and wondered again how dishevelled I looked. I walked up the passageway towards them, the violin bag banging against my shoulder. Heron and Esther turned. I gave them a smile. Hugh jerked his head, smoothed the shoulders of his coat meaningfully. I glanced down at white mortar dust, brushed it off.

"We cannot talk out here," Heron said sharply. "We must go in."

We trooped into a room off the passageway. It appeared to be the room Alyson had bespoken for himself. A newspaper, neatly ironed, lay unopened, on the table, together with an untouched jug of ale. Wearily, I pulled off the violin bag, put it down on a chair, caught Alyson looking at me and it. Well, no doubt we were both looking shabby. I decided to take the battle to Heron straightaway. "I didn't know you had business in town, sir."

Hugh choked, turned away to call for a serving girl. Esther said quickly, "Have you caught him – the girl's murderer?"

"Alas, no. Though we came to close quarters."

"During which encounter you were stabbed," Heron said. He was standing in front of the unlit fire, looking like a father about to punish a recalcitrant son.

"I admit I should have remembered the knife," I agreed.

Hugh was in the doorway ordering food and drink from the landlord; Catherine came back in to murmur to Esther. Heron met my gaze implacably.

"A mere scratch," I said.

"What I don't understand," Alyson said, frowning, "is why you're here at all. Did you come into town specifically in pursuit of us?"

"Yes," Heron said, uncompromisingly.

"My fault entirely." Esther smiled. "I simply could not sit at Long End and worry about Charles, so I persuaded Mr Heron to accompany me into town."

Charles, I thought, alarm bells ringing. I darted a glance at Alyson. He was frowning.

Esther put her hand on my arm. "Forgive me, Charles, it was foolish I know but this apprentice seems to be particularly vicious – "

I was still off-balance, distracted by the unexpectedly warm smile she cast on me, the softness of her tone. She was playing a game and I was uncertain as to what it all meant.

"But indeed," she said, "we have puzzled Mr Alyson. From the moment he came back from his walk and found us here, he has been trying to make sense of it." She turned to Alyson. "You must forgive a woman's weakness, sir, but I could not sit quietly by while my betrothed was in danger."

A silence. Heron was impassive, although I thought I glimpsed the faintest hint of a wry smile on his lips. Catherine was trying to control her grin. Hugh said brightly, "Breakfast will be here at any moment."

Alyson said incredulously, "Betrothed?!"

Heron took charge at once and Esther let him – after all she'd achieved her object; if others knew about the betrothal, it would be more difficult to call it off. Heron acted as if it was an everyday occurrence for a lady of quality to become betrothed to a mere tradesman. "Though I'm sure I needn't tell you, Alyson, that the matter is to be kept private."

"Until my relatives can travel from Norfolk," Esther said. "Family always come first, do you not agree?"

Alyson, as off-balance as I'd been, blustered. I let Heron deal with him, glanced at Hugh. He was finding great interest in the pattern of the upholstery on an armchair but he looked up and gave me a wicked grin. He said, "And have you named the day yet?"

It was a very good job I hadn't taken his bet.

Esther had the quietly satisfied air of a woman who has won the day; she said merely, "In a month or so, when the legal niceties have been dealt with."

The landlord swept in with serving girls in his wake and half a dozen trays of food. In the confusion that followed, Esther and Catherine went quietly out, to rearrange their hair or whatever else women do; Heron spoke to Hugh; from the few words I heard, he seemed to be gleaning the details of our abortive attempt to detain the apprentice.

Alyson came across to me. If he was attempting to emulate Heron's stern look, he was failing – he looked merely mulish, like a boy being forced to do something he doesn't want to.

"Damn it, Patterson," he said sharply. "You can't go ahead with this. It's simply not – "

I refused to help him out. I was pretty certain he was passing his mistress off as his wife and not in any position to lecture on morality.

"It's impossible," he said. "I cannot pay a man to entertain me when he's betrothed to one of my guests!"

To do him justice, this was clearly genuine outrage. I said, "You can rest assured that none of your guests need know the true situation. We've every intention of keeping the matter secret until after the wedding."

Was there any point in placating Alyson any longer, I wondered? The prospect of marrying Esther was becoming more and more inevitable, and in that case, did I really need to concern myself over a mere fifteen guineas? Mere, that is, compared to Esther's wealth.

Alyson seemed to be calming down. "You will undertake to guarantee secrecy."

I thought I could. I started, "I believe – " But we were

interrupted by a bright gleam that shot across our sight and hovered on the topmost point of a branch of candlesticks. "Mr Demsey?"

I gestured at Hugh, on the other side of the table. The spirit shot off towards him. "Aurelia Robinson," she introduced herself, a rather unusual proceeding for a spirit. "Daughter of Sir Matthew Robinson."

"Oh yes," Hugh said, obviously nonplussed.

"I have a message for you."

"Oh?"

"From Mr Bedwalters, the constable."

"Ex-constable," Heron said.

"He would be grateful, sir, if you were to go to Dog Bank."

"I've just come that way," I said, surprised. Alyson was looking puzzled; I said, "It's above All Hallows church – a respectable street."

"There's someone asking for you," the spirit said, single-mindedly concentrating on its message. "A dying man's last request."

"Who?" I demanded. "Who's dying?"

The spirit said, "Someone of the lower orders, I understand. A chapman – "

22

Many of the poorer buildings are neglected and are falling to pieces.
[Letter from Retif de Vincennes, to his brother Georges, 3 June 1736]

If Bedwalters was startled to see all four of us walking up the street towards him, he did not show it. He got up from his bench and waited calmly for us to reach him. Neatly dressed, ink on his fingertips as ever, thinner than previously, and with a look of peace about him I'd never seen before.

I was breathing heavily from climbing the hill. Edward Alyson was right to think he would not enjoy accompanying us; Dog Bank was respectable but it was poor, and stank. And this would probably be another of those dull 'talking' sessions; Alyson, I'd noticed, preferred occasions when there was running and shouting to be done.

He made me feel staid and middle-aged.

Heron and Esther greeted Bedwalters civilly; Bedwalters was polite in return, although Heron had treated him abominably on their last meeting. Hugh was anxious for news. "The chapman. He's been attacked?"

Bedwalters nodded. "Hit by a slate as he walked through an alley early this morning."

"A slate?" I said, startled. "One that fell from a roof?"

"Apparently so," Bedwalters said. I knew him well enough to know that he meant what he said, nothing less, and certainly nothing more. *Apparently*. "He was carried home but there was nothing to be done for him. The apothecary gave him something to dull the pain, and I was sent for. I did, of course, make it plain that I was no longer constable but they insisted. When I arrived, he was very weak, but I heard him mention your name, sir – " He glanced at Hugh. "And I understood him to mean he wanted to talk to you."

"Right," Hugh said. "Where is he?"

I took his arm. "I don't think there's any rush, Hugh." I held Bedwalters's gaze. "You said there *was* nothing more to be done."

He nodded. "He died a few minutes ago."

"Damn," Hugh said. "Damn, damn, damn…"

I went into the house, ducking through a door so low I suspected the house must have subsided at some point in the past. A smoky dark room held two or three ancient chairs, an unsteady table and a pot simmering over an open hearth. A ladder at the back of the room led up to what I presumed must be a bedroom, but they'd clearly been unable to get the sick man up there and had laid him instead on a mattress behind the table.

A woman sat on the floor beside the mattress, dry-eyed and still. She did not look at me, or move. I leant on the unsteady table and lowered myself to one knee beside the mattress.

The body lay on its back. He'd been a man in his late thirties or early forties, blond hair receding, leaving only a few wisps on his forehead. A weather-beaten man. A spare, lean fit man. The sharp end of the falling slate had laid his face open from temple to mouth, cutting over the bridge of his nose, down the length of his left cheek and ending just below his bottom lip. It was the kind of cut a butcher might make when cleaving meat from the bone. The smashed white skull was visible inside. Blood masked his face and drenched the front of his clothes.

I peered closer and reached for the wound. The woman, in a sudden convulsion, slapped my hand away. She stared at me with a fierce anger and possessiveness.

"Well?" Hugh asked.

I heaved myself to my feet, wincing against the twinge of pain in my side. "I can see traces of slate in the wound," I said, "flecks of grey."

"It must have been an accident, surely?" Hugh said. "A slate is hardly an effective murder weapon. To drop one on someone you'd have to climb up on the roof, push it down on him – he'd hear you and get out of the way, surely. And you'd have to have a damn good aim."

149

I hesitated over whether to give the woman a coin or two. Her fierce pride deterred me. It was the wrong moment. I went back out into the street. Bedwalters was just putting something into a pocket with a dull red flush of embarrassment on his face; Esther had apparently persuaded him to accept a little charity. I gave him a coin of my own and asked him to give it to the widow when the first shock of bereavement had died away. He said he would.

"Where was the chapman hurt?" I asked.

"Two or three streets away."

We all traipsed off in a procession led by Bedwalters. Heron engaged him in a quiet word or two; Hugh skittered along behind them like a man desperate to get everything done as quickly as possible.

Esther and I walked behind. It was the first time I'd had private conversation with her since our – *betrothal*. Good God, but we must talk about that! But instead, I found myself saying: "Why are you not wearing your breeches?"

She was startled. Her pale hair had been disordered by the exercise, and trailed out from under her riding hat; a fine sheen of perspiration shone on her face. She smiled. "I thought that if I am to be a respectable married woman, then I should behave respectably."

"I don't like it," I said curtly, and inwardly cursed. I sounded like a man thirty years married already. Esther said nothing. When I looked at her, I saw she was apparently idly regarding her riding gloves which she carried in one hand. *Apparently*.

The street in which the chapman had been attacked must be one of the narrowest in town, a mere cranny between houses, leading up from the Key in a series of steps separated by a yard or two of uneven cobbles. It was not a salubrious place. The houses on either side were almost all unoccupied – windows were cracked or broken, some doors had been stoved in. In one or two houses, a pile of rags suggested someone slept there. At the bottom, the street opened on to the Key; I saw a fragment of a boat, a few children running by, a stray pig snuffling at corners. Seagulls screamed overhead; the clear air carried the clattering rush of coal being tipped into a hold.

And here there was only a dark stain on the cobbles where a man had fallen in his death agonies. Fragments of shattered slate lay all around; pieced together they must have formed a massive whole.

"One of the biggest slates." Hugh kicked angrily at one fragment. "From the bottom edge of the roof. And it's my fault. I sent him to his death."

"It's the murderer's fault, no one else's," I said. I picked up a small piece of wood, about an inch long. The wooden peg that had once nailed the slate to the rafters. It looked undamaged.

Esther picked up another nail and handed it to me silently. I couldn't read her mood; she seemed unconcerned, not upset in the least by my sharpness. Heron was talking to Bedwalters, Hugh kicking about the cobbles. I risked a low "I'm sorry."

She looked up at me. "I am not unaware of the difficulties of the situation," she said. "But there is a natural law, Charles – the more unconventional the situation, the more conventional your behaviour must be."

"Damn it," I said recklessly, "then I'd rather settle for the situation as it was."

"You are calling off our betrothal?"

I felt like pointing out I'd never engaged in it in the first place. But a gentleman cannot call off a betrothal; only the lady can change her mind.

"Precisely," Esther said calmly, as if she'd read my mind. "Perhaps we should discuss this at a better time."

"I agree," I said feelingly.

Bedwalters was telling Heron how the chapman had been found. Despite his horrible injury, he'd managed to stagger to the top of the stair where he'd been found by a neighbour. This was probably a considerable time after the attack which, as far as I could judge, had happened while I was taking refuge in the other world. After the attack on me, therefore. The murderer had failed to catch me and had gone at once to eliminate another threat; he could not risk me talking to the chapman.

Which argued that the two men must have come very close as the apprentice ran from Mrs McDonald's house. Did he know Jas Williams and his customers had seen him too – were they also in danger? I thought not; they'd seen him in the shop, so they could probably label him a thief, but they could not directly connect him with Nell's murder.

The bloodstain lay at the top of a small flight of five steps; the chapman could hardly have stepped off the last step before he was hit. And – I sniffed – how odd; I could smell fish.

I glanced around. In the house nearest to where the chapman had fallen, the door hung on one hinge. Two steps led up into the ground floor room; I paused to let my eyes adjust to the semi-darkness after the brightness of the sunshine outside.

At the back of the room was a bright brand new skillet gleaming over the remains of a small fire; in the pan was a shiny fish, half-cooked, complete with fins, tail and bright watchful eye.

"It was a trap," I said.

Heron caught on quickest. "If the chapman came this way often, he would know this was an empty house. The smell of cooking, therefore, would make him stop to look in."

"The gleam of the new pan would have caught his eye," Esther said.

"And he would have presented an excellent target for whoever wanted to drop something on his head," Heron finished.

Hugh was already heading for the ancient ladder at the back of the room. "Not this house," I said. "Anyone on the roof of this house wouldn't have been able to see the chapman hesitating at the door because of the overhang of the eaves. But from the house opposite, the view would have been perfect."

Hugh relieved his feelings by kicking in the door of the house in question. He rushed towards the ramshackle ladder at the back as if he thought the villain might still be up there. The ladder led to a filthy room on the first floor, littered with the debris of casual occupation: rags, a chamberpot with a great section out of it, a pile of newspapers so ancient they were a sodden, rotting mass. Another ladder took us up into the roof-space; Hugh called back, "Be careful! It's dangerous up here."

From the top of the ladder, I saw the apex of the roof above me, and the rafters sagging away from it. Huge chunks of the lime and horsehair mortar that had lined the roof had dropped away; wooden nails and laths had rotted, and the slates had come crashing down on the joists below. The blue August sky was bright through gaping holes in the roof; seagulls wheeled over-head.

Hugh tottered across the joists to the largest hole in the roof; I followed, and found myself staring down at Bedwalters, Heron and Esther, standing in the doorway of the house opposite.

Immediately in front of us, the last, largest row of slates still clung to the rafters. One huge slate was missing from the rank.

"He could hardly have missed," Hugh said, leaning danger-ously out to peer at the alley below. "All he had to do was to yank out the nails, give the slate a gentle push, and nature would do the rest. Down it would go."

I nodded. "But he had to get the chapman to stop, so he'd have time to pull out the nails."

"It wasn't an attack in anger or fright," Hugh said distastefully. "The whole thing was planned. He had to buy the skillet and the fish, light the fire, cook the fish a little to get the smell going – "

"He had to know the man would come this way, and when," I added.

"I still don't understand!" Hugh protested passionately. "He doesn't have to stay in the town. He could simply flee to London. There's no need for all this killing!"

"The book," I said. "That's what keeps him here, though I don't have the least idea why."

I thought of telling Hugh I'd found the book but something stopped me. It would hardly profit him to know; only I knew how to come and go between that world and our own, so Hugh couldn't retrieve the book if the need arose. And it was best that he could genuinely claim ignorance if asked about it.

In the street, the others listened to what we had to report.

"It's an amazing crime," I said, staring at the bright eye of the fish in the shining new skillet. "So complicated and detailed."

"Well planned," Heron said.

"But done on impulse."

Hugh snorted. "Nonsense!"

I shook my head. "No one who'd paused to think would have done it this way. Apart from anything else, there's a huge element of good luck in it. What if the chapman had been so preoccupied he'd not noticed the smell of cooking and walked straight on? What if he'd met a friend and gone round another way? Think how much simpler it would have been simply to walk up behind and stab him."

"No," Bedwalters said. "There would have been a chance that the chapman would look round when he heard footsteps behind him. He might have seen his attacker. Alive or dead afterwards, he would have been able to lay the blame at the right door."

"And think of the blood," Esther said. "The murderer might have been covered with it – hard to explain away or wash out."

They had a dozen reasons why the murderer should not have come to close grips with his victim. But I still thought the whole affair very odd.

"It's an arrogant crime," I said. "Carried out by a man who thinks he can get away with anything."

"He has," Hugh said.

I shook my head. "Not yet."

I turned on my heels to survey the alley. A preposterous crime. It was as if the murderer was defying me to catch him. As if he was saying, *I can do the most far-fetched things and still you can't guess who I am.*

It was to be a duel between us, it seemed. Very well, I thought, so be it.

There would be only one victor.

23

Do not be offended if one of the lower orders greets you with
familiarity. This is merely the common conceit that any
Englishman, no matter how poor, is better than any foreigner.
[*A Frenchman's guide to England*, Retif de Vincennes
(Paris; published for the author, 1734)]

Alyson was prowling the parlour of the Golden Fleece; he
pounced on us as soon as we walked in.

"I've missed the excitement!" he cried with boyish indignation.
"The spirits have been telling me all about it."

"Cut to the bone," declared a male spirit, hidden somewhere
among the tankards on the table. "Flesh peeled back right down
his face."

"What happened?" Alyson's face was shockingly eager. I could
not forget that a man lay dead, a decent honest man who'd tried to
uphold the law, who'd tried to get justice for a girl he'd never met.

The cold meats and ale still lay on the table. Hugh looked on
them with distaste, flung himself moodily into a chair. Esther
hesitated, then poured herself wine. I looked at it all and found
myself suddenly viciously hungry. I'd not eaten since a very early
breakfast and it was now mid-afternoon.

I let Heron outline what we'd been doing, cut meat and bread
and bit deep into them. Esther asked me to carve her a slice of
beef.

"But you must catch the fellow!" Alyson said as Heron
finished. "A man like that can't be allowed to remain free! It's as
Ridley said – he began with the dregs of the town, now he's progressed to an honest but poor citizen. Soon he'll attack someone
of consequence!"

I cast a warning glance at Hugh. "I'll find him," I said.

Perhaps I had been too vehement; Alyson looked at me with
a frown.

"Good," Hugh said. "And I'll be first in the queue to line the fellow up and shoot him."

Heron strolled to the table and helped himself to wine. "Have you organised the horses, Alyson?"

Alyson was still staring at me. "What? Oh, yes."

"Then," Heron said. "I think we had better eat, then start off for Long End. We should have plenty of time to get back before dark."

"How the devil can you eat anything!" Hugh exploded.

Heron raised an eyebrow at his tone of voice; Esther said, "I suspect we will be back too late for dinner. Wiser to have something now."

"Long End?" I said. "We can't go back to Long End. The murderer's here."

Heron sipped wine and stared me out. "It appears the girl was killed because she knew of the book, and the chapman because he could identify the murderer. You were attacked last night because you found the fellow in his lair and nearly apprehended him. He must believe that if you are capable of finding his hideout, then you can find him. Therefore, you are in danger." He poured more wine and sat down, lounging at his ease in one of the hard chairs at the table, the very picture of the man in charge. "So we must remove you from the place of danger."

"I agree," Esther said.

"To Long End?" Alyson said brightly. "Good idea."

"I agree," Hugh said. "I'll stay here and see if I can find the fellow."

"Hugh – "

"You're not going to talk me out of it, Charles," he said obstinately. "I was the one who asked the chapman to keep his eyes open for the apprentice. I should have known how dangerous it would be. And now a good man lies dead and a woman and three children have no means of support. It's my fault, Charles! And I'm damn well going to do something about it!"

"What I don't understand," Alyson said, "is how the attack on Pattinson at Long End fits in."

"Patterson," Heron said.

"I'm in danger wherever I go," I said. Events suddenly seemed to be running away from me. I didn't want to leave Newcastle. This was where the book was (albeit in another world). I badly wanted another look at that book. "This town is where the heart of the mystery lies – I need to be here."

"Is there anything you are not telling us, Patterson?" Heron asked.

"No, of course not."

"There are no other witnesses to the murder?"

I thought of Maggie in Mrs McDonald's house. "None that can identify the man. Unless we can get him into the house for Nell's spirit to look at."

"No one else you have asked to look into the matter?"

I thought of Bedwalters. Of course!

"No. No one."

"Then it seems to me," Heron said, "that there need be no other victims. He has killed to protect himself and if there is no danger, then there will be no more killing. Therefore you may go to Long End with a clear conscience."

"You cannot guarantee he will not kill again," I protested.

Heron nodded. "There is certainly one person he will seek to eliminate. You. Which brings me back to my original point. You will be much safer at Long End."

He would not be moved from this logic. It was clear that it appealed to Hugh too, and to Alyson, who was becoming excitable again. "Heron's absolutely right," he said. "Newcastle's much too dangerous. There are too many people here, too many byways where you could be ambushed. At Long End we can control what happens. We can trap the villain!"

"That's a damn good idea," Hugh exclaimed, sitting up abruptly. "I'll come with you. I can prowl around and keep watch for anyone suspicious haunting the park."

"The justice will probably take you for a poacher and transport you," I said, wearily.

"Come and stay at the house," Alyson cried. "You can teach us the latest dances and keep an eye on Pattinson at the same time."

"Patterson!" Heron said.

Hugh struggled for a moment then gave way to his principles. "What will the fee be? For teaching?"

I left them haggling over terms and stepped out to find the landlord. It was plain I was to have no choice in the matter. I bought pen, ink and paper and scribbled a note to Bedwalters, telling him I was going back to Long End.

I hesitated before penning the last paragraphs.

It's plain, I wrote, *that the murderer has a good source of information, or perhaps several, because he's been one step ahead of us, more than once – he knew about the chapman for instance. So, I beg you, do not put yourself in any unnecessary danger – Nell has need of you now more than ever.*

I reconsidered that last sentiment, aware that it would only confirm Bedwalters in his decision to stay in Mrs McDonald's house. But I thought he was already determined on that, so I let the sentence stand.

He has lodgings in Pandon Chare – the lodging house on the corner – in rooms accessed by the back stairs. There's a spirit there – the spirit of the former landlord of the Old Man inn. He's of good character, and may be able to give you more information about the murderer. But do not, I say again, do not put yourself at risk!"

I was hugely frustrated as I rode out of town behind the others. I could not drag my thoughts away from the murder scene. I could picture the murderer waiting where Hugh and I had stood under the wrecked roof, hand poised above the wooden peg that secured the slate. Watching the chapman walking up the last few steps to his death, seeing him glance aside as he smelt the fish cooking, waiting for him to pause and peer in. And then the heavy slate grinding down the roof and dropping vertiginously. The chapman must have heard it, he must have turned, lifted his head to look up and –

Alyson dropped back alongside me, nodded at the violin bag that lay across my saddle. "Weapon, Patterson?"

I wondered why he got my name right sometimes and not others. "A few clothes."

We were going to the country, to idle through plentiful breakfasts and dinners, to play a few songs and deal a few cards, to read the latest marital scandals in the papers. And meanwhile the murderer swaggered free in Newcastle, free to kill. Nell went unavenged, and the chapman's widow had three children to raise and no wage to do it on. My only consolation was that the book was out of harm's way.

I stared at the passing countryside, blurred with the oncoming dusk. In front of me, Esther and Heron were riding side by side, talking quietly. They'd been talking a great deal at the rehearsal yesterday. They were plotting something – I was certain of it.

Probably arranging the wedding.

Esther was intent on behaving conventionally; was her departure from Long End in company with Claudius Heron – even chaperoned by Catherine – a conventional act? It would certainly have raised a few eyebrows.

Hugh brought up the rear of our party with a bag stuffed full of his best clothes and a kit fiddle slung over his shoulder. He'd not hurried over his packing – one reason we'd set out later than expected. He was still blaming himself for the chapman's death. And that picture came back into my mind. What kind of man would kill someone that way? So cruel, so extravagantly risky, and yet so completely successful.

The evening was gloomy as we clattered into the stable yard; torches had been lit. Grooms rushed to take the horses' reins, and to pet and cosset the tired animals. No one troubled themselves about us. Alyson escorted Esther into the house, with the gallantry of a man twice his age; Heron followed without a word.

Hugh heaved his bags over his shoulder; he'd decided to collect his other belongings from the inn tomorrow. He stepped back out of the way of a groom, eyed me perceptively.

"I know you're not happy with this, Charles. But he's going to make another attempt on you, and we'll have a better chance of catching him here. A stranger is always noticeable in a country district – he'll be far more conspicuous than if he was in town."

"You're underestimating him," I said. The book. The book was at the heart of the mystery; there was something among its tunes that made it so valuable a man would murder for it. I should have had a better look at it while I had the chance.

But I knew I'd looked long and hard at it and seen nothing.

It was late and I was too tired to think clearly. I went to my room, stripped off my clothes and fell into bed. I slept fitfully and was awake before Fowler scratched on the door. He came in with his shaving gear and a pot of green stuff that looked disgusting.

"My grandmother swore by this," he said. "Cures every wound imaginable."

"What's in it?"

"Marigolds."

"No, thank you," I said.

I submitted, of course – Fowler has a tendency to assume that no means yes. I let him smear the ointment on a wad of cloth and bandage the scratch on my side, then submitted to being shaved. He had every word of our adventures pat and only one person could have told him.

"Heron's asked you to keep an eye on me, hasn't he?"

"Did you expect anything else?" Fowler's lean face twisted into a grin. "Or anyone better qualified for the task?"

"Or more modest?" I murmured.

"You're not in the good books of the guests, you know," Fowler said, standing back to take a critical look at my face. "Wanted music and where were you?"

I couldn't imagine I'd been missed by anyone but the musical ladies. "If I'd been here, they'd all have been out massacring the local birds and hares."

"And the colonial gent has gone off."

I sat up sharply, to Fowler's annoyance. "Casper Fischer? Left?

Permanently?"

The book was his. And I'd only had his word that it was had been lost...

Fowler was obviously enjoying my consternation. "Gone off to this Shotley Bridge place."

I sank back. "To his cousins? Are you sure?"

"That's what he told Crompton."

"The butler?"

"Said he'd be back tomorrow. Staying overnight with them."

"His servant's gone with him, I suppose?"

"What servant? He doesn't have one."

I frowned. "Then who shaves him?"

"Never asked," Fowler said surprised. "None of my business."

"Has he left his belongings?"

"Don't trust anyone, do you?" Fowler said, finishing off his shaving with swift sure strokes. "Think he's done a runner?"

"Has he left his belongings?" I repeated.

"Don't know." He sighed. "I could ask, I suppose."

"Without raising suspicions," I said quickly.

I pondered on the implications of Fischer's disappearance. He was much too old to be the apprentice but Esther had seen the attacker in the wood meet another man. There were two men in this business, and there was no saying Fischer was not the second. I wondered where he'd been when I was attacked in the garden the first night at Long End.

Fowler started to pack up his shaving gear. "Crompton'll know. He'll tell me. Tell me more than he'll tell anyone else."

Wiping the last soap from my face, I stared up at him. "*You?* Oh God, Fowler, don't tell me – "

His grin was huge. "I won't tell you anything you don't want to hear. You know me, soul of discretion. Just say he's a *friend* of mine."

I remembered the looks the butler had given me, his quiet determination to do me favours – to make sure my notes were delivered, for instance. "Fowler! You didn't happen to tell him I was a – *friend* of yours too?"

"I said you were to be trusted."

Dear God, the fellow had probably got entirely the wrong idea about me!

"Knew him in London," Fowler said, "when he was working for Sir George Ellison. He's a good man. Honest," he added, "unlike me. And I don't take kindly to my friends being threatened."

"Someone's threatening him?" I didn't need to ask over what. "Has he told you who?"

"He's not said anything about it." Fowler lounged against the back of the ancient armchair. "But I know the signs. You learn 'em quickly," he said dryly.

"Any idea who it could be?"

"One of the other servants, for sure."

"But you don't know which one?"

He shrugged. "Could be any of 'em. They're all new barring the London coachman they brought with 'em."

"A servant," I mused, my thoughts suddenly skittering off in another direction. Esther had said that the second attacker in the woods was poorly dressed, like a servant. A servant would have found it easy to attack me in the grounds. Servants go everywhere and are never seen – ladies and gentlemen treat them as part of the furniture. And it was surely unlikely that there were two criminal servants on the staff – lawyer Armstrong had interviewed each of them himself. He was a shrewd man; it would be odd if he had been deceived once, out of the question that he should be deceived twice. So the servant involved in the plot against me was probably the one threatening the butler...

"Do you think you could get a name out of Crompton?"

Fowler shrugged. "Possibly." There was a reserved look in his eyes that made me wonder if he would tell me if he did know. "He's a good man, Crompton, but he doesn't have staying power. He can't *endure*. Troubles wear him down quickly. He's had to run from something like this before and there's going to come a time he doesn't have the spirit to do it again." He pushed himself from the back of the armchair. "Still, it won't happen this time. And when I know the name, I'll have the fellow in his grave in

162

minutes."

"Not before I've had a chance to talk to him first, I hope."

He laughed softly.

24

We have been confined to the house now for three days by the rain,
which has left miniature lakes in the roads. I suppose rain is the
reason the country is so fertile, but it is so lowering to the mind!
[Letter from Retif de Vincennes, to his sister, Agnés, 18 June 1736]

It was a frustrating day. It rained from morning to night, a thin fine
drizzle from overhanging grey clouds. Occasionally, the day grew
even darker and rain battered at the windows. The servants brought
in candles but the effect of lighting them in daylight was to make
the day seem gloomier still. The ladies languished in the drawing
room casting their eyes over magazines and novels in a desultory
way before tossing them aside. One or two pondered on why Esther
had dashed off to town the previous day. "And in the company of
Heron, my dear! Of course her maid was with her, but…"

The gentlemen repaired to the dining room to play cards;
from time to time, one would wander in to stare morosely out
of the window at the rain then wander back out again. Mrs
Widdrington suggested some music; Mrs Alyson pressed her
hand to her head. "I simply could not bear it!"

They bore it after a light luncheon. Hugh had been off to the
inn to fetch his belongings; I glimpsed him entering the hall on
his return, shaking the rain from his greatcoat and hat. By the
time he arrived at the luncheon table, he was dressed in his
favourite blue coat with a darker waistcoat enlivened by a hint of
embroidery, of such quality that he put every other gentleman
in the shade, including Alyson who'd come down in one of his
favourite bright colours, an oddly green shade of yellow. Within
minutes, half the ladies were swooning over Hugh; another half
hour, and it was firmly fixed that the afternoon should be spent
in dancing.

So the furniture was pushed back in the drawing room and I
was ensconced at the harpsichord all afternoon, playing dance

tunes as Hugh instructed the ladies in the latest imports from Paris. I reflected wryly on his instant success; he made a fine figure in his turquoise coat, with stockings whiter than any stockings have a right to be, and his black hair gathered at the nape of his neck.

Some of the gentlemen either thought Hugh too dangerously handsome to be left alone with the ladies or recognised an opportunity to get near the ladies themselves. Within a few minutes we were forming sets so large we had to open the drawing room doors so the dancers could gallop out into the hall and back. I was startled at one point to see Ord dancing with his wife – an unusual proceeding for any gentleman. But Lizzie was looking particularly fine in her enjoyment of the dance; her eyes were sparkling, and her hair had come loose and was trailing round her neck.

Midway through the afternoon, I gave the harpsichord up to the younger musical lady and went upstairs to my room for a piss and a few moments' rest. I was halfway up the stairs when I heard my name called and turned to see Fowler's head poking out of one of the doors to the servants' stairs. He beckoned me; I followed him into the narrow musty servants' passageway running behind the reception rooms.

He eased the door shut, so we were lit only by a single candle in a sconce on the wall. The air seemed immediately more stuffy; I sneezed. Fowler grinned.

"The American gent," he said. "He's left his bags. A big trunk and half a library of books, evidently. And a package of business letters too."

I was relieved – I rather liked Fischer. "Looks like he's coming back then." Not that that necessarily cleared him of involvement; he would have ridden through Newcastle to reach Shotley Bridge and might have found an opportunity to attack us.

"This weather'll hold him up but he could be back tonight," Fowler said. " Depends how chatty he gets with his cousins."

I nodded. "Had a word with Crompton yet? About the *other matter*?"

He gave me a reproachful look. "As if I'm going to raise the subject in the servants' hall!" He grinned. "I'll deal with it later."

"Tonight, no doubt," I said dryly.

"No doubt."

"In the butler's pantry."

"Not his pantry, no," Fowler said wickedly. I suddenly realised I must change the subject; the less I knew about this the better.

"Where's Heron? I've not seen him all day."

"Writing letters and reading some dead fellow that wrote poetry."

"Virgil?" I asked, recalling Heron's preferences.

"How should I know?"

A few minutes later I was scratching at Heron's door and hearing his voice call entry. I opened the door on to a room bright with candles. Heron was comfortable in a large winged armchair, browsing through a volume of what did indeed seem to be Virgil; a large, filled brandy glass stood on a table at his fingertips. He waited until I'd closed the door, then said, "Are you going to tell me what happened yesterday morning, before we met you at the Fleece?"

I laughed, accepted a glass of brandy and a comfortable chair opposite him.

Heron knows all about the world that runs alongside our own; on one occasion, he accompanied me there. He listened as I related my visit to the apprentice's lodgings, was grimly amused by my tale of being chased by cleaver-wielding butchers and nodded approvingly when I said I'd left the book in All Hallows churchyard in that other world.

"And there was nothing about the book that struck you as odd?" he asked after I'd finished.

"Apart from his version of *Winchester Old*, no. Oh, and the tunes were the Old Version."

"I don't think we are dealing with ecclesiastical controversies," Heron said dryly. "No marginal notes?"

"Not that I noticed. I need another look at it but I can only go to Newcastle a limited number of times before Edward Alyson decides I'm not value for money!"

"You need not concern yourself with that any more," Heron pointed out. "You are after all marrying a wealthy woman."

I gritted my teeth.

"I will, of course," Heron said, "give the bride away."

I went back to the harpsichord, to find the ladies and gentlemen lounging exhausted over refreshments brought in by Crompton and the footmen: macaroons, sweetmeats and wine. Hugh was chatting to a giggling Lizzie Ord but soon made his excuses and came across to where I was debating whether to follow Heron's excellent brandy – obviously brought with him – with one of Alyson's inferior offerings.

"I've been having a good gossip," Hugh said, grinning. "Devil take it, Charles, you never told me you were having so much fun!"

I sighed.

Hugh nodded at our host who was whispering something in his wife's ear. "The old uncle would have been horrified to see his nephew in charge here."

"You knew the old man?"

"Met him a couple of times at the Blackett country house." The Blacketts, I recalled, lived three or four miles nearer Newcastle. "He was a pleasant fellow, but he did have a biblical approach to behaviour. All *thou shalt not*."

"Not married himself, I take it?"

Hugh grinned. "His sister – Alyson's mother – soured him. She ran off with a ship's captain. Got married in Calais."

"I know – I saw the family Bible. Alyson's quite open about it."

Hugh looked surprised. "Not to his guests. I had it all from Ridley who knew the old man well. Strictly hush-hush, he said." He looked disappointed. "Damn it, Charles, don't spoil my surprises!"

"If the uncle didn't want him to inherit," I said, "he should have disinherited him in his will!"

"You don't disinherit family, Charles! Not unless there's something seriously wrong." His expression sobered; he glanced round to make sure no one was listening. "So what are we going to do?"

"About the murderer? I don't have the least idea."

"Damn it, Charles!" He stopped to allow a lady to pass; she smiled archly and wondered if the dancing was about to start again. He went off with her, only pausing long enough to whisper, "Damn it, we have to do something!"

I didn't need to be told.

I went to bed fretting. Nothing done, nothing learned. No way I could think of to get back to Newcastle to have another look at the book. And I was willing to bet Fischer would be back in a day or two, as innocent and honest as he'd always seemed.

My insistence that I would find Nell's murderer was beginning to look very hollow.

25

Every man knows his own history and can recite his ancestors for six generations at least. It is all very dull.
[Letter from Retif de Vincennes, to his wife, Régine, 1 August 1736]

The following day began rather better. At the door of the breakfast room, Crompton handed me a note with a polite murmur. This time his gaze did not linger on mine – he moved off at once. I wondered if Fowler had said something to him.

I went into the library to read the note. It was from Bedwalters. I've always respected the man and the note only increased my admiration. He'd been making enquiries about the apprentice; the spirit in the lodging house ('a very pleasant gentleman', according to Bedwalters) had referred him to other spirits; one or two local merchants had had a thing or two to say... Etc. Etc.

I regret to say I have not uncovered a great deal, Bedwalters began at the top of two pages of closely written information. *Some people believe the apprentice to be local but most do not. Many think he is a Londoner.*

That, I reflected, was what people generally say of someone not local.

One person, Bedwalters wrote, *believed him to be from Devon. He has an exceedingly bad reputation. Several local merchants suspect him of stealing goods.*

Here Bedwalters had listed six local tradesmen and the goods they believed to have gone missing. Nothing surprising on the whole: food, clothing, candles and so on. But one tradesman had missed two knives, which was alarming, as it meant the murderer might still have a knife even though he'd discarded the murder weapon. Another shopkeeper had missed several books, including, of all things, a Book of Common Prayer. Defoe's description of England had gone too – I wondered if the apprentice had turned straight to Defoe's description of Newcastle. Did that suggest he was a stranger to the area?

Something nagged at me – something I ought to remember…

He first rented the room in the lodging house three years ago, Bedwalters continued; *he paid his rent a quarter in advance and only once missed.*

In advance? I pondered on this. That suggested he was not short of money. But if he'd money enough to pay his rent in advance, why should he steal other goods? Out of sheer devilment? For the fun of it?

He does not appear to stay long in the town, Bedwalters wrote, in his impeccable hand. *He comes for a week or two, perhaps a month, then leaves once more. He told several people he had relatives in the area although he did not specify who or where. He has also said he has relatives in the Colonies and has been thinking of joining them.*

The Colonies. That was what had been nagging at me. Fischer had been reading Defoe! And the Colonial accent might at times be interpreted as being from the West Country. Fischer himself might be too old to be the murderer, but could it be a relative? One of the cousins at Shotley Bridge, for instance? No, if they were born and brought up in this country surely they would have local accents?

The murderer could have been the right age to be a son of Fischer. His periodic presence in the town might be owing to travelling backwards and forwards to Pennsylvania. I wondered if Bedwalters had managed to accumulate enough information to list the dates the murderer had been in town. If he had, I could see whether there'd been sufficient time between visits to get to America and back. But it was hardly a journey one would wish to do on a regular basis.

Suppose Fischer, at some point in the past, had sent his son from Philadelphia to recover his legacy. That would explain the connection of the book with this affair; perhaps an innocent search had turned into something disastrous. Had Fischer come to rescue his son after the debacle with Nell? No, he must already have been in England – and I'd swear he'd been genuinely surprised and distressed when I told him about the book's connection with Nell's death.

It was all a muddle. I folded Bedwalters's note, stowed it safely in a pocket and went for my breakfast.

I took one step into the breakfast room and stopped in surprise. The entire party of gentlemen were there, gathered round the table examining something I couldn't see, and all talking at the same time. As I approached the group, Claudius Heron, at the far side, saw me, nodded. His movement revealed the gentleman behind him. Fischer.

The American glanced round. "Patterson! My dear fellow! Come and see what I've gotten."

It was a sword. A gleaming, gorgeous, sparkling sword, plain but polished to within an inch of its life. No decoration on the hilt except for what looked like a small crest of intertwined initials. I bent to look more closely.

"MFF," Fischer said proudly. "Melchior Friedric Fischer. My grandfather's masterpiece. A little old-fashioned now, I agree, a little heavy, but still a fine piece of work."

I gathered my wits. "How did you persuade your cousins to part with it?"

This was plainly a story he'd told before, and the other gentlemen drifted into groups while he regaled me with the tale of his ride to Shotley Bridge, his confrontation with his cousins and his riding off with the sword, almost under the threat of attack, according to his account. He'd arrived back at Long End in the small hours of the morning evidently, and had been unable to sleep for excitement.

He broke off as Alyson lifted up the sword and hefted it experimentally. "Beautifully balanced," Alyson said approvingly. He made one or two experimental passes, one of which came unnervingly close to my nose.

"Isn't it?" Fischer agreed. "There was no better swordmaker in his time. I'm glad to have it, very glad. I have at least half my inheritance."

"And the most valuable part," Alyson said. "I know that book of tunes has sentimental value but better to lose that than this."

"I'd prefer to have them both," Fischer said ruefully.

"You went on your own?" I asked, as casually as I could.

Fischer looked surprised. "Indeed. Was that a problem?"

"The roads can be dangerous," I said. "Robbers. And it's easy to get lost, particularly when passing through Newcastle."

"A fine town," Fischer said enthusiastically. "I'm only sorry I did not have time to linger there. But I had excellent directions." He spread his arms. "And here I am, safe and sound, back again."

Alyson had reluctantly yielded the sword to Heron, who was looking at it with a critical eye. He made a pass with it and sparked off a technical discussion among some of the gentlemen. I looked at him in a new light; with the sword in hand, he'd looked positively dangerous.

"Well, my congratulations, my dear fellow," Alyson said, grinning at Fischer. "It's a prize worth having. I'll give you a hundred guineas for it."

Fischer was caught by surprise. "A hundred…"

"A hundred and fifty," Alyson said, clearly thinking Fischer was trying to beat the price up.

"It's worth twice that," said another gentleman scornfully; a third broke in. "No, no, nothing like so much. Beautifully made and balanced, I grant you, but old-fashioned, much too old-fashioned."

"I couldn't sell it," Fischer said. He was good-humoured but I fancied there was anger in his voice. "It's all I have of my grandfather."

"Memories," Alyson said, persisting when a more thoughtful and observant man would have retreated gracefully. "You have your memories."

"I never met him," Fischer said sharply and, with more adroitness than Alyson, changed the subject. "I'm impressed with the country hereabouts, Mr Patterson. The fast-flowing rivers – the coal – makes it ideal for industry, I would say."

Alyson was not in a good mood at breakfast. Fischer's rebuff had hurt his pride, I fancied – I rather thought he was considering ways to change the Philadelphian's mind. None apparently occurred to him; while I was dawdling over coffee, he accosted me and told me in a very curt manner that he wanted to rehearse the opera, and I should go into the drawing room and make sure the harpsichord was tuned. I went, but I did not rush. Given that not one of the ladies had risen from their beds, it was plain nothing was going to happen for an hour or two yet.

I tuned the harpsichord and played through the parts Hugh and I had copied, altering a few incorrect notes. Hugh, bleary-eyed, came down to breakfast, then took himself off for a walk in the gardens. Half an hour later, I heard him talking to one of the ladies on the terrace; half an hour after that, I heard the scrape of his kit fiddle from the library and the sound of women laughing over their own mistakes.

Then I heard another woman's voice, surprisingly loud, just outside the drawing room on the terrace. "It is such a lovely morning. I shall take my book to the rose garden."

Esther. I waited an impatient five minutes, closed and locked the harpsichord and hurried out to join her. Making sure no one saw me.

She had found a shady bower and was surrounded by white and yellow climbing roses. Her book was open on her knee but she plainly had no intention of reading it; she sat with her hands on her lap and her head cocked, listening for my approach. My heart turned over at the sight of her; the slender figure, the elegant neck, the cool amused look in her eyes. There were lines of age about those eyes – she was not a young woman after all – but they were lines which made me love her the more. If I had a free choice, if the world had been other than it was, if people were not so censorious and narrow-minded, I would have asked for nothing better than to marry her.

She held out a hand; I slipped my own into it, and sat down beside her. "If we're seen…"

"Then we will tell them the truth," she said composedly. "Do you think Alyson has not already told his wife, or that she will not pass the titbit on to Mrs Widdrington or one of the others?"

"She's more likely to order me out of the house," I said rue-fully.

I felt a ridiculous urge to kiss the hand I held. And the mouth that was curving with amusement...

I took a deep breath and told her about Fischer and his sword.

"Ah," she said. "So that is what it was. I saw them trailing through the hall excitedly insisting on 'giving it a trial' when I came down for breakfast. Even Heron was going with them."

I remembered Heron with the sword. Another man entirely, I thought.

I enlightened Esther on my speculations about Fischer. "Supposing he has a son, who was detailed to find the inheritance? Remember, Fischer said a correspondent had told him the book was in Charnley's shop? Suppose that had been the son – who found the task of retrieving the book too hard for him and called for his father's aid?"

"Have you asked Mr Fischer about his family?"

"The right moment has not yet arisen."

Esther laughed. "Then I will do it for you."

"Don't take any risks," I said involuntarily.

She shook her head. "My dear Charles, it will seem the most natural thing in the world. People always expect women to ask about their sons and daughters, and grandsons and grand-daughters. We are expected to have no other interests at all. Except, perhaps, a good recipe for beef gravy."

She stood and I, naturally, rose with her. She took her hand from mine to smooth down her skirts. "Is there anything else you wish me to ask him?"

"Ask if he stopped for a while in Newcastle on his way to Shotley Bridge," I said. "He might well have been there about the time the chapman was killed."

Esther turned her book over in her hands. "I cannot imagine Mr Fischer as a murderer."

"Nor can I," I said, adding ruefully, "It's a measure of my

desperation that I consider him at all!"

And then I did kiss her hand, raising it to my lips and touching the smooth, fragrant skin. Our eyes met...

Esther smiled and walked away, down the length of the rose garden, her pale gown rustling against the leaves of the plants. I turned to go back to the house –

And saw Mrs Widdrington regarding me with an arrested look.

There was nothing I could do but walk past her. She stood in the gap that gave access to the garden, and as I went steadily back towards her, she was patently waiting for me. She put out a hand and rested it on my sleeve. Her face was kind, like a woman who has children of her own and knows exactly how they think. She murmured, "A word of advice, Mr Patterson."

I stared into her smiling, gentle face, wondering what I could say, thinking it best not to say anything at all. "It is not wise to think of her so," she said, gently. "And if you are not careful, she will take offence and speak to our host about it. Then you will find yourself dismissed and without payment too."

My cheeks burned – there was so much to embarrass in this speech. Not least the lady's open acknowledgement that I was a mere tradesman dependent on the goodwill of my employers. And the suggestion that my attentions might be offensive to Esther. I had to remind myself that the warning was kindly meant.

"Besides which," she said, "I fancy the lady will not be unattached for much longer." Perhaps she saw my surprise; she added, "Mr Heron. I fancy arrangements are already being made in that quarter."

I did not trust myself to say anything.

"It will ease," she said, patting my arm. Her gaze shifted, as if she was looking into the past. "It will ease." She sighed.

I played through my entire repertoire of Scarlatti and Corelli in an empty drawing room. It at least saved me from thinking too much, and gave me some much-needed practice. Hugh's kit fiddle sounded still from the library; I saw gentlemen, talking excitedly, stride down the formal gardens into the distance, dogs yapping at their heels. Crompton came in to tell me luncheon was being served; I accepted his offer to bring me something to eat in the drawing room. Hugh's voice accompanied chattering ladies to the dining room.

Alyson popped his head around the door, as affable now as he'd been curt earlier. "Ah, my dear fellow. I thought I'd find you here. We're going to rehearse the opera this afternoon. Make sure the harpsichord's tuned properly, will you?"

As if it had not been tuned properly before.

"Certainly," I said.

I heard his footsteps receding in the hallway, sighed and reached for the tuning key. But I couldn't find it, even though I knew I'd brought it down with me this morning. Someone could have come in and purloined it while I was in the rose garden talking to Esther, I supposed. But why?

Or had I brought it down earlier? I thought I had. But it wasn't here now. The only thing to do was to check in my room. I climbed the deserted stairs, hearing laughter from the diners.

Something grated under the door of my room as I pushed it open. A fold of paper. I bent to pick it up.

Opened it on to seven words.

Return the book or the lady dies.

26

Decorum is the aim of all.
[*A Frenchman's guide to England*, Retif de Vincennes
(Paris; published for the author, 1734)]

One moment of cold hard fear, then I raged downstairs, note in hand, looking for someone, anyone, to take my anger out on.

There was no one. Conversation still echoed from the dining room; the drawing room was as empty as I'd left it. In the hallway, I almost walked into Crompton but whisked myself out of his way. It was all very well to turn a blind eye to Fowler's activities, but to be branded his *friend*, to have a servant think I was of the same persuasion – God, but that was dangerous ground! I stalked on.

Heron met me at the library door, took one look at my face and ushered me outside. We stood on the gravel of the drive with a thin rain spitting in our faces; he took my arm and guided me to the shelter of the nearest tree. Unable to trust myself to speak, I handed him the note; as he read it, his lean cheeks went dull. He said flatly, "This is abominable."

I outlined what had happened. Heron turned over the note as he listened, as if he suspected there might be some clue on it, some hint as to its author. He said finally, when I'd finished, "We must approach this in a sensible, logical frame of mind."

"Which is precisely what I can't do," I retorted. But I gripped a low-hanging branch and tried to be objective. "The fellow who wrote this note knows two things – that I have the book and that Esther's welfare is dear to me. Neither of those things is common knowledge."

"The betrothal is not," Heron said, "but your fondness for Mrs Jerdoun is. There has been gossip. And Alyson hints from time to time that he knows more than he is prepared to say."

"For heaven's sake!" I exploded. "Only yesterday he was eager to keep the whole matter quiet."

"He is a boy," Heron said dismissively, "with a boy's love of secrets. But the book is a different matter. Have you told anyone else about it?"

"No one but yourself," I said. "Given the danger, I didn't want to put anyone else at risk."

"So, logically, only one other person can know you have it."

"The murderer."

"Exactly." Heron waved the note. "Then we know that whoever sent this is indeed the murderer and must be taken seriously. And he clearly has access to the house…"

"He has an accomplice," I said. "Two men were involved in the attack in the wood. One could be a servant here. A servant would have little difficulty in pushing the note under my door."

"Or purloining the harpsichord key," Heron agreed, then looked exasperated at my puzzlement. "Really, Patterson, think! You did indeed have the key earlier today – I heard you tuning the instrument. The key was taken so you would go back to your room to look for it, thus ensuring you discovered the note. I warrant you the key's now back in the drawing room. Hidden in the stack of music perhaps?"

"Damn…"

"We must question the butler – he should know of the servants' movements."

"I've already asked Fowler to do that," I admitted. "I told him to be subtle."

Heron gave me a long measured look. "Then he will have to be more brutal. I will not allow this fellow to roam unpunished abroad any longer. This must be an end of it."

I knew he was thinking of something I wouldn't like – he had a familiar look in his eye, a look that said he was prepared to ride roughshod over all obstacles.

"The murderer will send you another note," he said, "detailing what he wants you to do. When you receive it, let me know at once. We will pretend to give in to his demands and set a trap to catch him."

My heart sank. "But I do not have the book here."

He gestured away the problem. "We will take one of roughly equal size and weight from the library."

"And when he discovers it's not the book he wants?"

"We will have caught him by then." He handed the note back to me. "Continue as if nothing is wrong. Wait for the murderer to give us further instructions. I will deal with everything else."

And he strode off before I could raise further objections.

Lizzie Ord was in the drawing room, looking about hesitantly. She was wearing a pretty gown and had dressed her hair less severely. She must have seen me glance at it for she said anxiously. "You do think I look well, Mr Patterson? It is a style Mrs Jerdoun suggested." She giggled. "She sent her maid to teach the style to my maid, and my maid was so frosty it was like mid-winter!"

I summoned strength to answer her in a natural manner. "It suits you very well."

She looked shyly pleased. "I am going for a walk in the gardens, but I was wondering..." Now she looked nervous. "I would greatly like to go on with my harpsichord lessons in the winter – "

"Of course," I said, smiling despite myself at her shy enthusiasm. "Shall we discuss it when we get back to town?"

"Oh, please, yes!"

She was more at ease now. She leant on the harpsichord as I bent to unlock it. "I have been looking at Mr Fischer's sword." She shuddered with delicious horror. "It is so beautiful – and frightening too. I'd rather look at the book."

So would I, I thought dryly. She stepped back so I could prop up the harpsichord's lid. "It's a shame it was so damaged. It must be the glue – I daresay it had been kept in a damp place. That's what makes the flypapers come away from the covers. And I do wish people wouldn't hook their fingers over the spines of books when they pull them off the shelf – that's how they get torn. Oh!"

Philip Ord had come into the room, immaculately, if

conservatively, dressed, and carrying a cane. "Are you ready, my dear?"

"Oh, yes," she said shyly.

And he gave her his arm and bore her off on to the terrace. It dawned on me that Philip Ord, brusque and no-nonsense gentleman of the world, with a new mistress every other month, was in the process of falling in love with his own wife.

I rifled through the music. The tuning key had been pushed between two songs – it had been done in a hurry, for it had torn a page. A second note was wrapped round it.

Tonight. Midnight. Leave the book on the parapet of the ornamental bridge and return to the house. Tell no one. Come alone.

I was furious. Not just at the notes but at the way I'd been manipulated, sent running round the house while the murderer or his accomplices sauntered in and out of rooms and carried out their plans unmolested. I was on the verge of summoning Crompton and demanding he line up every servant for me to question. A moment's thought told me I couldn't do it. *Tell no one.* I couldn't defy the fellow's instructions; Esther's safety was more important than my pride.

I heard a noise at the door, looked up – and there was Esther regarding me steadfastly. She looked particularly fine in a gown of the palest green spotted with tiny flowers; her fair hair was drawn up and two little ringlets allowed to fall over one shoulder. And she was wearing one of those hideous caps.

She wasted no time. She left the door open and came across the room, with a challenging look in her eyes. The sun drifted in through the window and touched her with brightness.

"I've been talking to Mr Heron," she said.

"Indeed?"

"He told me you received a note this morning, threatening me."

"Damn the man!" I exploded before I could stop myself. "I beg your pardon – I meant –"

"You were not going to tell me?"

"I was not," I said forcibly.

I knew what she was going to say. She was going to demand a part in tonight's plotting, in whatever Heron had in mind. And that was out of the question.

"Oh really, Charles," she said in exasperation. "So I am to know nothing of a threat against me? What if I decide to walk alone in the rose garden, or to ride out across country to the village, totally unprotected, unconscious of any danger?"

"I would hope you'd have your maid with you at least!"

"Yesterday you were railing at my decision to wear a respectable riding dress rather than breeches," she said irritably. "Do be consistent, Charles. Do you wish me to follow the conventions or not?"

I scowled.

"Exactly," she said. "Now I am aware there might be some danger to me, I can take precautions. I can make sure that indeed I do not go out alone. And I can have a loaded pistol at hand at all times. Is anything the matter?"

I was staring at her.

"Yes," she said. "I do know that you must have some sort of plot in hand to catch this man."

"And you don't wish – "

"I do not wish to set the whole of society in uproar," she said. "And the people here have contacts with almost all of society – or at least that part of it that is significant. If our marriage is to be accepted, Charles, we must be cautious about our behaviour from now on. And it is not appropriate for a lady to take part in this kind of activity."

She swept from the room.

Leaving me unhappily ambivalent. I was glad to have Esther safe, to ensure she was not involved in anything dangerous. But I missed, oh how I missed, her no-nonsense disregard for convention where it was at its worst. Even a week or two ago, she would unhesitatingly have insisted on accompanying me – she'd ridden out to protect me from that attack in the wood only a few days ago. But now we were betrothed and Esther was insisting on acting the conventional wife.

And I hated it.

More than hated it.

And why did it make me itch? As if there was something I was missing, some crucial detail...

27

Entertainment is looked for at all times.
[*A Frenchman's guide to England*, Retif de Vincennes
(Paris; published for the author, 1734)]

I have a great respect for Heron – indeed, a sneaking liking. He's cynical, overbearing and exacting, but he can be an excellent conversationalist and I've spent many a pleasant evening in his company. But if he chooses to take charge of any matter, there is no gainsaying him. When I told him of the second note, he was swift to lay plans. He, Hugh and I would deal with the matter between us. I would obey the instructions and leave a substitute book on the parapet. Hugh was to hide in the shrubbery, Heron in the rose garden – Heron among the roses for heaven's sake! – and leap out to apprehend the villain when he came for the book. He prowled about the drawing room, dizzying me as I sat at the harpsichord, planning every detail with minute precision.

"The approach to the canal bridge is across grass," I said at last, when he paused for breath. "The rose garden and the shrubbery are a considerable distance off – you'll be seen the moment you leave their shelter. There's no possibility of catching this fellow by surprise."

"There is, I think, a wood on the other side of the bridge." Heron stared out of the window. "I wonder if we should place someone at the far side in case the murderer flees that way."

"I've walked through that wood. There's an access on to the road certainly, but also into the kitchen garden, and back to the house. We can't keep an eye on them all."

"Then we will stop him at the bridge," Heron said decisively.

He was off without another word, leaving me staring at the pages of one of Mr Scarlatti's abominably difficult sonatas and wondering if there was any prospect at all of bringing the matter off. If the murderer did escape, he'd discover the book was a substitute – would he not then take his anger out on Esther?

None of this brought us any nearer to uncovering the identity of the villains. A young man and an older man, according to Esther. I could still not discount Fischer. He could have left the notes; he could have been in Newcastle to attack the chapman. But surely he'd not have been fit enough to chase me up Butcher Bank? That might have been a hypothetical son. But if such a person existed, he probably had attacked the chapman too and it didn't matter whether Fischer was in town at the right time or not.

And I'd swear Fischer had known nothing of Nell's death until I told him.

My thoughts turned to Crompton. He had secrets that could send him to a noose if they were known, and was being threatened with exposure. He could easily have left notes in any part of the house; he could have attacked me in the grounds. He had no motive that I could think of, but perhaps he was acting under duress. But of course he couldn't have killed the chapman – he could never have left the house for any length of time.

And there was Fowler, who'd been reluctant to promise me the name I wanted. Had he even questioned Crompton? Was he protecting a man for whom he must inevitably have all the sympathy in the world? Was he protecting himself? He and Crompton were more than – *friends*.

The door opened; Alyson sauntered in with an easy grin. He had the book of the opera in his hand, a finger between its pages.

"My dear Patterson!" He lounged against the harpsichord. "Do tell! What's going on?"

I didn't have a chance of feigning innocence; he bent towards me. "Now don't deny it. I've just seen Heron creep into the library and come out again with a book of architectural drawings. And only a few days ago he was telling me rebuilding this house was a fool's errand and he didn't have the least interest in it!" He winked at me. "Come on, Patterson, tell me all."

184

He had my name right, I noted, and wondered if he'd taken care to do so because he wanted information out of me.

"It's the murderer, isn't it?" He glanced round conspiratorially as if suspecting someone was hiding in the huge winged armchairs. "I'd like to help," he said wistfully. "I really would."

I couldn't resist his boyish enthusiasm. "It will be dangerous," I said, somewhat lamely.

"More reason to have all the help you can."

I told him, briefly and in outline, what had happened. He was outraged to hear of the notes and was all for summoning the servants and threatening to dismiss them unless the culprit confessed. The uproar – and the later resentment of the servants – would be tremendous and all for no possible result. And the murderer might take revenge. *Tell no one.* I talked Alyson out of the idea but he went on to an equally unwelcome topic. Why was I using a substitute book?

"I don't have the original," I admitted.

He looked bewildered. "But you said you did."

"Did I?" I frowned. "When?"

"In Newcastle. At the Golden Fleece. I'm sure you said you'd found it."

I couldn't remember. "Everything was so confused."

"I thought you had it in your bag."

"No, that was just clothes."

"But you do have it? Simply – you don't have it here?"

I was forced to admit this was true.

"We could send one of the servants for it!" he said eagerly.

We could not, I thought. Besides, the only servant I trusted fully at this moment was Esther's maid, Catherine, and I wasn't about to expose her to danger.

"I'm afraid that's not possible," I said. "I'm the only one who can reclaim the book."

Alyson pondered on this for a moment. "Then the only thing we can do is go ahead with the plan and make quite certain we catch them."

We?

"Midnight," Alyson said thoughtfully. "I'll be there. In the shrubbery with Mr Dobson." He grinned hugely. "Mr Pattinson, I am so glad I met you. I'd no notion that life could be so exciting! Meanwhile –" He brandished the opera book. " – we'll carry on as usual, to lull the murderer's suspicions. We've let this opera project drop and I am determined to get back to it."

The rest of the day I spent in an agony of anticipation. The opera project was seized on with eagerness by all as if it was something entirely new. Alyson had the inspiration of including dances in the opera which provoked a general exodus in the direction of the library, and repeated demands that I should accompany the dancers. Moving the harpsichord was out of the question – it would be horribly out of tune instantly – so I fetched my fiddle and stood for hours playing through every dance tune I could think of.

After an hour and a half of this, I'd a great deal of sympathy with the renegade spirit who was bemoaning the destruction of his usual peace and quiet, and threatening to escape to one of the attic rooms.

"Do so," I said wearily. "I would love to join you."

Hugh was trying to coach the ladies in a complicated step; I said, "The old man – the uncle – did he die here?"

"No one knows exactly where he died," the spirit said. "Went out for a ride, put his horse at a fence and came off. Caught his foot in a stirrup and the horse dragged him a mile or more. If you want my opinion," it added, "he did it deliberately. He once said that if he died in the house he'd be listening to that nephew of his spending all his money and he'd had enough of that in life."

"Did you ever meet Alyson before the old man died?"

"Lord, yes. Came here two or three times. Always dressed up to the nines and saying he needed money."

"Did he get it?"

The spirit cackled. "The old man told him to sell his clothes! Mind you, there was always a little something missing after he'd gone."

"He stole things?" I said incredulously.

"Caught him once," the spirit said. "Putting one of the old man's mother's necklaces in his pocket. Said it would come to him in the end anyway. And it *was* an ugly old-fashioned thing."

Well, I reflected, that bore out Fowler's story of Alyson pottering off to the country for more money. But the 'trustees' had not existed. "Did you tell his uncle?"

"He knew," the spirit said.

"I'm surprised he didn't will the property away from his nephew."

"Didn't make a will. Kept saying there was plenty of time."

"And Alyson was the only living relative?"

"No, there are cousins somewhere. Scotch cousins." The spirit, to my astonishment, giggled. "Mind you, young Mr A is getting paid back in his own coin, so to speak."

"You mean – "

"A few of his silver spoons gone already. And a couple of min-iatures."

"The servants?" I asked, suddenly alert.

"Well, I never caught anyone yet," the spirit said, "but I have my suspicions. That butler for instance. Oh Lord…"

And to my annoyance Hugh yelled for music, and the spirit shot off, presumably to take refuge in the attics.

Just before dinner I accosted Fowler outside Heron's room, and asked him to find time to go down to the village tavern and ask if they'd seen any strangers in the past few days. I couldn't make up my mind whether the notes had been left by Fischer or Crompton or someone else entirely, but one at least of the plotters was outside the house. The man who'd killed Nell and the chapman, and who'd attacked me in town, had freedom of movement and was neither servant nor guest.

Fowler agreed to the errand with such alacrity I wondered if there was anyone in the village who'd caught his eye. But when I warned him to be careful, he merely looked exaggeratedly patient and said, "How do you think I got to be this old?"

"Have you spoken to Crompton about whoever's threatening him?"

"In my own time, Patterson." A wolfish grin spread across his face. "In my own time."

"That man could be our murderer!"

Fowler shook his head. "It's one of the servants and none of 'em was missing yesterday while you were off enjoying yourselves in town. Think I didn't ask?"

And he sauntered away with a swagger.

I was distracted during dinner, which suited Casper Fischer very well; he had a fine time laughing at his cousins' peculiar ideas about Pennsylvania. Lizzie Ord enjoyed his tales; Philip Ord, who'd manoeuvred himself into the seat next to his wife, glowered and continually tried to distract her attention with titbits of food. From time to time, he cast fulminating glances at Mrs Alyson, whose weary air led her to murmur more than once about 'provincial' lack of sophistication.

Heron was not pleased when I told him, in a quiet moment over the brandy, that Alyson was intent on helping us. He had strong words about the naïveté of youth, and I almost recommended he chat to Mrs Alyson. Then I had to explain our plans to Hugh who was rather too eager for my liking.

"Devil take it," he whispered – we were surrounded by adoring ladies in the drawing room – "Once I get my hands on him, he'll wish he'd never set foot in Newcastle."

"Hugh – " But the ladies were wanting more of Hugh's tales about his last trip to Paris. Was the court as magnificent as everyone said? Were the fashions really better than English fashions? I watched him flirt outrageously with every one of them. At least, I reflected, he was, like most dancing masters, an excellent fencer, and Heron had looked dangerous with the American's sword.

Maybe tonight would not be a disaster after all.

28

**I rose this morning to find the house in an uproar – some
chambermaid had lost a shilling or something of the kind. What a fuss!**
[Letter from Retif de Vincennes, to his brother, Georges, 11 July 1736]

The man who'd sent me that note knew nothing about the
gentry. Expecting a houseparty of gentlemen to go to sleep
before dawn was about as likely as expecting them all to give six
guineas to a beggar at the door. Or welcoming a musician as the
husband of a lady with money and aristocratic connections.
When I went softly down the stairs and hesitated at the door to
the servants' quarters, there were at least five or six gentlemen
still roistering in the dining room, including Alyson who, in the
splendour of a midnight blue coat and breeches, was either
looking for something on the floor or had fallen down dead
drunk. It looked unlikely he'd be sharing the shrubbery with
Hugh.

I pushed open the servants' door as quietly as I could; it was
well-oiled of course – no servant must make any undue noise.
The lively chatter drifted to me from the kitchen, and a quieter
conversation nearer at hand – from the steward's room, I
thought, or the butler's pantry.

The door to the stable yard stood ajar. To peer round it
cautiously, then hurry out with a wrapped parcel under my arm
would seem suspicious in the highest degree. So I took a deep
breath, pushed the door wide and strode out across the cobbled
yard to the gate to the gardens.

The gate led into the walled kitchen garden with its neat rows
of vegetables stretching into the moonlit distance. I stared
gloomily at the brightly lit paths. Moonlight is wonderful for
travelling but the very devil if you're trying to conduct an illicit
encounter. My opponent would be glad of it, I supposed; it
would enable him to see if I was being followed. Hugh and

Heron had both retired early and must, I hoped, already be concealed in the bushes.

An ornate gate from the kitchen garden led on to a path of beaten earth. Rose bushes flaunted fragrant blossoms on every side, subtly different shades of grey in the moonlight. Choosing a path leading directly ahead, I came eventually into the great formal garden in front of the house, with its tiny box hedges and complex patterns of flowerbeds.

To my left the old house displayed its silly little corner turrets and multiple windows. Candles gleamed behind windows on the upper storey; on the ground floor, the dining room was ablaze – I could see the gentlemen there, still carousing. The door was open on to the terrace and one man, blurred against the bright light, came out on to the terrace, pissed into an ornamental flowerpot and went back in again.

I walked down the path to the bottom of the formal gardens. The water of the canal gleamed pewter in the moonlight as I approached; the trees of the wood beyond were dark and impenetrable. As I crossed the grass, I almost slipped on a patch of mud, and paused, heart thumping, to regain my balance. Somewhere far off a sheep bleated in panic, followed by the bark of a fox.

I started off again, taking more care where I walked. The grass had been recently scythed and stood up in little spikes. Ahead of me, the stone bridge gleamed in the moonlight; its parapet was wide but had a rounded top. How the devil was I to get the book to balance on top of that?

It was ludicrous. The whole thing was ludicrous. If it hadn't been for the fact that Esther had been threatened, and the fellow had killed twice already, I'd have gone straight back to the house –

A hand landed in the small of my back, pushed. I slipped, flung out my hands to regain my balance. The book was plucked from under my arm.

Then I was plunging into stagnant, stinking water.

29

Highway robbers can be very audacious.
[*A Frenchman's guide to England*, Retif de Vincennes
(Paris; published for the author, 1734)]

I pushed myself on to hands and knees, coughing, and spitting out water. Someone was running over the bridge. The slightest of figures, dressed in black – a flapping greatcoat, a cloth of some kind draped round head and face, a hat.

I splashed about, trying to get free of the trailing weed. A second man ran across the bridge, the sword in his hand flashing in the moonlight. Heron. For a man in middle-age he was fast, sprinting off the bridge, leaping a mess of mud and water and coming within touching distance of the attacker just as he reached the margins of the wood.

The attacker stumbled – I heard a gasp, high and incoherent. Heron shouted in rage, brandished the sword –

A second greatcoated figure stepped from the wood, tall, slim, masked. Something was raised in his hand – a club or cudgel. I yelled but it was already too late. The club came down hard. At the last moment, Heron twisted, tried to take the blow on his left shoulder but the club glanced off his temple.

He went down as if poleaxed.

I struggled across the wide deep water – it came up to my thighs and made walking like wading through mud. The second attacker tossed down his club which looked broken – he stooped to take up Heron's sword, hefted the elegant blade in his hand.

I shouted, thinking he intended to run Heron through. For one moment, his eyes, behind the folds of black cloth, met mine.

He was laughing at me. I knew he was. He was laughing, and challenging me to catch him.

He lifted an arm – and tossed the sword away.

He took off like a hare behind his accomplice, greatcoat flapping. I knew even then that I couldn't catch them.

I dragged myself over the crumbling edge of the canal, crawled a yard or two. I staggered upright, sodden clothes dragging me down. The water poured off me. I stumbled across to Heron.

He lay face down, blood pouring from a wound on his left temple, matting his fair hair and running down into his eye. It looked worse than the injury I'd received the night I was attacked. But I could still hear his breathing, ragged and uneven. Next to him lay the two pieces of the branch he'd been hit with; it had been rotten in the core, thank God – that must have lessened the force of the blow.

Someone was calling my name. Hugh was racing across the bridge, in shirtsleeves, pistol in hand.

"Where the devil have you been!"

Hugh gasped for breath. "Heron told me not to come! He said the plan was off."

"Why the hell should he tell you that?" I dragged at my cravat – something had to be done to staunch the flow of blood. It was sodden. Hugh wrenched off his own dry cravat.

"He left me a note, I tell you! Pushed it under my door. I found it when I went back to my room tonight."

I wadded up the cloth, pressed it to Heron's head, tried to tie it on. Heron groaned. "Have you ever seen his handwriting?"

"No, but – " Hugh swore. "The villain got wind of the plan, didn't he? Took steps to reduce the odds against himself. And I fell for it – in heaven's name!"

"Themselves," I said. "There were two men, Hugh."

"You got a good look at them?"

"Not a chance. All wrapped up in greatcoats with scarves about their faces." I dragged myself upright and tried to squeeze some of the water out of my coat. "We've got to get Heron back to the house."

He was a dead weight. We heaved his arms over our shoulders and half-carried, half-dragged him across the bridge, staggering under the burden, then up the formal gardens. My sodden clothes were becoming unpleasantly clammy.

"Front door or back?" Hugh asked.

"Whichever's quickest."

"Dining room window's open."

We manhandled Heron up the steps to the terrace. The wad about his wound had slipped. Blood was blossoming across Hugh's shirt sleeve.

Alyson stared at us from the terrace. He looked befuddled, clearly drunk; his hands hesitated at his breeches as if he'd come out here to piss. Then he seemed to come to his senses; he ran back into the dining room, yelling for servants. We stumbled in, brushing past him without ceremony. I left grimy marks on the curtain that fell against my arm, and footprints on the expensive rugs.

In the dining room, two gentlemen were fast asleep with their heads down on the table; a third was being sick in the chamber-pot that was kept in the sideboard. Alyson yelled again for Crompton. The butler hurried in from the hall, stopped dead when he saw Heron hanging between our arms.

"Send for the sawbones, man!" Alyson yelled. "Quick!"

Crompton hesitated, then swung back for the servants' door. We struggled out into the hall. A clatter of footsteps. A great shout, and Fowler came racing down the main staircase. He thrust me aside, grabbed Heron's arm, hauled it over his shoulder. "I'll sort him."

"You'll need help – " Hugh began.

Fowler shouted him down. "I said I'd do it! Get out of my way!"

And he dragged Heron up the stairs, yelling down all the curses of hell upon us.

We stood at the foot of the stairs looking up. "Now I remember why I don't employ a servant," Hugh said.

"Heron'll be safe," I said. "Which is more than can be said for the rest of us, when the murderer discovers that book is not the one he wanted."

Damn the conventions; I scratched on Esther's bedroom door. She had to be warned she was in danger. But it was Catherine who slipped out.

"She's asleep," she whispered.

"Then lock the door and put a chair behind it," I said, "and make sure the pistols are loaded. And she's not to go out of the house tomorrow. Understand?"

She nodded silently.

"And if anyone tries to get in," I said, "shout the place down!"

30

Never tell any complicated tale – for if it can be confused, it will be.
Within two hours you will not recognise it.
[*A Frenchman's guide to England*, Retif de Vincennes
(Paris; published for the author, 1734)]

There was a furore among the ladies at the breakfast table. I helped myself to eggs and ham and bread and listened to their tales. Heron had apparently been ambushed by six men while he was engaged in an amorous encounter with a chambermaid from the local inn. Fowler had evidently been procuring the lady's services – Heron was of course too well-bred to approach the maid himself – and had fought off the villains with Heron's sword, Heron being incapacitated by a blow from a duelling pistol.

All this was of course couched in delicate language. The chambermaid was 'a certain person', Fowler was 'Heron's man', Heron's supposed purpose was 'dalliance'. As the only man in the room – apart from the servants, of course – I was applied to for my supposedly greater knowledge of the affair. I sat down opposite Esther, saw her lips set in a thin line of anger.

"And why should Mr Patterson have knowledge of the affair?" she asked in a voice so tight I hardly recognised it.

"Oh, my dear Mrs Jerdoun," an elderly lady said in girlish reproach. "Gentlemen are told the truth of these matters – the ladies are always protected from the worst of it." She cast a significant glance across the table at Lizzie Ord, who was nervously biting into a piece of toast as quietly as she could. "And quite rightly, too."

Esther looked contemptuous. Lizzie hesitated then said, "But how are we ever to develop strength of mind if we are to be forever protected from anything unpleasant?"

A horrified silence reigned. I waited for Esther to say something in Lizzie's support but she merely looked, if possible, even more severe.

A lady tittered. "You will be suggesting next that we play our part in such things!"

I glanced at Esther, who had played her part more than once in a desperate situation.

"Oh no," Lizzie said with serious earnestness. "Quite apart from anything else, men are so much stronger than we are. But I do not think we should ignore such things and pretend they do not exist. And things like politics too – "

Several ladies started talking at once, disclaiming all interest in such boring topics.

"I don't think it's boring," Lizzie said. "I think Mr Walpole – "

I intervened hurriedly. Whether Lizzie approved of Mr Walpole or not, she was certain to offend someone. "As a matter of fact," I said, "I was there."

There was uproar. All the ladies exclaimed at once. Lizzie said anxiously, "You were not hurt?"

I laughed. "No, just very wet!"

Amid more exclamations, I spun them the tale I'd carefully fabricated overnight. I'd been unable to sleep, I said; I'd gone for a walk in the gardens and met Heron who was pursuing an interest in astronomy. The ladies nodded sagely; this clearly seemed the idiotic sort of hobby a gentleman like Heron would have. We'd strolled down to the canal, I went on, and had been ambushed there by two villains apparently intent on robbery. I'd been pushed into the canal; Heron had gone at them with his sword, and Hugh had run out to help, having seen everything from his bedroom window.

At the end of my tale, the ladies took it into their own possession. Someone remembered the attack on me on the first night of my stay, someone else mentioned poachers. A third had heard of a highwayman. Five minutes later, a new arrival was told I'd been held up by a giant who'd tried to drown me by holding me underwater and who'd been run through by Heron. Lizzie's faint protests went unheard.

Esther remained silent, breaking up toast with tiny angry snaps and drinking coffee as if she could hardly bear to swallow. Under cover of the ladies' chatterings, I said softly: "What's wrong?"

"Nothing!" she said. She signalled to a servant who poured her more coffee.

"I thought – "

"It is none of my business," she said cuttingly. "Men's business."

"Indeed, indeed," said her next neighbour approvingly. "But – " in a sudden change of mood, "Seeing it was Heron, my dear – "

Esther and I both looked at her blankly. She said coyly, "Oh, my dear, you cannot deceive me. I know how you feel about the gentleman. Indeed, when you went off to Newcastle together, I was quite convinced you would come back married."

"There is nothing between Heron and myself," Esther said with such vehemence that the lady tittered. Her neighbour on the other side immediately wanted to know what was going on; watching the two ladies put their heads together, I suspected that by the time the tale reached the other side of the table, Esther and Heron would have been married six months.

I went upstairs to enquire after Heron's health. I scratched on his bedroom door; after a long wait, it was pulled open with some force. Fowler glared at me.

"Oh, it's you." He looked as if he was about to deny me entry, then grimaced. "You'd better come in."

The heavy shutters had been closed over the windows and the room was almost completely in darkness, except for one candle on a table by the unlit fire. A glass of wine and a newspaper also stood on the table; a chair beside it had been pulled back – presumably that was where Fowler had spent the night. The bed curtains were closed and there was no sound from within.

"Has the doctor seen him?"

"I won't have him," Fowler snapped. "What will a doctor do but bleed him, and he's bled enough. He'll be well enough if he has rest and quiet. No thanks to you."

"It was his idea!" I said indignantly.

He bared his teeth at me. "And you didn't try and talk him out of it?"

"How the devil could I do that?"

He brooded in silence. "You might at least have brought back his sword."

"His sword?" I echoed, startled. "Damn! I never gave it a moment's thought."

"It'll be halfway to London by now," Fowler said. "It's Spanish – worth a fortune."

I saw again the attacker, a greatcoat buttoned over his clothes, a cloth about his face, a hat rammed down over his hair. Sword lifted, ready to run Heron through with his own weapon. (I was not going to tell Fowler that!) And the moment our eyes met, it was as if he had said, *Not this time. Not now.* But later?

And the sword had gone arcing into the undergrowth.

Was all this – a challenge? A contest to see which of us would be the victor?

"Well?" Fowler said sourly. "You going to look for it, then?"

The man really was obnoxious. His familiarity grated, his insolence irritated me beyond measure. The only thing I couldn't object to was his loyalty to Heron. "Did you find out anything in the village."

"And that's another thing," he said. "Sending me off when Heron needed me." He bit down hard on his anger; his lean face looked harsh. "I asked. But you'll not like the answer."

"No strangers?"

"Not for months. Not for years. Not in the village or round about it." Some of the tension went out of him. "This place would drive me crazy. Most excitement they've had this year is when Mrs A snapped at the schoolteacher on Sunday. Swore like a man, they said. Oh, and the London coachman and all the footmen are light-fingered. Which wouldn't surprise me in the least. Now get out of here and get me that sword!"

"*Please* would be welcome," I said.

"That's supposing I wanted to be polite," he said. "And I don't. I've known nothing but trouble ever since I met you."

"Funny," I said. "I was thinking the same of you."

He grinned though there was sourness in the twist of his

mouth. He was venting his fury and helplessness on me – and why not, if it made him feel better?

"Look after Heron," I said.

"What the devil do you think I'm going to do?"

As I went downstairs to retrieve the sword, I knew I was missing something. The look the attacker had given me… It had been so oddly intimate. As if the fellow knew me. Indeed, why should he challenge me otherwise? But did that suggest it was someone I'd offended? Or who had a grudge against me? Had Nell and the chapman had been killed as a part of that challenge? Surely not. Nell's death had been the catalyst for this affair; any 'duel' with me was the result of her death, not a cause of it.

Conversation drifted out of the breakfast room. William Ridley was again expounding on the woodland dispute, his grumbles this time aimed at the iniquities of the English legal system which demanded facts, facts and more facts "when everyone *knows* what happened!" Fischer was doing his best to divert Ridley with tales of Philadelphia, but failing. I heard another man mutter; Philip Ord said sharply, "My wife, sir, is a very sensible woman." High praise, I thought.

I went into the dining room, intending to make my way out into the gardens. I expected to see the room still in uproar after the revelries of the previous night but the glasses and the cards and the used chamberpots had been removed, and vast quantities of fresh flowers brought in, probably to disguise the smell of piss and drink. One maid still lingered, on her hands and knees, rubbing furiously at the Turkish rug. A line of muddy footprints.

She looked me up and down and snapped, "Mind out the way." She brushed damp hair out of her eyes. "I don't want you messing up what I've already done." She went back to her work, the hair falling across her face again.

I studied the muddy footprints. From their outline – clearer in some places than in others – I could see they started at the window and came across to the door where I stood.

I was the one who'd made those footprints. Sodden and

dishevelled, I'd traipsed in all the mud and water from the canal. There were fainter traces of other prints, perhaps made by Hugh or Heron.

"Well," the maid said. "Are you coming through or not?"

"I'll go round the other side of the chairs," I said. "To keep out of your way."

"Yes. Well," she said, sitting back again. "If you find the gent that did this, you can tell him from me, I don't take kindly to him. They don't pay me enough to do this sort of thing."

The table had been pushed back to give her better access to the rug. I edged round it – and came to a sudden halt, just as I was about to push between two close-set chairs.

There were more footprints, fragmentary – just an outline here and there but still unmistakable. A lump of mud had been deposited by an occasional table, with a fragment of dark moist leaf still attached.

"There are more footprints round here," I said.

The maid shrieked and leapt up. And while she was swearing and complaining and condemning all gentlemen to their own cleaning up, I was staring at the prints and pondering on their significance with equal intensity.

Hugh and I had gone straight from the window to the door. We'd not come anywhere near this side of the room. These prints had been made by someone else entirely. Someone who'd also been out in the gardens last night.

The murderer?

31

**And then of course the ostler took my sixpence and never
brought me the journal I requested. Never trust a servant!**
[Letter from Retif de Vincennes, to his brother, Georges,
10 August 1736]

I looked down from the bridge into the canal; the water was a
muddy brown, as if my fall had stirred up all the silt at the bottom.
I shivered. It was one of those days when clouds chase each other
across the sky and warm sunshine is followed by chill shade.

There were a few patches of dried mud on the bridge, bearing
fragments of footprints, too slight to be informative. Two darker
spots were almost certainly Heron's blood. The path beyond the
bridge, leading into the wood, had patches of obdurate mud on
it, suggesting that in wet weather it was a mire. I remembered
Heron jumping over one of those patches –the murderer must
have trodden in one and trailed the mud back into the house.

I sat down on a fallen tree at the edge of the wood, with a
magnificent view of the old house, looking across the rather too
formal gardens to the odd corner turrets and the small windows.
Efforts to modernise the house had left it lopsided. Those
big doors on to the terrace in the drawing and dining rooms
certainly made the rooms lighter but were entirely out of
character. It was an amazingly old-fashioned place and I couldn't
blame Alyson for wanting to pull it down and start again.

The murderer had been out in the mud and trailed it back in.
But that meant he'd boldly walked into a room full of gentlemen, any one of whom could have noticed him. But of course, if
he was a servant, not one of them would have seen him. Even if
he was not, the gentlemen had probably all been so drunk they
would not have noticed a bull trampling through the room.
Except possibly Alyson. But it was still a huge risk to take.

Had he sneaked in later, after all the gentlemen had gone to bed? Surely the window would have been locked? It had still been open well after midnight when Hugh and I dragged Heron back in but Alyson had called Crompton, and the butler might well have seized the opportunity to lock up. After all, one of the guests had just been attacked in the grounds – it would be logical to secure the house against any marauders still wandering about.

I needed to talk to Crompton. Fowler was patently procrastinating on the matter.

I realised I'd been watching, without really seeing, a figure make its sedate way through the gardens, dropping out of sight for a moment behind the fountain then coming into view again. The slim figure of a woman in a gown of pale green billowing slightly in the breeze. Fair hair was piled up on her head except for two or three small ringlets; the lappets of that appalling cap danced about her neck. She was glancing from side to side as if sight-seeing, but I knew that purposeful walk all too well.

Esther was coming to talk with me.

Her gown – her expensive, hand-embroidered, voluminous gown with dozens of yards of expensive material in it – swished against the upright of the narrow bridge; the trailing material caught briefly on a splinter then came free. Esther stood over me, as I stumbled to my feet.

"I've come to apologise," she said.

Startled, I began to protest but she shook her head.

"I was unforgivably rude at breakfast. I was worried. I had been hearing ridiculous speculation about what had happened, and Catherine told me you had instructed her to lock the door and barricade it. And then," she said with smiling severity, "you had the audacity to be well and uninjured!"

I smiled back, then hesitated. "I remember when you wouldn't have needed to ask what had happened – you would have been there."

"And you would have been trying to persuade me to retreat to somewhere safe, and let you take care of the matter."

I grimaced. "I don't claim to be consistent!"

She lifted a hand, smoothed the cloth of my coat. Her hand

was warm and heavy on my chest. I looked down into her sombre face, raised my own hand to touch hers.

"Charles," she said patiently, "I am trying to reassure the ladies and gentlemen that marrying you will not cause society to collapse in chaos!" Her tone was playful but when she raised her grey eyes to mine, I saw an obstinate steely determination. "Putting my breeches away and abjuring expeditions like last night's is a small price to pay."

"I think it too high a price," I said on impulse and went recklessly on. "And what must I do? A gentleman does not earn his living. Am I to put aside my music and sit at home all day managing your estates? Because I tell you now, Esther, I cannot do it! I will ruin you and myself at the same time. I have not the least idea of the workings of estates, and to ask me to give up music is like tearing out part of my soul."

I stopped, breathing heavily. Esther stood, her pale hair touched by sunshine, her face set and hard. "We will marry, Charles," she said. "Only I can break the betrothal. And I will not."

I watched her walk away, sedately, calmly, back across the bridge and up the long central walk of the formal gardens. Lizzie Ord, accompanied by a severe-looking middle-aged maid, was peering into the dry fountain; she waved at Esther and the two women met, overshadowed by the statue of the nymph. So different. Esther with hair of light gold, Lizzie with dancing brown ringlets. Esther in green as pale as the nymph herself might have worn, Lizzie in delicate blue with darker blue flounces. Esther calm and grave, Lizzie excited and chattering.

I did not want Esther on the terms she offered. I wanted the woman I'd fallen in love with – the cool, collected woman who didn't care a fig for what anyone else said, who adopted or rejected the conventions of society according to whether she found them convenient, not according to the dictates of other people. And I thought that no amount of conventional behaviour would reconcile society to our marriage.

But Esther is as obstinate as Heron. It must be something in the upbringing the gentry give their children.

I pushed through the brambles and wild roses at the foot of the trees in an effort to find Heron's sword. I had visions of him demanding I pay for a replacement if I couldn't find it. I snagged my clothes on thorns, stained my fingers with red blackberry juice. I kicked over a fallen branch and disturbed a nest of ants. At last I caught a bright glint among the bushes and brushed away a layer of dead leaves and broken twigs. Heron's sword had been driven almost to the hilt into the soft earth; I pulled it free.

Damp soil and mud dulled the weapon, but it seemed undamaged – no nick in the edge. I lifted the blade to peer along it, in case the light caught a scratch. It was slim and elegant and felt lighter in my hands than Fischer's had. And yet Alyson had been willing to pay highly for the old thing. Still, I was no judge of the matter.

I was hardly halfway up the formal gardens when I saw Hugh, magnificent in a dark plum coat and pale lilac waistcoat, hurrying down the path towards me.

"Where have you been?" He was out of breath. "No, never mind. There's the devil to pay. They've found the book!"

"Good God," I said blankly. "Oh, you mean the substitute book. The one the murderer took. Where?"

"Crompton had it! Devil take it, Charles, the butler ambushed you and Heron!"

32

The crucial thing, I find, is never to be frank and honest in speech –
it causes so much trouble. The English are not used to it.
[Letter from Retif de Vincennes, to his brother, Georges,
10 August 1736]

Alyson had braved the servants' quarters. When Hugh and I ran
into the passageway that led to the cellar and the butler's pantry,
the servants were standing in doorways – the hall, the kitchen,
the scullery – all looking black as thunder. One or two moved
back quickly when they saw the sword I held.

We heard Alyson twenty yards away. He was shouting at the
top of his voice, cursing, demolishing Crompton's character,
threatening transportation or hanging. The door to the butler's
pantry was wide open; I caught a glimpse of a chair and table, a
coat hung on a hook. Crompton was in shirtsleeves and waistcoat, an impressive man, strongly built and towering at least six
inches over the slight Alyson. But he looked red-faced and dull-
eyed, defeated.

On the table behind him was a brown paper wrapping, opened
to show a book.

I strode in. "Alyson, what's going on?"

He stopped in mid-rant, stared at me. His gaze flickered to
the sword. I had the impression he'd been expecting me – he
looked resigned.

"Demsey tells me you think Crompton stole a book."

Alyson gestured towards the table. "Not *a* book. *The* book."
His face was flushed and excited. "The one Heron chose as the
substitute for last night's trap! The villain seized it from you, did
he not? He ran off with it. And today I find it in Crompton's
pantry!"

I looked Crompton up and down. "He wasn't one of the
two who attacked us last night. Much too tall and heavily built.

205

The two villains were slender and only of medium height – indeed, one was quite short."

"Then he's their accomplice!" Alyson began to pace the room, ignoring the pale-faced butler and the other servants at their cautious distance. "There must be a servant helping these villains. Who else could have left the notes for you?"

"That's true," Hugh said.

I looked at Crompton. He shook his head almost imperceptibly.

"How did you know the book was here?" I asked Alyson.

"Pure chance!" His face glowed. "I couldn't help you last night, Pattinson, but I thought there must still be something I could do. It was obvious a servant must be in on the plot." I heard mutters of resentment at that from outside. "So I thought I'd check their quarters. And by pure good luck, I found it the first place I looked!"

"How fortunate," I said. "But I repeat – Crompton was not one of our attackers last night. Anyone could have put the book here."

"The room's locked every night."

"But opened every morning?"

Crompton found his voice, said hoarsely, "Yes, sir."

"It's gone midday," I said. "There's been plenty of time for someone to slip the book in here."

Alyson was plainly unwilling to give up his theory. "But why should they?"

"Once the attackers discovered the book was not the one they wanted," I pointed out, "they had to get rid of it. It obviously wouldn't be long before someone decided to search the house for it. By putting it in someone else's room, they divert suspicion away from themselves, lead us off on the wrong track altogether."

Alyson's eyes were alight with laughter. "My God, Pattinson, you're well versed in this game of deceit, I see!"

"It's not a game," I said. "Two people are dead."

Alyson tried to look sombre but his mouth still quirked with amusement. "Of course, of course. Are you saying then, Pattinson, that we can draw no conclusion at all from finding the book here?"

"None at all," I said, then added, "Except that Crompton is therefore probably the least likely person to be our murderer."

"Could be a double-bluff," Alyson said wickedly, clearly unaware of the way Crompton's cheeks paled again.

"I don't think our attacker is that clever," I said.

Alyson grinned. "Nonsense, Pattinson." He swept up the book into his arms. "What do you say to a bet? I'll wager you fifty pounds that the fellow gets away with it!"

I didn't have fifty pounds. Fifty pounds was around my average income for the year.

"I don't like to take your money," I said.

He crowed with laughter. "Don't spoil the fun, my dear fellow! Let's set a date. It's now August; let's say that if the fellow's still not caught by the end of the year, we'll assume he has escaped for ever and I've won. No, no – " He lifted a hand to forestall me. "You can't back out of a bet, you know, not the done thing at all! Well, I shall go off and give the matter some serious thought. Maybe I can come up with some clue that will lead us to the truth."

"Even if by so doing you lose your bet?"

He grinned. "Even so. My dear Pattinson, I would not miss this for the world!"

"Patterson."

He nodded and went off whistling.

"Pompous, ignorant, conceited ass," Hugh said, after having first made sure Alyson had disappeared through the door into the family part of the house. "Betting on something as serious as this!"

I closed the door; Hugh stood by it to make sure the other servants did not eavesdrop. Crompton sank down into a chair and buried his face in his hands.

"What happened?" I asked.

He looked up at me, his face strained. He cleared his throat.

"Mr Alyson accosted me in the hall, sir, and insisted I accompany him to this room." He looked round as if it all seemed rather alien to him. "He lifted the cushions in this chair and showed me the parcel. I don't know how it got here," he insisted.

"I know how it got here," Hugh said, grimly. "Someone put it here."

"You didn't see anyone acting suspiciously?"

"No, sir."

I hesitated. "Crompton, I must ask you. Is there anyone with a grudge against you? Anyone who might want to get you into trouble?"

He went very still. He lifted his head, met my gaze and said in a clear calm voice. "No, sir."

I thought him a fool, but I could not deny there was a great deal at stake. A conviction for theft could get him transported, but his other activities might land him on the gallows.

"Well," I said. "If anything occurs to you, you will of course let me know?"

"Of course, sir."

I took a risk. "Heron's manservant, Fowler, will get a message to me if necessary."

He clearly took my meaning; if anything, he looked paler. "Yes, sir." He didn't look as if he was about to act on my advice.

"He'll not say anything," Hugh said as we emerged from the servants' door into the main house. "Damn it, we're no further forward! What now?"

I showed him Heron's sword. "I'm going to return this."

"And what do I do?"

"Continue to teach the ladies. And make damn sure Esther's in sight every moment. Our murderer might try and exact revenge."

When Fowler opened the door of Heron's room to me, it looked much as it had before. But I saw from Fowler's face that something had happened; the anger had subsided into irritation, the fear into mere fussing.

"No, you can't talk to him," he said straightaway as if I'd asked.

"He's sleeping."

I held out the sword. He looked at it for a moment without taking it. "You could have cleaned it."

I shook my head. "And have you tell me I've used the wrong stuff and scratched it to blazes?"

He bared his teeth, in what was probably intended to be a grin.

"I need you to talk to Crompton," I said.

"Talk to him yourself. I've got better things to do."

"I've already tried. He won't say anything."

"Maybe he doesn't like talking."

"Hardly surprising," I said dryly. "Fowler, I know what the pair of you are so desperate to keep quiet. I've known for several months in your case and never uttered a word about it. But someone else knows too, about Crompton at least, and that someone has just done his damnedest to get Crompton accused of theft, assault and murder. I want to know who is threatening Crompton. Because that person had the book and is therefore implicated in the murder of the girl and the chapman. I would remind you that that person is very likely the one who injured Heron last night."

"I haven't forgotten," he said sourly.

"I need his name, Fowler."

He said nothing.

"I'll find him," I said, "I *will* find him. And if you try to obstruct me, you'll have to take your chances on being caught up in whatever debacle follows!"

And I walked away from him without another word.

I went back to my room, more to compose myself than to do anything purposeful; I lay down on my bed, in the hope that rest would clear my thoughts. But the things I knew, or thought I knew, simply went round and round in my mind uselessly, making no more sense than they ever had. More often than I would have liked, I saw the look the attacker had given me as he stood over Heron with the sword. Had he really intended to kill

Heron? And would he take revenge on Esther?

He could not do so, surely; once he did that, he had no more hold over me.

I sat up, rubbing my eyes. I'd missed something. I could see the fellow standing in front of me. I'd been focused on that sword, on that look, but there'd been something else about him that troubled me. Something I'd seen, but not understood.

It was no use. Perhaps I should play some music – music always clears my mind.

The drawing room was empty, the window on to the terrace standing open. I bent to unlock the harpsichord and realised that the volume of Scarlatti's sonatas had been separated from the rest of the music and set on the closed harpsichord lid. There was a note on top of it with my name elegantly subscribed; a blob of red sealing wax, unmarked, closed the paper.

The handwriting was Esther's.

Inside, the note said, *Rose garden*.

I heard voices as I went cautiously down the steps from the terrace. Women's voices. I hesitated, then went on quietly. Two ladies were sat on a shady bench, under the trailing stems of a climbing rose. As I came softly along the walk behind them, I heard Esther say: "I often find the countryside dull. There are not the attractions there are in town."

"The attractions of town are very much overrated," Mrs Alyson said, obviously bored. I could just see her profile; her head was lifted, and she was staring down the length of the rose garden. She seemed very stiff, I thought.

"I generally find one takes pleasure from a concert or theatre performance in due proportion to the effort one puts into it." Esther delivered this rebuke with infinite civility and with boredom at least equal to Mrs Alyson's. I wondered if this was a conversation I'd had been intended to overhear, or if Esther had anticipated being on her own and wanted private words with me.

Mrs Alyson said indifferently, "You may be right." And then with sudden startling passion, "But what else is there for women to do but to sit and look pretty and gossip and fan themselves in rose gardens!? Oh now pray, Mrs Jerdoun, you are about to talk of reading, or sewing, and of course a married woman has other *duties*. But can you see any point to it all?"

"To what?" Esther asked, in evident confusion.

"To existing at all!" Mrs Alyson's head turned; I saw her insolent contempt. "Oh, please do not talk about love, Mrs Jerdoun. Do you and Heron talk of love?"

Esther said nothing.

"And don't talk of God either," Mrs Alyson said without a breath. "There is no God. There is nothing but mere dull existence."

"I find that a dispiriting point of view," Esther said composedly. "Is there nothing you enjoy?"

"Oh yes," Mrs Alyson said, with a tiny tight smile. "I enjoy setting everyone else at sixes and sevens. I enjoy scandalising people."

"Even if they don't know it?" Esther's gaze was steady. "I refer, of course, to the fact that you are not married."

Mrs Alyson laughed. "Oh, but I am. Just not to Edward. My husband, madam, wanders the remains in Italy and sends me back learned epistles on how the ancients behaved, and the duties of a good wife. He was, many years ago – before I was born, in fact – tutor to the Archbishop's sons, and he can write a sermon better, or worse, than any man living. And no, madam, he does not know what I am about, and I do not feel the slightest need to enlighten him."

Esther considered. "Of course, if you did, you would lose the allowance he makes you?"

"Exactly so. And money does at least make the dullness comfortable."

A pause. Mrs Alyson said, "No comment, Mrs Jerdoun? No homily of your own to give me? No threat to tell the other guests? No? You are correct, of course. You have no proof – how could they believe you?" She leant forward, said, "Do you know what I find most infuriating of all, Mrs Jerdoun? Self-satisfied, smug, middle-aged spinsters who think they have the right to poke their noses in wherever they choose!"

She was on her feet before I had time to do more than catch my breath in fury. I heard the rustle of her skirts as she walked away down the length of the rose garden, to a gap in the trellis and into the formal garden. A slender elegant figure walking faster than a woman generally thinks appropriate.

Something stirred in my memory...

I rounded the rose trellis, looked at Esther, who was still seated on the bench, with her hands in her lap. She looked at me quizzically. "Calm yourself, Charles. You cannot say I did not bring that insult on myself."

I stood looking down at her. "I arrived when you were defending the attractions of town. She'd clearly said something earlier to annoy you."

She winced then sighed. "She said that it was not *edifying* to watch you mooning over me."

I sat down beside her, said indignantly, "Mooning? I've never mooned in my life!"

She laughed, laid her hand on mine; her touch was warm and sent a frisson of pleasure through me. "Oh, what a mess this is!" she said ruefully. "But I did not ask you out here to overhear my argument with Mrs Alyson. I wanted to tell you I have talked to Casper Fischer and discovered the entire history of his family. He has four daughters, three sons-in-law and six grandchildren. But no sons. And the sons-in-law all sound too old to be our murderer." She sighed again. "There seems to be no solution to it all!"

I was still haunted by that nagging feeling and it was beginning to take shape. I looked down at Esther's hand, lying on the skirts of her pale gown. I still regretted those breeches. "Well," I said, "shall we do something so totally dull and conventional that it will relieve everyone's anxieties."

"Charles," she said, laughing. "What are you talking about!?"

I smiled. "How would you like a picnic?"

33

It seems to me sometimes that the English have two responses to
trouble – the lower orders revel in it, the better sort ignore it.
[Letter from Retif de Vincennes, to his wife, Régine, 16 July 1736]

A footman brought me a note from Bedwalters. It was short and
sounded dispirited. He'd found plenty of evidence of the killer's
petty theft, of his taste in fine clothes; he'd found someone who'd
lost money to him at cards and was convinced he'd cheated. But
there was no sign of the fellow in town at the moment.

Of course there wasn't, I thought; he was hanging around
Long End in the hope of getting the book from me.

I needed to get back to Newcastle and look at that book. Every
answer must lie in its pages. But simply to ride off would have two
undesirable effects: firstly, it would result in Alyson dismissing me
– and I was still determined on payment for my work – and
secondly, the murderer or his accomplice would follow me back
to town. Or, worse, one would follow me, the other would stay
within reach of Esther.

Whatever I did, I had to take Esther with me, to watch
over her safety. But how was that to be managed without scandalising the ladies and gentlemen? I laughed over Mrs Alyson's
determination to outrage society. She was doing nothing of the
sort; she was sitting quietly at home, guarding her secret,
making sure no one knew she was not married. She obviously
found pleasure in that but it was a safe pleasure. Our marriage
would be acknowledged.

I climbed the steps back up to the terrace and was surprised
to find Heron seated there in the sunshine, impeccably dressed,
a glass of brandy and a folded newspaper at his side. His eyes
were closed but he opened them when he heard the sound of my
footsteps. A dark bruise disfigured the left side of his temple.

"Yes, perfectly well," he said irritably. "And if you start

fussing like Fowler, I will take myself straight back to town and to the devil with all of you!" He straightened. "I know that look, Patterson. You know who our murderer is!"

I shook my head, sat down beside him. "Not know. Suspect. Though I still don't have the least idea why the book is so important."

"Are you going to elucidate?"

I hesitated. There was the sound of conversation in the drawing room behind, loud voices – one, I thought, was Alyson's, the other Fischer's. I couldn't hear what they were saying but they sounded heated. I lowered my voice – I could not be explicit under the circumstances but I could hint.

"Why do you tend to dress in light colours, sir?"

He looked startled. "Who can account for personal preference? Fashion has a part in it too, I daresay. And practicality – I wear darker colours when I am out riding."

"Our attackers last night were wrapped up in greatcoats, hats and scarves."

"To disguise themselves, obviously."

"I was watching one of them closely – the one who hit you over the head. He was wearing dark clothes underneath his greatcoat. And," I added, reviewing my memory of the events, "shoes more suitable for the house than the gardens."

Heron frowned. "If he was an outsider watching the house, he would have been in boots of some sort. But you have been suspecting one of the servants, have you not?"

"There were also muddy footprints in the dining room. Made by the murderer certainly. *While the gentlemen were still there.*"

He studied me for a long moment. "I saw them on my way out," he said finally, "They were all drunk. Alyson was prostrate on the floor. They would have seen nothing. But the murderer could not guarantee that, so he would not have risked being there unless he had a purpose. As a servant would."

"I think there are three of them," I said.

Heron was startled. "Three?"

"Our assailants last night were both slight, were they not? Yet

Esther witnessed the attack on myself and Alyson in the wood, and she says the attacker took his horse from a *burly* man."

"God help us," Heron said. "A conspiracy? But why?"

"I'd lay odds the burly man is the servant."

"The butler?"

Shouting behind us. Heron twisted round. The next moment Fischer erupted from the drawing room. "Patterson. Patterson!"

He looked distraught; I automatically rose and he seized hold of my coat. "You must find it, Patterson! Find it!"

Alyson was behind him, gesturing helplessly.

"What's happened?"

"The sword!" Fischer cried. "The sword has been stolen!"

Between us, we got a whole story out of him. Heron gave him brandy; Alyson put in what he'd already been told. The sword had been in Fischer's room; it had disappeared while he ate breakfast – about the time, Alyson said, that he and I had been questioning Crompton.

"One of the servants?" Heron suggested, glancing at me.

"Most of them were gathered outside the butler's pantry."

"But not all?"

I shook my head. "I can't tell. It's unlikely the outdoors servants would have been there – the grooms and the stable boy, for instance."

"Why is this?" Fischer demanded. "Is someone waging a war against me? First the book, now the sword!"

"There is some anti-Colonial feeling in this country," Alyson said doubtfully.

"I'd lay odds the sword was stolen for its monetary value," I said.

"The servants," Fischer said. "It must be the servants. No lady or gentleman could sink so low. You must search the servants' quarters."

I saw Alyson flinch at this. Given the reaction to his search of Crompton's rooms, I fancied he suspected he'd find himself without any servants at all if he tried the same thing again. But there was a noise at the drawing room door, and Crompton emerged in his scarlet and gold livery; behind him was a stocky man, in serviceable outdoor clothes.

"My coachman, Hopkins," Alyson said to us. "Well, what is it?"

"The sword, sir," said the coachman, obviously embarrassed to be the centre of attention. "Mr Crompton says a sword's missing and wanted to know if any of us had seen anything. I thought you should know. I went down to the village this morning and when I was on the way back, I saw a fellow running off through the woods."

The coachman had a London accent to rival Fowler's; I presumed he was the one who had driven his master and mistress north.

"Could you see what he looked like?" I asked.

He shook his head. "Too far off, sir. A slight fellow, that's all I'd say."

"What colour clothes was he wearing?" Heron asked with a trace of humour.

The coachman looked bewildered. "Dark, sir."

"Was he carrying anything?" I asked.

"I thought it was a stick, sir."

"My sword!" Fischer moaned.

"This is a matter for the local constable," Alyson said. "And the justice. If the fellow is roaming the countryside, he may have been seen. Indeed, it may not yet be too late to set the hounds at his heels. Fischer, we will ride into the village to see what can be done. Crompton, ask the grooms to make two horses ready."

"Sir." Crompton bowed his head. He looked strained, I thought.

"As a matter of fact," I said, before Crompton could go, "while you're doing that, could you ask for Mr Heron's carriage too? He wishes to take the fresh air."

"Indeed," Heron said, without a trace of surprise. He had that faintly amused air again.

"A picnic, perhaps?" I said. "Could you provide a hamper, Crompton?"

"Yes, sir."

"I believe you said you wanted to visit an old friend. Where did you say Mr Blackett lives?"

"A couple of miles from Newcastle," Heron murmured. "A long time since I saw him. He is old and ailing now, I regret to say. And he loves to talk. We had better stay the night and come back tomorrow." I had to admire his quick wits; he'd plainly understood what I hoped to do.

Alyson looked unsettled, as if wondering whether this was an insult to his hospitality.

"Patterson has already agreed to accompany me," Heron said.

"And Mrs Jerdoun too," I murmured.

Heron looked at me impassively; Alyson raised his eyebrows. The coachman was smirking.

"I see," Alyson said. Unlike the other guests, of course, who seemed to think Esther and Heron would make a match of it, Alyson knew she was betrothed to me. I wondered if he thought this was a ploy to carry out the ceremony in secret; he'd no doubt be worrying that I'd go away an employee and come back the husband of a guest. But he merely nodded at the butler.

"Crompton, ask the grooms to prepare my carriage – the new one we bought for jaunts around the countryside. Hopkins, you will drive of course."

"I have my own coach and coachman," Heron said.

Alyson laughed. "You can't take a travelling carriage on a pleasure jaunt! Much too uncomfortable, particularly with a lady on board. Too stuffy. I had this one made for my wife – it'll be ideal. And my coachman has been familiarising himself with the local roads, precisely so he can drive the ladies about. He's a perfectly safe driver – no less an exacting critic than Ridley will witness to that. My dear Heron, I do feel guilty all this has happened on my land – it offends my idea of how a host should look after his guests. At least allow me this small gesture of compensation!"

Heron conceded gracefully; there was nothing else he could have done.

Alyson nodded to Crompton. "The horses for Mr Fischer and myself, and the carriage for Mr Heron. Do you plan to go straight away?"

"In an hour, perhaps," Heron said.

"And tell my wife where I am going, Crompton."

"I believe Mrs Alyson has just gone out riding, sir."

"Very well. Then give her the message when she returns."

"Yes, sir."

The servants withdrew. Alyson took Fischer's arm and guided him inside. Heron and I were left alone on the terrace.

"I take it," Heron said, "that the purpose of the exercise is to allow you to ride on to Newcastle to examine the book without the fact being widely known."

I nodded. "And Esther must come for her own safety. We cannot risk the killer attacking her."

And I mused again on the look the murderer had given me as he stood over Heron. He wanted to make a game of it but I would not play by his rules. The important thing was to gain justice for Nell – and justice she would have.

Alyson's new carriage was painted a tasteful powder blue, the Alyson coat of arms on the doors. I saw Heron grimace at the ostentation of it all. It didn't please Fowler either, when he came out with a rug for Heron's knees.

"An open carriage!" he demanded in outrage. "He can't go out in that! What if it rains?"

I looked up at the cloudless sky. "I don't think that's likely. And he's dressed sensibly." In dark brown, I noted.

"There'll be a draught. The wind'll whistle by when you're driving at speed!"

"That's undeniable."

"And that coachman looks the sort to go at a ridiculous rate round every corner – he'll probably turn the carriage over before you get out of the grounds!"

"He drove the Alysons up from London – I think he's competent enough."

Fowler glowered. "Our own coachman's perfectly capable – why go for this fellow we don't know?"

But Heron was calling for the rug and Fowler handed it up to him, clearly wanting to fuss, but not being allowed to. Behind us, Hugh came out of the house and exchanged a few words with Alyson. Hugh was in a smart, dark-coloured coat, with a snow-white cravat, black breeches and strong riding boots; Alyson, in yellow, was looking critically at the carriage horses.

Fowler was muttering irritably. "I've just to get my greatcoat and I'll be ready."

"You're not coming," I said.

I'd never been afraid of him, but seeing the look on his face at that moment, I knew he was a dangerous man.

"You have to talk to Crompton, remember," I said. "I want to know who's threatening him."

For a moment, I thought he'd defy me. Then he said, "You let him get hurt again and you won't live long enough to regret it."

And he strode back into the house.

34

The countryside is very pleasant but I do not wish
to linger in it. There are too many flies.
[Letter from Retif de Vincennes, to his sister, Agnés, 18 June 1736]

A footman stowed a huge hamper under one of the carriage's
seats. Then Esther arrived with her maid, Catherine, who was
armed with another rug. There was a great deal of fussing to get
her settled in the carriage – plenty of time for me to admire her.
She was dressed in a gown of palest amber, with a sprigging of
tiny green leaves, and falls of lace about her elbows; her shoes
were dark green, high-heeled and beribboned. She was wearing
a fortune; the yards of material that went to make up the skirt
draped over the hoops had probably kept the mercer in food for
a week. And all that was supposed to be mine if I married her.
All that wealth, given to a man who was accustomed to living on
sixty pounds a year.

How the devil do you keep the accounts straight when you're
dealing with so much money?

We were ready at last. The grooms had brought Mercy round
for me while Hugh was seated on a grey that looked half-asleep.
We rode out of the park safely enough, despite Fowler's gloomy
prediction, turned for Newcastle, went through half a dozen
hamlets. In the carriage, Esther and Heron conversed; Catherine
looked at the countryside but seemed troubled. Hugh and I
clattered along behind. Hugh was in a good mood, whistling a
Scots dancing tune; I noticed, however, that among the folds of
his coat thrown across the saddle in front of him, something
glinted. He'd brought his pistol.

Dogs barked at us, sheep scattered in panic, hay carts refused to
budge. I was on edge, waiting for an attack, scanning every hedge,
every wood we passed through. The plan was for us to have our
picnic then drive on to Blackett's house. Hugh would stay with

Esther and Heron to counter any threat to them. I would push on to Newcastle. If we didn't linger too long over the picnic, I should arrive in Newcastle before dark.

The coachman said he knew of a pleasant place for a picnic not far off the road, about three miles north of Newcastle and one or two miles from Blackett's house. He didn't tell us it was approached through trees down a potholed track of half a mile or so; the carriage bounced unpleasantly – I saw Heron's hand tighten on the carriage door. Esther leant forward to speak to Catherine, who was beginning to look ill.

We came out of the trees at last. A wide meadow stretched ahead of us, with a slight rise to our right and a faint track leading through the grass. I heard the hum of a river close by. Hugh and I tied our horses to the back of the carriage and pulled open the door.

Esther looked at me doubtfully. "Catherine is not at all well." The maid tried to protest, but it was obvious that she was sickly pale.

"Just a little travelsick," the coachman – Hopkins – said cheerfully. "A bit of a sleep'll do her a world of good. Tell you what, I'll take her on to the inn. Got to take the horses on anyway – can't have them standing around. When d'you want me to come back for you?"

"Which inn?" Heron said.

"Black Pig, sir. Just a couple of bends further down the road. Half a mile maybe. Tumbledown cottage next to it. Respectable place – landlord's wife's the schoolmaster's sister."

Catherine was feebly refusing to leave her mistress; Esther might be unconventional but Catherine knew her duty was to chaperone her. Esther hushed her. "You'll be a great deal better if you can lie down."

There was some consultation and an exchange of money so Catherine could pay for a room for an hour or so and whatever refreshment she wanted; Hopkins was given money by Heron for beer and stabling the horses. Hugh and I manoeuvred the hamper out of the carriage and took one of the rugs, leaving the other for Catherine. Hopkins turned the horses expertly and started the carriage down the potholed track through the trees again. I wondered if Catherine would make it to the inn before being sick. Esther was unhappy. "I should not leave her. There is nothing worse than being ill on your own."

Hugh and I carried the hamper along the faint track through the grass; Heron and Esther came behind, Esther leaning on Heron's arm. Her high heels were not suitable for walking on grass; several times she turned over her ankle. Once she muttered, then caught my eye and straightened with her best aristocratic air.

At the top of the rise, we looked down on a kind of dell, or little valley, bisected by a stream that fell over small rocks with a pleasantly musical murmur. One side of the dell was bordered by a wide and slow river; on the far side of the water, cows came down to drink in a meadow filled with wild flowers.

"Very pretty," Heron said with such a lack of expression I couldn't tell if he was being ironic or not.

Esther was hobbling. The wide skirts of her gown were already grass-stained. She had difficulty negotiating the slope of the dell down to the flatter land near the stream where Hugh was laying out the rug, but when I went to help she gave me an irritable look. Conventional clothes were evidently taxing her temper. She had some difficulty positioning herself on the rug but once she was settled she looked very elegant with her skirts billowing around her. One of the few trees in the dell sheltered her from the worst of the sun.

Hugh threw open the hamper. Crompton had thought of everything. Beneath a tablecloth were wine glasses, two bottles of wine, cloth-wrapped ham, cheese and bread, and a parcel of chicken legs. Small individual dishes held rich, sugary desserts. There were plates to eat off, napkins to wipe our hands.

And, nestling in the bottom of the hamper, a pair of duelling pistols.

"Do you think he knows more than we do?" Hugh asked as Heron capably loaded the pistols with the ammunition

Crompton had also thoughtfully provided.

I handed round glasses of wine. Crompton must have raided Alyson's own private cellar; the wine was a cut above the fare we'd enjoyed up to now. "Crompton? He knows who the servant is."

"Which servant?"

I was reclining in the sun and it was making me sleepy. Sleepy and content. To sit in comfort with friends, drinking excellent wine and enjoying desultory conversation seemed to me at that moment to be the height of pleasure. With difficulty, I dragged myself back to the present. "The murderer's accomplice. Or one of them."

"Patterson thinks there are three villains," Heron said.

"God help us!" Hugh muttered.

"My sentiments exactly."

"A servant could have left the notes for you," Esther said. "And intercepted the letter you sent to Mr Demsey."

I nodded. "I mentioned Fischer's book in that note – I suspect our murderer was still hoping at that stage that we wouldn't connect it with the book Nell was killed for. The note told him we hadn't yet made the connection – but it must have worried him that we might."

"There is an anomaly here," Heron said. "If a servant made the muddy footprints in the dining room, he must have been one of the attackers in the wood. But the attackers were slight, and I believe you said the servant is probably burly – judging by the man Mrs Jerdoun saw in the wood."

"Two servants?" Esther suggested, frowning.

"And he has to be a *house* servant too," Hugh said. "One of the outdoor servants – a groom, for instance – wouldn't have been able to walk about the house unchallenged."

"Then we are back to Crompton," Esther said. "He is surely the most likely candidate. Why are we not questioning him?"

"I have," I said. "But he won't say anything. I've asked Fowler to talk to him."

Heron raised an eyebrow. "Do feel free to order my servants

around as you choose, Patterson."

"And the servant involved in the plot will of course know who the apprentice is!" Hugh said, triumphantly.

"There is no apprentice," I said. "According to the spirit in the lodging house, he is little more than a vagabond, coming and going as he chooses. We were misled. If you think back to what Maggie said and what the chapman said, I think you'll find they assumed he was an apprentice because of his youth and his bad taste in clothes."

"Clothes," Heron said, sipping at claret. "Why are you so interested in clothes, Patterson?"

"Consider the situation," I said. "It was a warm evening – no one needed to wear a greatcoat. Someone from the house flung one on to disguise his clothes, but he had to act in a hurry or he would have changed his shoes too – he was wearing shoes where boots would have been more suitable."

Esther contemplated her smart, beribboned, high-heeled, muddy shoes. "Alyson's livery is ostentatious. If you'd seen someone in scarlet and gold you would have known it was a servant."

"The attackers weren't wearing scarlet and gold," I said. "Or I would have seen it when their greatcoats flapped open. They were dressed in dark clothes."

"So the servant changed his clothes," Hugh said.

I shook my head. "Then why didn't he change his shoes too? And he would never have passed for normal when he went into the drawing room. If he was to pass unnoticed, he needed to be in livery."

Hugh chewed on a drumstick. Esther said uneasily, "So you don't think it was a servant after all? You are suggesting one of the guests is involved?"

I accepted more wine from Heron. "A guest could have dealt with the notes as easily as a servant."

They were all looking bewildered; I said, "Let's go back to basics. Everything that's happened is because of Fischer's legacy."

"What is so special about that legacy?" Esther asked. "Why

should someone steal both book and sword?"

"I think we're dealing with two separate crimes," I said, "although they may have been committed by the same person. The book, I think, was originally disposed of by Fischer's cousins – they thought it of no value, and it made its way eventually to Charnley's shop from where it was stolen. I think the thief at that time had no idea it belonged to Fischer. It was merely suitable for his purposes."

"And the sword?"

"That's more simple," I said. "It's valuable. Someone has stolen it to sell."

"But why should anyone steal a severely damaged book?" Hugh mused.

"Ah," I said. "Now that's one thing of which I'm absolutely certain – thanks to Lizzie Ord."

"Enlighten us," Heron said dryly.

"*Because* it's damaged. According to Lizzie, the spine's hanging by a thread and the glue's giving way. The covers were coming away from the boards."

Esther stared at me. "Oh, no. Charles, tell me it is not so simple!"

I nodded. "Leaving room for a document to be slipped between the cover and the boards. Then the hiding place could be sealed up – "

"What kind of document?" Hugh demanded.

"That's why I want to have another look," I said. "But if you ask me to guess, I'd suggest it's a map. An accurate surveyor's map of a piece of woodland currently in dispute."

They stared at me. "Good God," Hugh said. "You're not telling me William Ridley's behind all this!"

35

There is nothing more pleasant than a stroll in the early evening,
but confine yourself to your host's grounds, or you will be
importuned by every poor man in the area.
[*A Frenchman's guide to England*, Retif de Vincennes
(Paris; published for the author, 1734)]

We chewed the matter over for a few minutes. Esther and Hugh
were incredulous although Heron said that in his opinion Ridley
was capable of any dishonesty he thought he could get away
with. I gathered there'd been talk of a coal co-operative whose
members would share the cost of producing, transporting, and
shipping the coal south, and Ridley had in effect sabotaged the
entire affair to gain some advantage of his own.

Esther was, however, adamant Ridley wasn't involved. "I saw
the two men who attacked you in the wood, Charles! The one
who ran away was young and fit. The one who held the horse
was older and I admit I did not get a close look at him, but he
was by no means as plump as Ridley! Taller, too, I would say – a
well-built man, not a fat one!"

"Sounds like Crompton to me," Hugh said. "Charles, why
don't you see he's the one!"

The conversation became unprofitable, going round and
round over the same ground. The sun was sinking down the sky,
and Esther shifted out of the increasingly chill shade of the tree,
to sit in a pool of sunshine. It was about time the coachman
returned; I got up and climbed the slope out of the dell to the
point where I could look down on the track.

No sign of the coach. I jogged back down to the others. Was
there any polite way to ask Heron how much money he'd given
the coachman and whether it was likely the man could have got
roaring drunk at his expense?

"I think we need to get going," I said, "and the coach isn't back yet. I'll walk to the Black Pig and turn the coachman out."

"Want me to come with you?" Hugh asked.

"No, no, I'll be quicker on my own."

Esther glanced up. "If Catherine is not recovered, or if she is worse, do not make her move. Tell the landlord to give her a chamber and everything she needs, and we will call for her on our way back tomorrow. Tell him to call out the doctor or apothecary if necessary."

I agreed, although I doubted I could persuade Catherine to desert her mistress. She's a determined woman and I suspect she'll probably be on her deathbed before she gives in to weakness.

Heron called to me as I was turning away. He was holding something out to me – one of the duelling pistols Crompton had packed in the hamper. "It would be foolish to take any risks," he said.

"Is it loaded?" I'm nervous around pistols, all too aware of my incompetence.

"It is my experience that pistols are generally pointless when they are unloaded," Heron said, dryly. "Unless you are facing a very gullible adversary, which these plainly are not."

I took the pistol from him gingerly, surprised by how light it was – or how well balanced. "Careful," Heron said. "It will fire if you so much as twitch."

I gave him it back in a hurry. "Thank you, sir, but I have an even better weapon in my armoury – I can run very quickly."

"Charles can't hit a barn door!" Hugh said grinning. "He may have a good sense of rhythm but his sense of direction is dreadful!"

I left them with dignity, climbing up the rise then jogging across to the track. I was beginning to regret the picnic almost as much as I'd enjoyed it. Sitting in the warm sunshine with good friends and the woman I loved had lulled me into a kind of warm sleepiness from which it was difficult to return. But I was going to have to stir myself – get myself ready for the long ride into town and the *stepping through* into the other world. To put an end to this mess once and for all.

The track was longer than I'd remembered. The trees kept the worst of the sun off my head although the air below them was thick with midges that itched on my face and in my scalp. I waved them away. The sun was lower than I'd anticipated – how long had we indulged ourselves?

At the road, I turned left – we'd come from the right and I knew there was no tavern that way. If the coachman was roaring drunk, sobering him would take some time. I'd have to make arrangements for Catherine too. In heaven's name, why had we delayed so long?

Tall overblown hedges on either side were rampant with cow parsley, honeysuckle and reddening rosehips, tall seeding grasses and trailing brambles. The road was potholed and rutted, the hard earth surface disintegrating in the dry weather. We'd had one of the hottest Junes in living memory, and it hadn't rained a great deal since. The road twisted and turned in the peculiar way country roads do; I glimpsed sheep in the fields and one or two wilting, yellowing crops. I started at shadows, and rabbits rustling among the brambles.

A pair of geese strutted out into the road in a sudden rush, necks held stiffly. I hesitated – in my admittedly limited experience, a goose can be extremely unfriendly. But they flapped off into bushes and I rounded a corner to see a spread of buildings in front of me.

The Black Pig, the tumbledown cottage – they were both there, with a barn besides. But they were all ruined. The roofs had fallen in, bar a few rotting rafters over the cottage; the windows of the Black Pig were broken, and a sturdy rowan tree had grown up inside, pushing its branches through gaps in windows and door. All that was left was the ghostly presence of letters painted across the façade, and a half-rotted sign that must once have swung above the door. The sign had fallen into a water butt and the paint had long since mostly peeled away, leaving just the pig's snout and a tree in the background. It looked as if it had once been someone's prize pig, fat and bloated and complacent.

I stood under an oak tree and contemplated the ruin. The coachman, Alyson had said, had been familiarising himself with the country roads – he'd found the picnic site easily enough. So why had he not known the Black Pig was a ruin, and had been, by the looks of it, for twenty years or more? And if he hadn't known, why hadn't he returned as soon as he found out, to tell us so and make new arrangements?

One of the servants in Alyson's house must be in on the plot. And if a guest was involved too, the servant didn't need to be an indoor servant. The coachman was stocky – and he was the only one of the servants good honest careful lawyer Armstrong had not personally interviewed and approved.

And he had Catherine.

I started running back along the road.

36

Ancient ruins can be very picturesque places –
take your drawing pad with you at all times.
[*A Frenchman's guide to England*, Retif de Vincennes
(Paris; published for the author, 1734)]

A whine. Something flicked past my eyes. I stumbled to a halt. Geese squawked furiously. Dear God, the geese! Something – someone – had spooked them. Someone in the hedge, in the field, among the old ruins.

Someone shooting at me.

And I was standing stock still like an idiot! But if I ran, I'd be an easy target…

I flung myself at the hedge. A second shot, high above my head. He had two pistols. At least I'd startled him into firing too quickly, before he could aim properly.

I crashed through a rotting, broken-down fence into a dense tangle of saplings. This had once been coppice; the spindly shoots grew up in dense bundles from low stumps. The attacker was further away than I'd thought. By the wall of the ruined barn, in deep impenetrable shadow, I could just see his movements as he furiously reloaded. I had seconds to reach him and it wouldn't be long enough. I shouted and ducked down. The fellow was excitable; he loosed off another shot. The ball went over my head again.

I ran at him, tramping through brambles that caught at my clothes, scrambled over another, more sturdy fence. He must realise he didn't have time to reload again; he turned and ran. A lithe, slender figure, in dark coat and breeches. At the corner of the barn, I tripped over something, grabbed a tree trunk to steady myself. He'd abandoned one of the pistols.

The squeal of a horse. Hooves clattering on a road.

I heard the thud of the horse's hooves receding into the

distance as I came out into a farmyard. Tavern and cottage on my right, barn on the left. Weeds sprouted through cobbles, stunted, distorted saplings twisted from broken-down walls. Suddenly conscious I was exposed, I retreated to the deep shadows of the barn.

Nothing. No one. The attacker must have been alone.

I went back to the coppice, twisted one of the saplings from its stump and prodded cautiously at the abandoned pistol. It was a cheap affair, nothing on it to identify its owner, no convenient coat of arms. I left it, afraid it had been abandoned because of a misfire.

The low sun was in my eyes as I ran back along the road. We needed to find shelter. Somewhere we could easily defend. And our problems multiplied if we had to spend a night in the open. We had food and drink, and pistols, but we were not warmly dressed, least of all Esther. And no one at Long End would miss us until late tomorrow – they all thought we were staying the night with the Blacketts.

The track loomed up ahead. My scraped side was aching where I'd been stabbed; I was labouring for breath. Midges swarmed around me. The track seemed endless and –

There was movement behind one of the trees. I spun – and saw Hugh, sighting at me along his cocked pistol.

He lowered the pistol. "We heard shots. What happened?"

"The Black Pig's ruined. Has been for years by the look of it."

"The coachman's one of the plotters?" he asked instantly.

I nodded. "There's one of the others here too. Shot at me, then rode off. Where are Esther and Heron?"

They were still in the dell, close behind the tree that had sheltered Esther. She'd draped the rug over her shoulders to hide at least part of her pale dress, and held one of the duelling pistols; Heron, beside her, had his sword drawn. I would have run a mile rather than face him with that look on his face.

"I brought this on myself," I said. "I thought I was being clever using our outing to cover my visit to Newcastle. But we've walked into a trap."

"What about Catherine?" Esther said in horror.

I had no answer to that. "We need shelter," I said. "And somewhere no one can take us by surprise."

"A local farm?" Hugh asked.

"Too risky. How could we be sure we could trust their occupants?"

"But what's the alternative? We can't walk." Hugh was looking at Esther's shoes; if she had to walk more than across a room, they would probably cripple her. And that unwieldy dress was made for an elegant turn or two in a drawing room, not for a hike down country lanes.

Heron said unemotionally, "I do not believe I will be able to walk far either." A muscle in his cheek worked as he spoke; it plainly cost him to admit this weakness.

"I think the best thing to do is to take shelter in the Black Pig ruins." I cultivated a tone as cool as Heron's to try to discourage argument. "With several pistols and a sword, it may prove defensible. I'll walk on, try to find help. If I can get hold of a horse, I can ride on to Blackett's house, and bring him back with a band of his servants."

"You're not going alone," Hugh said.

"I am. You're staying with the others."

"Damn it – "

"It does make sense," Heron said. "In my present state of health, I doubt I'd be a match for a young fit assailant. And Mrs Jerdoun cannot match a man for strength."

"I don't like it," Hugh said obstinately.

"Neither do I," I agreed. "But what else is there to do?"

We filled our pockets with the more portable foodstuffs and followed the track back to the road. Heron walked slowly, and I thought that determination alone would probably carry him through. Esther was a different matter – she was limping after only a few yards.

The lowering sun didn't reach between the tall hedges on either side of the road; we seemed to be walking along a tunnel of rapidly gathering gloom. I walked in front, the loaded pistol uncomfortable in my hand, anxiously scanning every possible place someone might hide. Hugh brought up the rear, pistol cocked and ready to fire. Between us trudged Heron and Esther. We made slow progress – by the time we reached the Black Pig, the sun touched only the very tops of the trees.

I looked at the ruins with growing trepidation. Was this a good idea? Once we were inside the buildings, there would plainly be no escape. I gestured to the others to wait, climbed the fence into the coppiced wood and followed the flattened trail I'd made earlier until I came to the second fence. The empty yard stretched ahead of me: the tavern on my right with the tumbledown cottage attached to it, the ruined barn on the left. The yard seemed to debouch on the far side on to a track running at right angles to the road; when I reached the track, I saw that it joined the road to the right – to the left it ran along the edge of fields towards a distant glimpse of the river.

The ruins were deserted.

The tumbledown cottage looked the best bet for shelter; most of the roof in one corner seemed to be intact. I pushed open the door. Windows in the far side were blocked with planks of wood. Broken remnants of ploughs and harness glinted under the sunshine coming through the slateless rafters; in the corner where the roof remained intact, one heap was covered with a horse's blanket. Underneath the blanket was an odd assortment of goods – two bottles of wine, a hunting gun, a bag of money, a battered goblet that looked as if it might even have come from a church. A wrapped parcel turned out to hold bread and cheese. Someone had been using this as a hideout.

I fetched the others; we crowded into the cottage. A mouse ran across one corner even as we looked around. Esther sighed.

"I'll get started," I said. "The sooner I'm on my way the sooner I'll be back – "

We all heard the noise at the same time, paused, listening.

"Animals?" Heron whispered.

Hugh trod silently to the door, eased it open. Voices. From the road. "Friend or foe?" he whispered.

I signalled to Esther and Heron to stay where they were and sidled out into the yard. Hugh slipped out after me. The voices were a distant mumble. The soft sigh of a horse, the rattle of harness.

At the corner of yard and track, I peered round the cottage towards the road. Hugh flattened himself against the wall behind me. I glimpsed the rear end of a horse, the spread of a greatcoat over its back, a man's head turning...

I drew back.

"Well?" Hugh demanded.

"It's the coachman," I whispered. "And there's someone else with him."

"Who?"

"Can't see."

"What are they saying?"

"Shh."

It was no good; it was all a mumble – they were keeping their voices low. But I suddenly heard the coachman say, "Well, don't blame me." The horse shifted. I ducked back.

"They're moving."

A clatter of hooves dying away. Had they gone? I risked another look round the wall and ducked back, grabbing Hugh. "Quick – move! The coachman's coming this way."

We dived back for the cottage; Esther and Heron were at the door and I bundled them back in.

"Hide! Quickly!"

Heron pushed a pistol into my hand. "It's loaded. Take care." This time I took the weapon; positioned myself to one side of the door. Hugh took the other side, Heron stood behind me. Esther retreated to the far corner of the cottage, pulling the rug as closely around her as she could. It barely covered half of the wide hooped skirts.

I eased the door open, watched the thin slice of cobbled courtyard visible through the gap. A dirty-coloured grey horse came into view, ridden by the coachman, who was wearing a heavy coat of the type such men usually use to protect themselves in bad weather. As he swung himself down from the horse, I caught a glimpse of a pistol in his belt.

He reached to unfasten something from the saddle. Then he was striding for the cottage. I pulled back, gestured to the others to be quiet. Through the narrowest of slits, I watched him approach. He'd dropped the humble air, was purposeful. Looking at his sneering face, I wondered how we'd ever thought him anything but a thug.

He pushed at the door. He saw me at once. I brought up my pistol. "Stand still!"

He lunged at me. Sunlight glittered on a knife. I smelt his breath, all beer and onions, saw him snarl –

Then he threw up his hands with a strange gasp. The knife clattered to the floor.

Heron pulled back his bloodstained sword.

37

I beg you not to tell my wife, but we were held up on the road
yesterday by a fellow who demanded our money. I lost
three guineas by it and another traveller lost a hundred!
[Letter from Retif de Vincennes, to his brother, Georges, 16 July 1736]

Heron was remarkably cool considering he had just killed a
man. As we all stood in shock, he bent stiffly to pull at the coachman's coat. "Help me take this off him. It will cover Mrs Jerdoun's
dress."

I laid my pistol safely on the floor and Hugh and I manhandled
the coachman. Thankfully, there was not much blood, but he was
heavy and unwieldy and we struggled to turn him over. The coat
was bloodstained but Esther hung it about her shoulders without
hesitation. It covered her back but her wide hooped skirts still
showed palely at the front.

"You could remove the hoops," Heron suggested.

Esther shook her head. "Then there would simply be yards of
loose material hanging to the ground."

Hugh nudged me aside. "What now?"

"We must get out of here. The other conspirators may come
back and when they find this fellow dead – sir, what are you
doing?"

Heron was crouching beside the body and unfastening a bag
from the coachman's belt. I heard the chink of coins. He slipped
the coins into his own pockets. "If he is found with his belongings
rifled, it will look as if he was killed by a robber."

"What about the horse?" Esther asked. "A robber would take
that as well."

"I need that," I said. "I can use it to get to Blackett's."

"No, you can't! If you're caught with it, it will be assumed you
killed the coachman."

"We'll have to hide it!" Hugh said. "Put it in the barn."

236

I shook my head. "There's no door. I'll turn it loose in the fields."

"Take its saddle off," Heron recommended. "A saddled horse running in a field will attract attention, an unsaddled animal will not."

"Meanwhile," I said, "get the body under cover of the blanket with the other stuff – it won't deceive anyone for long but seconds might be vital."

I left them dragging the body across the floor and went outside. The horse was restless but docile and let me unfasten buckles and pull the saddle from its back. I hid the saddle in the barn and led the horse off towards the coppice. I intended to cut through the coppice into the field beyond but I'd forgotten the fence; rickety it might have been but my attempts to break it down failed miserably. Worried over the length of time it was all taking, I led the horse down a narrow gap between the barn and fence, hoping to find a gate or broken rail.

Behind the barn were the ruins of a wall, surrounding what looked to be an overgrown orchard of apple trees, laden with fruit. I found a gap where a leaning tree had broken down the fence, gave the horse a slap on its flank. It cantered off into the field.

I heard a shout from the cottage.

I went back at a tearing run, plunging through nettles between barn and fence. Two figures were struggling in the dusk-shrouded yard. Heron was one of them – the other, a smaller, slighter figure, was wrapped up in greatcoat, hat and mask. They were punching at each other. Or trying to, rather. Heron connected with one blow but the fellow twisted away and took it on a shoulder; the villain himself was merely swinging wildly.

I stumbled over Heron's sword, lying at some distance – it must have been knocked out of his hand. I dipped for it, and ran at the pair, roaring. Heron stepped back nippily; the other fellow took one look at me bearing down on him and fled towards the coppice. I ran after him. He was supple, vaulted the fence and crashed through the trees.

I was clambering over the fence when I heard Hugh yelling. He was running across the yard from the track. Esther was in the doorway of the cottage, pistol in hand.

"More!" Hugh gasped. "A man on the road! We've got to get out of here!"

"Can we not defend the cottage?" Esther demanded.

"There are holes in the roof," I said. "They could climb the walls and fire down at us. We'll have to run."

Hugh glanced involuntarily at Esther, in her hooped skirts and high heels. She said, "I *cannot* run."

"You'll have to." I handed Heron back his sword. "Hugh and I will distract them. Head down the track towards the river. See if you can find help."

Heron was still breathing heavily from his fight. He was damnably weak, I thought, and wondered how much exertion he was capable of. He nodded silently.

I jogged to the corner of cottage and track, Hugh hard on my heels. Peering round the corner, I realised how fast the dusk was gathering – the trees around the road were gloomy and impenetrable. There was a horseman on the road, wrapped in greatcoat and hat; he was staring back down the road towards the coppice. Then he kicked at his horse's flanks, urged the animal on along the road, out of our sight.

I turned and gestured wildly at Heron and Esther to run. We watched in near despair as they stumbled away down the track. "They'll never get away!" Hugh said.

I turned my attention back to the road. Esther and Heron needed us to delay the villains as long as possible. I could hear voices – further along the road by the coppice. "They've met up," I whispered.

I gestured to Hugh to stay where he was and sprinted up the track to the road. A flourishing rowan tree grew on the corner; I crouched and peered through its branches.

Our assailants were at the far end of the ruined tavern, roughly at the point where I'd been shot at. The horseman was leaning down to the other fellow. They were both wrapped up; even though the horseman had pulled down his mask to talk, the shadow of his hat still hid his face. I glanced back over my shoulder, saw a flash of amber far down the track. Then it was gone and there was no more hint of Esther and Heron.

By the time I looked back to the road, the horseman was turning his mount, the other fellow was climbing the fence back into the coppice.

They were going to attack us from both sides.

Hugh was peering round the corner of the cottage. I gesticulated wildly, trying to warn him he would be attacked from behind. He seemed to take my meaning, and pulled back round the corner of the cottage.

There was only one thing to do. I shifted into the open, stood, lined up my pistol on the advancing horseman. The pistol felt horribly awkward in my hand. The villain saw me – he pulled back on his horse's reins, came almost to a halt. I had the uncomfortable feeling that he was waiting, daring me to shoot him.

I took careful aim. I had one shot and I had to make it count. I fired.

Ridiculously, I hit the fellow. I saw him jerk back and topple from the horse's back on to the road. It was only a slight wound, plainly; his hand flew to his arm and he struggled up at once. But it had two desirable side effects – the horse reared and bolted, and the second conspirator reappeared at the fence, screaming alarm.

I ran back down the track towards the yard.

Hugh was nowhere to be seen. Where the devil was he! I pulled open the cottage door. Empty. I started across to the barn. Empty. I retreated, uncertain what to do. I couldn't leave Hugh but –

The two attackers were standing at the junction of track and road. The taller one had bent his left arm against his body; I saw blood dripping from his fingers to the ground, drop by drop. The shorter one had a swagger, an arrogant tilt of the head. Under those masks, I thought, they were grinning.

They both had pistols. Mine was empty and they knew it.

The taller one lifted his weapon and took aim.

38

There is much attractive woodland here,
enough to make hundreds of warships.
[Letter from Retif de Vincennes, to his brother, Georges,
10 August 1736]

No sound, no movement. Just the pistol pointing at me, the round muzzle and the shot lurking deep within it. One of the thugs shifted – I heard the rustle of clothing as if it had been a thunderclap.

A horse shrieked. The men swung round. The thunder of hooves on beaten earth. Then the runaway horse crashed into them. The slighter figure went down, rolled, scrambled to get out of the way of flailing hooves; the taller figure grabbed for the flapping reins, caught them, dropped them again as the horse pulled away.

Someone was yelling at me. Hugh – racing across the yard. "Run. Run!"

I fled, sprinting ahead of him down the track towards the river. Hugh caught me up, panting hard. "Hit the brute hard. Panicked it."

We ran, gasping for breath. Behind us, the horse was still neighing but seemed to be calming down. The track ran straight for a hundred yards, then took a sharp turn to the right, cut across the corner of a field and wound into an oak wood, a narrow strip that ran between river and fields. I stumbled over protruding roots, slid in muddy patches. At one point, Hugh grabbed me to prevent me pitching down a steep slope. Suddenly there was a gorge alongside the track, restricting the river and making it flow fast, white with froth over hidden rocks.

Ahead, a pale blur showed us where Esther and Heron were waiting, under a large oak tree. Heron looked pallid and haggard. Esther's hair had pulled free of its pins; strands hung about her neck, tangling with the lappets of her cap.

Hugh doubled over, gasping for breath. "What now? Stand and defend?"

"We have only one sword and three pistols," Heron said. "Not enough."

"And I've fired mine," I said.

Hugh straightened. "I'm a tolerable shot – I'll undertake to take at least one of them out."

"Surely we'd hear if they were following." Esther scanned the wood over my shoulder. "Will they risk coming after us?"

"They have to," I said. "They can't know which way we'll go in this wood. There might even be a ford, or stepping stones across the river."

"One thing's for certain," Heron said. "We cannot go out into the fields. They would see us straightaway."

"But damn it!" Hugh said. "We have to do something! It'll be dark soon and if we're still trying to tramp through this wood, we'll break our necks."

"All the more reason to get moving then," I said, and pushed between Esther and Heron.

The path was difficult to see. It was merely a thin line of beaten-down earth and grass, probably made by sheep; in the encroaching gloom it soon became indistinguishable. I kept on, trying to find the easiest route, winding round trees, pushing through tangles of shrubs, using tree roots as 'steps' to climb up or down slopes. Behind me, Heron was breathing raggedly, Esther cursing.

Hugh called out. I turned to find Esther's skirt caught on some thorns. Heron was leaning against a tree as Hugh crouched to pull at the trailing material. He was trying to disentangle the gown without damaging the material; I said, "Tear it." Esther glanced up at me. Without a word, Hugh tugged. We heard cloth rip.

We went on. I nodded to Hugh to go first. Heron stumbled as he pushed himself away from the tree. I knew better than to offer to help. I went back a few yards to see if I could spot our attackers.

No sign of them. But they were wearing dark clothing and would be difficult to spot. And Esther's pale gown would be a ghostly blur even in the dark, giving away our position. We needed to take the initiative – send our pursuers off on the wrong track, perhaps, or trap them as they'd tried to trap us. But how?

When I went back, a tiny square of amber fabric still hung on the thorns. I bent to pull it off.

On, through grey trees and dark shadows that might have held anything. The river frothed over the rocks below. The wood could not go on for ever, I thought; sooner or later we'd find its end, and be faced with the merciless exposure of the fields. Thank God the moon hadn't risen yet!

Hugh called from a little way ahead. He was standing on the edge of a deep-cut little dell; the land dropped away beneath his feet and plunged to a tiny stream tossing over rocks and falling into the river. I peered into the gloom. The dell seemed to run right back through the oak wood into the fields between us and the road.

"There's no way Mrs Jerdoun can get down there," Hugh said. "We'll have to go round. Into the field and then cut back to the river."

"Too risky," I said.

"But – "

A branch cracked behind us.

39

One of the rare virtues of the English is that they have a firm idea of
the true order of society: wife defers to husband, lower orders to upper.
[*A Frenchman's guide to England*, Retif de Vincennes
(Paris; published for the author, 1734)]

Esther swore, softly, fluently.

"This is my fault," she said. "If I had not been wearing this
ridiculous dress and shoes, we could have been well away."

"No point in apportioning blame," I said. "We have to do
something."

I peered into the gloom of the wood behind us, trying to see
something, anything. Could the noise have been caused by an
animal? A shadowy blur of movement. Too high up to be an
animal, too far off the ground. "Go on. I'll distract them."

Esther took my arm. "No, *I* will." I looked at her in astonishment. "This is my fault, Charles. I will put it right."

"No," Hugh and Heron said at the same time.

I tried to speak calmly. "They won't spare you because you're
a woman." The whole idea was out of the question. Unthinkable.
It was not going to happen. I had to convince Esther of that fact.
Quickly.

"I agree," Heron said. "*I* will do it."

"Sir – "

"I can't go any further!" he snapped through gritted teeth.
"Now give me your damned pistols and get out of here!"

I met his gaze, remembered that glimpse I'd had of him when
he handled Fischer's sword. All the same, what could one man
do against two attackers who'd already proved themselves ready
to kill? "Very well," I said.

Silently Hugh handed over his pistol; Esther glanced at me
before doing the same. I pushed them ahead of me. I wanted to
say something to Heron but even as the words formed on my

lips, he shook his head. "You have much the worse task, Patterson. You will have to explain to Fowler what has happened." His hand fastened on my arm, warm and heavy. "And for God's sake, don't let him get himself hanged! Now, go!"

He slipped into the shelter of a tree, started to work his way back along the path towards the place where we'd seen the movement. I could not bear to watch him, and turned away. Hugh was already slipping and slithering down the slope of the dell, trying to find footholds in the rocks and the grass; he went down the last few feet in a rush, cursing, twisting aside at the last moment to avoid crashing into a tree.

Esther tossed the coachman's coat down to him and fearlessly launched herself over the edge. Her pale skirts billowed out around her. Almost at once, they snagged on a rock, and pulled her off her feet. As she stumbled, I went after her, headlong, recklessly, grabbing for her. The cloth tore; her arms windmilled wildly. I almost caught her, felt her arm slip through my fingers then she was rolling away from me down the slope. I heard her cry out as she grazed a rock, then she was still, lying half-in half-out of the stream.

Hugh got to her before I did, but she was already struggling up. Her hair was down around her shoulders; her cap torn off, her skirts ripped and hanging in tatters. Her shoes had disappeared. I seized hold of her. She pushed me away. "Don't fuss!"

High above, we heard a shot.

We froze. Esther was clutching my arm. Hugh swore. Relief at Esther's close escape faded instantly. "Damn it!" I said. "I *can't* leave him. Go on. Both of you!"

"Charles!" Esther cried.

I was already running, sprinting along the length of the dell, stumbling on rocks hidden in the gloom and almost falling. I clutched at an oak sapling to save myself. How could I have left Heron? He'd been generosity itself to me, in his friendship and support, and I'd just let him go to his death!? Devil take it, I would not!

At the end of the dell, I hauled myself up and out by clutching at trunks and branches. I found myself in an open field stretching, grey and gloomy into the distance.

A horseman was galloping down the field towards me.

Another shot. From the wood. Our attackers must have separated – one had come through the wood, the other along the road. Well, he'd seen me now – he was altering his course to come straight for me. I sprinted along the edge of the field, dived back into the wood. I could hardly see anything. I blinked furiously, trying to penetrate the gloom.

Two shots. Pray God it had been Heron firing. But in that case he'd now be defenceless except for his sword. And if his attackers got close enough for hand-to-hand fighting, he'd not have the strength to last long.

I started forward, tripped over a root and went down, banging my knees. I hunched, desperately peering around. The thudding of the horse's hooves in the field came ever closer. I crept on, from tree to tree. There was something up ahead. A long low hump under an oak. Dear God, it was a body. And up ahead, more movement among the low shrubs.

I felt in the grass, set my hand on a heavy stone, prised it out of the ground. The movement resolved itself into a figure. No, two. Slight, slender figures coming towards me. Then who the devil was on the horse?

I hefted the stone – and threw it as far as I could into the river below. It bounced off rocks with a huge crack. I saw the figures spin round –

And in that moment the horse and rider crashed into the wood. A low-hanging branch whipped aside and back, and caught the horse across its neck; it screamed and reared. The rider dragged it back, held it rigidly on course. I saw the rider lift a hand; a pistol glinted faintly. Then there was a gunshot so close it almost deafened me. Someone shrieked. I scrambled forward trying to get to the body under the tree. The rider had another pistol, aimed and fired again – I saw the flash of fire in the darkness.

I laid my hand on Heron's shoulder. His head shifted slightly; he said irritably, "For God's sake, Patterson, keep down!"

But I could already see we were safe – the two figures were crashing back through the wood, making the most tremendous noise as branches cracked and dislodged stones tumbled down into the river. I thought I heard one of them gasping in pain and panic.

Heron and I looked up at the rider on the horse, high above us.

"You missed," Heron said. "I thought you never missed."

Fowler bared his teeth in a snarl.

40

**I am unfashionable, I agree, but I do like to be up
early in the morning and get my business done.**
[Letter from Retif de Vincennes, to his sister, Agnés, August 1736]

The first light of dawn was breaking. On the Keyside sailors
hurried to and fro, loading the last supplies, making ships
seaworthy; the tide would begin to ebb shortly and the ships
would sail with it. The bell of St Nicholas chimed a quarter hour;
a cock crowed.

I climbed Silver Street towards All Hallows church. It had been
a long night and I saw no prospect of sleep for a few hours yet.
Fowler had been in the devil of a mood, cursing everyone – for
undertaking such a stupid expedition, for not leaving word where
we were going, for not going properly armed, for insisting he stay
behind. He'd managed at last to wheedle the name of the servant
out of Crompton, only to find he'd let us go off with the fellow.

"He did at least give us two pistols," I pointed out.

"Just salving his conscience," Fowler said savagely. "So he
could say he did something to help. Someone's going to throttle
that fellow soon, and there'll be no mystery – it'll be me!"

Heron had stood quietly by, making no attempt to moderate
Fowler's behaviour or language as he told us what had
happened. Perhaps he judged it wiser to let Fowler work out
his frustration. Armed with Crompton's information, Fowler
had ridden out after us on the fastest horse in Alyson's stables;
eventually, after a great deal of searching, he'd found the coach.

"No horses," he said. "Looks like they hid them somewhere, to
sell maybe. But the girl was still in the coach. Sleeping her head
off."

Catherine, it transpired, had been given a drink by the
coachman, to 'settle her stomach'. It had patently been drugged.
When Fowler found her, she was just waking and, being a

sensible woman, had been able to give him a good description of where we'd been left for our picnic. Fowler had discovered the abandoned hamper and the dead body of the coachman, and had been methodically quartering the land in search of us when he heard the first shot.

The telling of the tale calmed him down; he stood breathing heavily, looking at me with a great deal of resentment; when Heron turned to ask Esther whether she felt able to carry on, he hissed at me, "I told you what I'd do if you let Heron get himself into danger."

"Save your anger for our attackers," I recommended. I expected a swift retort, but he merely looked at me for a long moment, before turning back to answer something Heron said. Bit by bit he regained his old manner, became again the respectful servant, anxious to assist.

We rescued Catherine whom Fowler had left with the carriage – she was hiding in trees when we arrived. Then we descended on the first farmhouse we could find. The farmer was just preparing for sleep; Heron dispensed a purseful of guineas, bought food, and a dress and shoes for Esther from the farmer's wife, hired the farmer's carriage and horses, and left the household giddy with excitement. We drove on to Blackett's house, Esther and Heron in a brand-new lady's carriage painted a particularly fetching shade of puce, while Hugh and I rode alongside armed to the teeth with almost every weapon the farmer had possessed. Fowler had reloaded his pistols and rode at the rear, as ramrod straight as a soldier.

Heron and Hugh remained at Blackett's house. Heron was not capable of further exertions and knew it; he'd accepted my suggestion without comment. Hugh had been more difficult to persuade but had eventually agreed – I wanted him to question Blackett, to glean what he could about the dispute over the woodland. Blackett would certainly know all about it – he was an inveterate gossip. With everything settled, I went out to the stables for the horse Blackett had agreed to loan me, knowing that at least the others would be safe – our opponents would hardly raid a house full of servants and securely shut up for the night.

Fowler was in the stables, lounging against the wall with his hands in his pockets and a sour expression. He looked at me, said, "Heron's always saying I talk too much."

"You were anxious for him."

Another long look. "You'll do," he'd said at last, heaved himself off the wall and went back into the house. I'd supposed that meant we were on good terms again.

The light straining into the sky dimmed the bright full moon that still rode high. I sat on the churchyard wall, unwrapped the cloth I'd brought with me and broke apart the bread and wedge of cheese inside. I was, I realised, ravenously hungry.

A seagull screeched. I was desperate for sleep, but tried to remain alert. I could hear footsteps, echoing, as sounds do in the quiet of the dawn. I glanced down Silver Street and saw someone walking up towards me. A slim figure wearing a greatcoat over dark breeches, topping the outfit with a wide-brimmed country hat.

My heart turned over. As she came closer, I saw that Esther was smiling. I'd not been able to persuade her to stay at Blackett's and I'd not tried particularly hard – I wanted her by me, I trusted no one with her safety but myself.

"Sensible boots," she said, with a gesture, "nothing more than a greatcoat flapping around me. I cannot tell you how good it feels!" A few pale strands drifted from the hair tucked up under the hat. "To have the freedom to stride out rather than to mince along in a ladylike fashion... Wonderful!"

"You've given up then on convention," I said, teasing. "You're abandoning respectable ladylike behaviour?"

"Convention," she said ruefully, "is much overrated." She sat down beside me, took the bread from my hand, broke it apart and gave me half back. Her scent of roses tantalised me. "Convention could have killed us last night."

"It was my fault," I said. "I underestimated our opponents. I thought they'd follow to try and retrieve the book before attacking us. Instead, they decided to take us by surprise."

Esther contemplated the bread in her hands. Her scent was making my senses reel. And the breeches. She knew it too; she cast a sideways glance at me. She frowned. "Does that mean – " She glanced around. "Are they following us now?"

"Footsteps echo in the quiet streets," I said. "You think it's merely your own steps until you stop, and the echo continues. Yes, they're here somewhere, watching."

She raised a cool eyebrow at me. The thought that she might have been killed last night seized me, a wild panic. I said, "Marry me. Please," then reddened. Of all the gauche, embarrassing, awkward ways to propose...

She was smiling. "Yes," she said. "Of course."

I took her hand –

And at that moment, the door to a house opposite opened and two servants came out gossiping. We snatched our hands away. Esther started to laugh. "I suppose convention is not so easy to cast off!"

I sighed. "I suppose we'd better be about our business." I stood, held down a hand to help her up. This time she accepted my help, with a smile. I folded the cloth around the remains of the bread and cheese and stuffed it in my pocket.

"You know who they are," she said.

"Yes," I agreed. "The breeches were the clue."

She dusted herself down. "The fact that they were dark?"

"The fact that they were there at all," I said.

I pushed open the churchyard gate, allowed Esther to precede me. She was frowning. "I suppose I will make sense of what you say when we find the map in the book. But will they not attack us as soon as we have it?"

"Not in the street," I said. "He wants to kill me, but he wants to get away with it too, and that requires a little privacy."

The grass in the churchyard was wet with dew. The day was beginning to warm; a few lazy clouds drifted overhead. "We're in danger of forgetting Nell," I said. "If she'd not been murdered, none of this would have happened. And her murder was because of that book."

I shut the gate behind us; we started along the path, side by side. "Nell's spirit told me the murderer gave her sixpence for keeping the book," I said. "But when I searched her room, the money was not there – she had only three pennies and two farthings. *He took it back*, Esther. I know there's nothing a spirit can do with money, but nevertheless it was rightfully hers and he took it back. That act of meanness is almost worse than all the rest."

The paths crunched under our feet; a bird flew up, startled. In the strained light of dawn we skirted the tall tombstones, carved with angels and curlicues and eternal protestations of love and remembrance. Nell's grave was still raw earth, still had only a rough wooden cross at its head. Esther looked down with a murmur of regret. "I never knew her. What was she like?"

I considered. "Young. And constant in her love for Bedwalters."

I had a moment's forewarning, and drew Esther's arm through my own. A little thrill of cold; I shivered, Esther gasped. Then I blinked as daylight bright enough to dazzle flooded the grave-yard. And there was the sombre stone – *Loving and beloved…*

I looked round for passers-by. Esther was clutching my arm; looking down, I saw a faint alarm on her face but she said nothing.

I led the way across the graveyard towards the undercroft behind the church. The sun drifted into the shadow of a darkening cloud; I felt a spot of rain on my face. I was mentally uttering a prayer that the book would still be there. I knew from past experience that time moved at a different speed in this world – months might have passed here where only days passed in my own world. I could only hope I'd hidden the book well enough to escape notice, and that no one had found it.

At the back of the church, we found the entrance to the under-croft. I went down three steps to it, checked its metal grill. The lock was rusted through and the door swung outwards; Esther held it open for me as I fumbled in my coat pocket for my tinderbox, struck a spark and lit a candle stub. The light danced over the stones of a passageway and the crumbling mortar of a barrel vault.

I had to stoop although Esther was just able to stand upright. Holding the candle in front of me, I made my way to the end of the long passage, to a cave-like room held up by one thick clumsy pillar. Boxes and barrels were piled along one wall. "Contraband?" Esther asked evidently surprised.

I handed her the candle stub; she held it high as I went to the wall where I'd hidden the book. I counted bricks left and right, up and down, and found the loose bricks easily enough but nearly broke my fingernails trying to remove them from the wall. When I'd originally hidden the book, I'd gouged out the loose mortar with a key and the bricks had come out easily, but they resisted me now for several minutes before they tumbled out with a rush. I pushed a hand into the dark cavity behind, felt with relief the edge of the book. As I eased it out of the cavity, something fell from the top of it – a stalk of grass, with a feathery, delicate seed head. The grass was green and bright, as if it had just been picked; perhaps, I thought with a shiver, I'd just missed myself putting the book in here...

I unwrapped the paper, angled the book so that as much light as possible fell on it. The spine hung by two or three threads, the hard covers of front and back were battered and rubbed.

I opened the book and laid it, pages down, on top of a barrel. I tugged gently at the damaged front cover. It gave a little, but the glue that bound it to the board below was still good. I turned the book round and eased a nail under the back cover. With a dry crackle, the cover shifted and came away. And between cover and board –

Esther peered over my shoulder as I struggled to remove the extra sheet of paper without damaging it. It slid a little way, then stuck. I could get only the very tips of my fingers to it and it was painstaking work. I edged it from side to side, gently easing it out.

"Music paper," Esther said. "Hand-ruled."

It was not what I'd been expecting. I'd been expecting a map, or a legal document at the very least. The paper had been folded into four; I opened it carefully. It was not new paper but not very old either. There was music on it; the writing – both words and musical notation – was neat, rather unformed, obviously that of a young person.

It was a song, a melody line with words underneath, and a figured bass for the harpsichordist to play from. Esther squinted at the words. "Sweet Damon, when asleep you lie…"

"Damon and Thyrsis," I said. "I penned an ode about that pair when I was eighteen or so. My first serious composition. I use the word *serious* lightly. I've done my best to lose it."

"It's explicit," Esther said, with a trace of disapproval. "Hardly suitable for a young girl to write."

"A young girl?"

"Read the title, Charles." Esther pointed at the words. *To my dearest beloved, Edward Edmund Alyson on his eighteenth birthday, 21st August 1730. From yr own love, Margaret.*"

I stared at it for a long moment then burst out laughing.

"Charles!" Esther said irritably. "What *is* the matter?"

"The date," I said. "Look at the date!"

41

They have found the fellow who held us up and have slapped him in prison to await the Assizes. He will hang, I guarantee it, he will hang!
[Letter from Retif de Vincennes, to his brother, Georges,
10 August 1736]

I looked about the small room with distaste. I couldn't bring myself to sit on the straw-mattress in case it was bug-infested so I propped myself against the window sill instead. From outside the lodging house came the sounds of the Key, the rattle of coal being poured into a hold, the cry of an apple seller, angry shouts from a drunk.

"I blame myself," the spirit said. It was hovering on the back of the unsteady chair. "I should have taken notice of what was going on, instead of chattering away like an old woman."

"You weren't to know he was a murderer." I wiped white mortar dust from my sleeve. Those crumbling stairs were highly unpleasant.

"I *knew* there was something wrong with him," the spirit retorted. "I *knew* he was up to no good. I should have acted on it."

"There are plenty of petty thieves about. They don't all turn into murderers."

"I didn't look," the spirit said sadly. "You have to live with them, you see. If you're at outs with fellows living in the house, it gets so uncomfortable. And they move on so quickly as a rule. They come for a few months, go somewhere else. Why fight them? Leave them alone and they'll go, and it'll be peaceful again."

"You're not the only one," I said. "I wager there were other people who didn't look."

"You looked."

"He killed someone I knew. I couldn't not look."

There was a sound below, at the foot of the outside stair.

"Hide!" I whispered. "Quickly!"

The spirit slid down the chair leg and disappeared into a crack between the floorboards.

The steps creaked worse than ever – I wondered how long they'd last. The whole place was on the verge of disintegration; every time I came up the stairs I thought they were leaning further into the wall. And that the wall was leaning too. I waited.

He emerged from the stairwell, hesitated in the doorway. Then he smiled at me, winningly, charmingly. "No more subterfuge, eh, Pattinson?"

"I have it now!" I said. "You mangle people's names when you want to establish some sort of authority over them, to put them at a disadvantage. Well, two can play at that game, Mr *Allinson*."

His fist clenched on his sword. He was dressed for travel, I noticed, but his clothes were still bright, a rich summer sky blue. A sword was entangled in the skirts of his coat and he stood legs apart with his hands at his sides like a man ready to fight. There was no sign of our contretemps last night, or of that shot I'd put through his left arm. It had probably been only a graze. He still had that arrogant tilt of head, that faintly amused smile.

He was still confident of victory.

"The spirits gave you my message, then?" I said.

"My dear Pattinson," he said, smiling. "You know I'm always delighted to chat to you. But I'm very much afraid your fifteen guineas is gone for good."

"I have the book," I said. "The one you killed Nell for."

His smile widened. "I thought you had. But you hid it so well!"

"And I have what was secreted in its pages." I held up the music paper.

He took a step forward, stopped. It was the first sign of unease I'd seen in him.

"You couldn't bear to throw it away," I said. "Not since it was written by your beloved Margaret."

Perhaps I sounded cynical; he said, "You wouldn't know what love is. You're just after that woman's money." He was still smiling, still unbelievably confident. Did nothing dent his arrogance?

"I know how the constable felt about the girl," I said. He nodded encouragingly so I went on. "Keeping the music was dangerous, so you stole a damaged book and hid the song between its covers. But you were still concerned it might be found. When you met Nell you thought it a good opportunity to hide it where no one would think to look – just for a few days until you could make a hiding place for it. But then you worried she might have seen the song, so you killed her too."

"I discovered the constable was one of her regular customers," he said grinning. "So, yes, I decided to kill her. Once she was a spirit and confined to that house, all I would have to do was stay clear of the street and I'd be safe. She was just a whore," he added, amused. "Was she one of your haunts too, Pattinson?"

I bit back anger; I'd not win this battle if I lost my temper. "And the chapman? He was a decent honest man."

Alyson shrugged. "He was in the way. And are you alone, Pattinson? No dancing master hidden in the wainscoting to leap out at me? No servant to rush to your defence? I object to your attempts to suborn my butler, by the way."

"And I object to your attempts to threaten my betrothed," I returned. "And while we are on the subject of ladies – what about your mistress?" I waved the song at him. "The 'lady' married to an archbishop's tutor now permanently in residence in Rome. Isn't she just a whore?"

He had the sword half-out of the sheath before he recollected himself and slammed it back down. I was relieved; I'd been beginning to think I would never shake that self-assurance. "I rather think," I said, "the lady didn't know about Nell's death until afterwards – you had an argument over it at Long End, didn't you? But after that, she threw herself into the fray with gusto. A pity she isn't a better shot – she wasn't supposed to hit you in the woodland attack was she? I was the target that day. Were you trying to kill me, or just deter me from investigating further?"

"You were so damn persistent!" he said with mock outrage. He looked like a man relishing the situation. "But do tell, my dear Pattinson, what gave us away?"

"The clothes," I said. "It all came down to the clothes. On the various occasions we saw our attackers, we saw two men. But we were fooled. Your wife wore breeches." I of all people should have known better, I reflected. "Once I realised our attackers were a man and a woman – that, naturally, narrowed the field of suspects somewhat."

"Naturally," Alyson agreed. "You don't seem particularly scandalised, Pattinson – and I thought you were a deeply conventional man. But Ridley did tell me you and he had seen Mrs Jerdoun in breeches – perhaps you like the idea. I wondered then if you'd make the connection."

Poor William Ridley, I thought. I owed him an apology for suspecting him of involvement in this affair.

"And you made an error in respect of clothes, too," I pointed out. His face darkened – clearly not a man who liked criticism.

"That night on the bridge over the canal," I explained, "you wore shoes suitable for the house, not boots – hardly surprising as you had to get back to the dining room and pretend to be too drunk to know what was going on. Boots would have been out of place. But you should have cleaned your shoes off before traipsing mud in."

"I thought you'd assume it was a servant." He was grinning again.

"No, that was out of the question. The attacker wore dark clothes under his greatcoat and the servants have gold and scarlet liveries." I gestured at his blue coat. "You yourself usually wear bright clothes, but for the first time you were wearing dark ones that night."

"Very clever," he said, but there was an edge in his voice.

"I admit I got sidetracked by the idea of a servant being involved," I conceded. "Who else could have left the notes? Those were your doing of course. You tried to take advantage of that misapprehension by putting the book in Crompton's room."

Alyson was still grinning broadly but his hand was tight on his sword. "You have it all worked out, I see. And I suppose you must have worked out that while you and I were arguing over that last matter, Margaret was purloining the Colonial's sword from his room?"

"Are you that poverty-stricken?"

"Not at all. We simply thought we ought to do the job properly. We'd inadvertently stolen one half of the gentleman's inheritance – why not all of it?"

"For the fun of it?"

"For the *satisfaction*," he corrected. "But you haven't explained it all yet. What about that time here, when you and I were both attacked by the murderer?"

"You faked it," I said. "You sent Hugh round to the front of the house out of the way. Then you went up the stairs before me – you had the only light. You took advantage of the turn in the stairs to blow out the candle without my seeing you do so, then shouted and came back down against me in the darkness. With a knife in your hand. Your aim was just as poor as your wife's, of course." He didn't like that insult; his smile slipped. "You pretended to chase someone – you had enough time to get into the yard before Hugh and I came on the scene."

He shifted an inch or two. "So," he said, as if it was a matter of no real importance. "Tell me why we did it? Why is that song so important?"

I unfolded the music paper.

"*To my dearest beloved Edward Edmund Alyson on his 18th birthday, 21st August 1730.*" I looked up at him. "Families are so troublesome, aren't they? They can let you down so badly. Even before you're born."

He said nothing, continued to smile. But there was an extra tension in him. It would not be long before he made his move.

"You yourself showed me the family Bible," I reminded him. "You were trying to be clever, were you not? Daring me to work it out. You pointed out that your parents married in January 1713. You told me your month of birth too, didn't you? August, you said, inviting me to guess the scandal. And, as you'd intended, I assumed you meant the August *after* the marriage. But you were misdirecting me." I waved the song at him. "If you were eighteen in August 1730, then you were born in August 1712. *Before* your parents' marriage."

His smile broadened.

"You're illegitimate," I said. "Which means you cannot inherit your uncle's estates."

He started to laugh. "You're too clever by half, Patterson. I keep hearing your praises sung – I'm told you can untangle every mystery known to man! But compliment me a little at least! Did my antics not tax you even for a moment? And I worked so hard to confuse you! With the help of my wife, of course. And Hopkins. You remember Hopkins? The coachman? Who even now, by the way, is keeping watch downstairs."

It was his first slip and I was fiercely exultant at it. They hadn't discovered the coachman's body. Alyson had come alone. Of course he had – he would have done so in any case. He'd challenged me – it was an argument between the two of us. One he was so confident of winning.

"Hopkins is dead," I said. "In that derelict cottage."

His head lifted; he clearly didn't know whether to believe me or not. "And don't look to your wife to help you either," I added. "Mrs Jerdoun and the new constable have gone to find her."

He was shaken. "You won't find her," he snapped. "You'll never find her."

The spirit startled us both by shooting up the wall to the little shelf. "Golden Fleece," it said. "Parlour on the first floor. Drinking wine and waiting for you. Just like she was waiting for a morning call. Well, she was. She's off to the prison now with the lady and the constable."

"You should have brought her with you," I said, taunting him.

"This is between you and me," he snarled, drawing the sword. Fischer's sword.

"No," a voice said behind him. "This is between you and *me*."

Alyson swung round. Bedwalters stood calmly in the doorway. He was thinner than he had been but he still carried with him that new air of ease. "You have apparently forgotten," he said courteously, "that Nell is a spirit now, too. She received a message telling her what was going on here. Did you think, Mr Alyson, sir, that I would sit back and let you wreak yet more havoc?"

The sudden vehemence in his voice took Alyson by surprise. He flinched. And in that moment the spirit shifted, shooting across the intervening space of ceiling, and latching on to a cobweb. The cobweb swung into Alyson's face – I heard the spirit slap on skin.

Alyson broke. He dived for the doorway. Bedwalters put out a hand, caught him by the right arm. Alyson tried to swing the sword but Bedwalters tightened his grip. Alyson gasped; the sword dropped from his nerveless fingers and went clattering down the stairs.

As I started across the room, Alyson swung his left fist – but the constable was used to dealing with refractory drunks and swayed backwards out of reach. I seized Alyson from behind. He kicked out a foot. Bedwalters shifted but the foot caught his ankle, swept his feet from under him. He gasped, let go of Alyson, wavered at the top of the stairs, fell.

He landed on the top step; the old wood snapped like a gunshot. I had an arm round Alyson's chest, struggled to pull him down. He jerked his head back, hit my nose with a thump. I felt blood flow at once. I clung on, spluttering with pain. Bedwalters scrambled up and lunged at Alyson.

Everything seemed to happen at once. Alyson disconcerted me. I was braced to stop him jerking forward but he fell back against me instead. I fumbled my grip, lost my balance, grabbed at the door jamb to stop falling. Blood was running down my chin, dripping on to my waistcoat.

Alyson flung himself at the stairs, Bedwalters grabbed at him.

With a rumble and a screech, the stairs gave way.

A snowstorm of plaster and mortar descended on me. Fragments of brick stung my cheeks. Alyson screamed – I saw him tumble, bounce down the top steps then crash into a great gap where the treads broke apart.

Bedwalters went with him.

He'd had a grip on Alyson's arm but let go almost at once. It was not enough to save him. His forward momentum took him down.

I grabbed for Bedwalters, caught only a handful of his coat skirts. It slowed his fall but I heard cloth rip. The door jamb was breaking away from the wall. I wrapped my arm around it.

"Grab my hand!" I yelled.

The snowstorm of plaster was still falling. More solid objects now too – whole bricks. I could hardly see for the dust. Blood from my nose dripped into the fallen plaster like roses among snow. But I felt Bedwalters's fingers curl round my wrist.

His full weight jerked at my arm. I slid down the wall, felt myself being dragged over. I managed to get on the floor, lying at full length, let go the door jamb, struggled to get my other hand around his wrist. His weight was well-nigh pulling my arm out of its socket.

The spirit shot over my head. "Hold on, hold on! They're coming! I've sent for help. Hold on!"

They came, five burly keelmen in yellow waistcoats, who clambered over the rubble below, taking no notice at all of the bricks and plaster falling from the disintegrating walls. They took Bedwalters's weight, handed him down to safety then found a ladder and encouraged me down it. We'd hardly got out of danger before the entire outside wall of the stair went down in a huge flurry of dust and a roar that must have been heard all over town. It pulled part of the eaves away and we ran from the lethal rain of slates.

And all of it came down and buried Edward Edmund Alyson, and the spirit slid down the wall and rushed across the surface of the rubble, crying out in triumph.

42

**When all is said and done, nothing must disturb
the natural order of things.**
[Letter from Retif de Vincennes, to his wife, Régine, August 1736]

Bloodied and dust-covered, I sat watching the sailors and labourers sifting through the rubble of the staircase. Bedwalters stood a little way off, speaking to the new constable, Phillips; the two men looked to be on the best of terms. I'd already overheard Bedwalters spinning a tale about Alyson and myself coming back to look for clues to the murderer's identity. The sword was under all that rubble too, and I'd dropped the song in my hurry to apprehend Alyson. I wondered if Fischer would still be so eager to have his inheritance, given its recent history.

A scent of summer flowers drifted to me and I heard the swish of skirts. I looked up. Esther was walking towards me, dressed once more in a gown of palest green, halting in sudden shock as she took in the blood and the grime and the bruises which were rapidly forming.

"Do you have her?" I asked.

She took a deep breath, nodded. "She's hysterical. I left her to the attentions of the law – I couldn't tolerate her any longer." She cast a critical look over the stairs and the men rigging up a pulley to remove the heavier blocks of masonry. "He is dead, of course."

"I can't see how he could survive."

"*Sweet Damon…*" she murmured. "They had an odd idea of love."

"Love conquers all," I said flippantly.

"I wish it did." She turned to regard me in a measured way. "Do you know what Claudius Heron said, that night in the drawing room at Long End?"

"I assumed he was planning the wedding."

"Oh, he has done that," she agreed. "He has already taken steps to procure the marriage licence. But he was more concerned to make sure I knew what kind of a marriage I was making. He told me I would never stop you getting yourself into trouble." She gave me a wry smile. "He was right."

I gestured helplessly. "Until last year, I led a blameless life. Dull, but blameless."

"Until, in fact, you met me."

"A coincidence, no doubt."

She stood looking at me for a moment. I enjoyed looking back – at her slender figure, flattered by the pale gown, at the golden hair that drifted about her neck in the faint morning breeze. And I loved her calm air, her matter of fact acceptance of life, her exasperation with my obstinacy, her ability to find a solution to any problem.

There was no help for it, I knew. I'd probably be a married man before the month was out.

There was nothing, I thought, that I wanted more.

"Charles," she said.

"Yes?"

She sighed. "We will, I know, set the town gossiping when they hear of our marriage. I am resigned to that. But," she smiled, a trifle maliciously, "I do draw the line when it comes to walking through the town with you in that state! Dinner, Charles. Don't be late."

I watched her go, with a grin. Then I heard one of the labourers shout. They had found Alyson's body. *Plainly dead*, someone called.

I glanced over at Bedwalters. His face was flushed. He nodded to Phillips and, calmly, unhurried, walked off.

HISTORICAL NOTE

Every effort has been made to be geographically accurate in a depiction of Charles Patterson's Newcastle. In the 1730s, Newcastle was a town of around 16,000 in population, hemmed in by old walls, and centred on the Quay where ships moored to carry away the coal and glass on which the town depended. The single bridge across the Tyne, linking Newcastle with its southern neighbour Gateshead, was lined with houses and shops, a chapel and even a small prison; from the Quay, the streets climbed the hills to the more genteel (and cleaner) areas around Westgate and Northumberland Street. Daniel Defoe liked the place when he visited in 1720, but remarked unfavourably on the fogs that came drifting up the river. Places such as Westgate, High Bridge, the Sandhill and the Side did (and still do) all exist, although I have added a few alleys here and there to enable Patterson and his friends to take short cuts where necessary, and invented a stylish location for Esther's house, Caroline Square.

Musically, Charles Patterson lives in an atmosphere that the residents of Newcastle in the 1730s would have recognised instantly. The town had one of the most active musical scenes in England, after London, Bath and Oxford. From 1735, inhabitants could hear music in a weekly series of winter concerts (and occasionally during the summer too), listen to music in church (plain simple music if you went to St Nicholas, much more elaborate and 'popular' music at All Hallows), attend the dancing assemblies in winter, and listen to the fiddlers, pipers and ballad singers in the street. Nationally and internationally famous soloists often visited, but sadly there is no evidence to support the story that the most celebrated musician of the period, Mr George Frideric Handel, ever visited Newcastle.

The summer musical party around which *Sword and Song* takes place is based on the house parties held by George Bowes of Gibside in County Durham. Bowes was rather more ambitious than Edward Ayrton, and a great deal wealthier, and entertained his guests each year with an Italian violinist, who brought not only music with him but also macaroni and mineral water. The German sword makers of Shotley Bridge also really existed, although their family connections with Philadelphia are fictional.

A number of real people fleetingly appear in Charles Patterson's world. Solomon Strolger, organist of All Hallows for 53 years, is one, as is another organist, James Hesletine of Durham Cathedral. Thomas Mountier, the bass singer in *Broken Harmony*, was a singing man at the Cathedral for a short while until drink intervened. The Jenisons and Ords were real families with a particular interest in music but the specific individuals who appear in these books are fictional.

Charles Patterson is entirely fictional, but the impoverished situation in which he finds himself would have been entirely familiar to musicians of the time. If he has an alter ego, it would be Charles Avison, a Newcastle-born musician and composer who was well-known in his time and who dragged himself up by his own efforts from obscurity to wealth and respect, even being invited by local gentry to dine at their tables. If Patterson's career follows the same path, he will be extremely happy.

CHARLES PATTERSON'S NEWCASTLE

Key

1 Town walls
2 St Nicholas's Church
3 St Andrew's Church
4 St John's Church
5 All Hallows' Church
6 Castle
7 Guildhall
8 Caroline Square

9 Chares
10 Bigg Market
11 Fleshmarket
12 Sandhill
13 Sandgate
14 The Key
15 Tyne Bridge
16 The Side

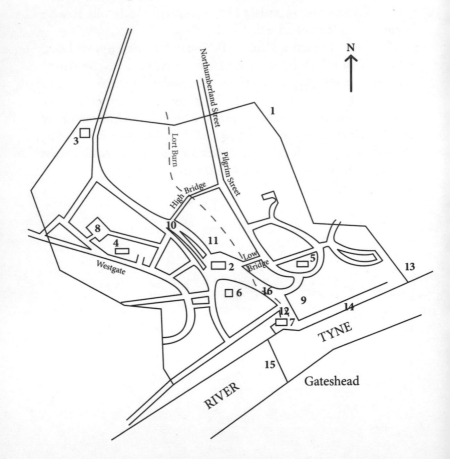

Meet Charles Patterson again in

CRIMINAL TENDENCIES

a diverse and wholly engrossing collection of short
stories from some of the best of the UK's crime writers.

£1 from every copy sold of this
first-rate collection will go to support the
NATIONAL HEREDITARY
BREAST CANCER HELPLINE

*She lay on her face, as if asleep. I turned her over and saw the deep
wound on her brow...*
– Reginald Hill, *John Brown's Body*

*...she was shaking badly. Terror was gripping her; the same terror she
previously experienced only in her dreams...*
– Peter James, *12 Bolinbroke Avenue*

*His lips were thin and pale. "She must be following us. She's some sort
of stalker."*
– Sophie Hannah, *The Octopus Nest*

*When he thought he was alone, he squatted down and opened the
briefcase. I was interested to see that it contained an automatic pistol
and piles and piles of banknotes.*
– Andrew Taylor, *Waiting for Mr Right*

*Avengers, that's what we are. We're there to avenge the punters who pay
our wages.*
– Val McDermid, *Sneeze for Danger*

The job was a real peach. Soft, juicy, ripe for plucking.
– Simon Brett, *Work Experience*

ISBN: 978-09557078-5-8 £7.99

CATCH UP WITH THE EARLIER ADVENTURES OF
CHARLES PATTERSON
HARPSICHORDIST, CONCERT ARRANGER
AND ACCIDENTAL INVESTIGATOR
by
ROZ SOUTHEY

BROKEN HARMONY

The 18th century – a different world…
But theft, blackmail and murder never change…

In Newcastle-upon-Tyne in the 1730s, life is not easy for an impoverished musician.

For Charles Patterson, violinist, harpsichord player, composer and would-be church organist, it's about to get a whole lot harder.

First he is accused of stealing a valuable book. Then a cherished violin belonging to his flamboyant professional rival Henri le Sac disappears, rapidly followed by le Sac himself. And when the young apprentice he inherited from his rival is gruesomely murdered, Patterson starts to feel out of his depth.

Strange goings-on at the elegant home of capricious Lady Anne leave him in fear for his health and sanity, and the lady's cousin, Esther Jerdoun, seems to be trying to warn him about something.

The mystery deepens as the death toll mounts, and it becomes clear that things are not quite as they appear…

ISBN: 9780955158933   **£7.99**
Also available as an ebook.

…a masterpiece of period fiction that delights while it provides an intriguing puzzle that keeps the reader riveted until the end.
– Early Music America

CHORDS AND DISCORDS

Music may be the food of love…
But it doesn't fill an empty belly

Winter is not a good time for jobbing musicians in early 18th century Newcastle. The town has emptied for the season, and Charles Patterson, harpsichordist, concert arranger and tutor to the gentry, is down to his last few shillings.

But Patterson has another talent: solving mysteries. When an unpopular organ builder thinks his life is in danger and a shop-boy dies in dubious circumstances, the offer of a substantial fee persuades him to seek answers to some difficult questions.

Like, who stole the dancing-master's clothes? Why is a valuable organ up for raffle?

And will Patterson escape whoever is trying to kill him?

ISBN: 9780955707827   **£7.99**

a very unusual historical mystery, and… quite a page turner
– Eurocrime

SECRET LAMENT

Italian actors...
French spies...
At least the thugs are English...

Charles Patterson is not happy. It's the hottest June for years; he's stuck in musical rehearsals with a family of Italians; some local ruffians are after his blood; and someone is trying to break into the house of Esther Jerdoun, the woman he loves.

When a murder is discovered he fears Esther may be next. It's time to ask some tough questions.

Who is the strange man masquerading under a patently false name? Are there really spies abroad in Newcastle? Why is a psalm-teacher keeping vigil over a house in the town?

And can Patterson find the murderer before he strikes again?

ISBN: 9780955707865   **£7.99**

... a tremendous feel for the era: her characters are likeable and her plotting is immaculate.
 – Sarah Rayne, award-winning author of *Tower of Silence*

NEW
CRÈME DE LA CRIME
PERIOD PIECES

THE BROKEN TOKEN   Chris Nickson
Pickpockets, pimps and prostitutes:
All in a day's work for the city constable –
until work moves too close to home…

When Richard Nottingham, Constable of Leeds, discovers his former housemaid murdered in a particularly sickening manner, his professional and personal lives move perilously close.

Circumstances seem to conspire against him, and more murders follow.

Soon the city fathers cast doubt on his capability, and he is forced to seek help from an unsavoury source.

Not only does the murder investigation keep running into brick walls, and family problems offer an unwelcome distraction; he can't even track down a thief who has been a thorn in his side for months.

When answers start to emerge, Nottingham gets more than he bargains for…

Debut novel from well-known music journalist.

Published May 2010   **£7.99**
ISBN: 9780956056610

DEBT OF DISHONOUR   Mary Andrea Clarke

Even a highwayman has friends –
sometimes in unexpected places

London society is outraged when charming, popular Boyce Polp is murdered on his way to an evening party, apparently by one of the highwaymen who make travelling even a few miles such a perilous business.

But Miss Georgiana Grey, herself no stranger to peril, has her own reasons for doubting the version of the tragedy which is soon the talk of the town.

She uncovers a darker side to Polp, and though her probing makes her as unpopular as the Bow Street Runner who is investigating the case, Georgiana is determined that justice will prevail.

Third adventure for the Crimson Cavalier.

Published August 2010   **£7.99**
ISBN: 9780956056641

The Crimson Cavalier also rides in:
The Crimson Cavalier   ISBN: 9780955158957
Love Not Poison   ISBN: 9780956056603

CRIME FICTION FOR ALL TASTES FROM CRÈME DE LA CRIME

by **Linda Regan**:

Behind You!   ISBN: 9780955158926
Passion Killers   ISBN: 9780955158988
Dead Like Her   ISBN: 9780955707889

Regan exhibits enviable control over her characters – Colin Dexter

by **Adrian Magson**:

No Peace for the Wicked   ISBN: 9780954763428
No Help for the Dying   ISBN: 9780954763473
No Sleep for the Dead   ISBN: 9780955158919
No Tears for the Lost   ISBN: 9780955158971
No Kiss for the Devil   ISBN: 9780955707810

Gritty, fast-paced detecting of the traditional kind – The Guardian

by **Penny Deacon**:

A Kind of Puritan   ISBN: 9780954763411
A Thankless Child   ISBN: 9780954763480

a fascinating new author with a hip, noir voice – Mystery Lovers

by **Kaye C Hill**:

Dead Woman's Shoes   ISBN: 9780955158995
The Fall Girl   ISBN: 9780955707896

… a welcome splash of colour and humour – Simon Brett

by **Gordon Ferris**

Truth Dare KILL   ISBN: 9780955158940
The Unquiet Heart   ISBN: 9780955707803

If It Bleeds   Bernie Crosthwaite   ISBN: 9780954763435
A Certain Malice   Felicity Young   ISBN: 9780954763442
Personal Protection   Tracey Shellito   ISBN: 9780954763459
Sins of the Father   David Harrison   ISBN: 9780954763497